AND YOU THOUGHT YOUR WORLD WAS HARSH

DARRIN ADAMS

Palmetto Publishing Group, LLC
Charleston, SC

For more information regarding special discounts for bulk purchases,
please contact Palmetto Publishing Group at
Info@PalmettoPublishingGroup.com.

ISBN-13: 978-1-944313-57-9
ISBN-10: 1-944313-57-5

CHAPTER ONE

JASON SAT SILENTLY, contemplating his surroundings, as he continued to write in his notebook. He had spent a little over four years looking at the same faces and the same dirty concrete walls. Always the same expressions as he walked the halls. Always the same noise. Everything was always the same.

Silence.

He continued to write, feeling others' eyes on him. Every night he woke up sweating, shaking, and gasping. He came to the library daily, trying to make sense of the visions that flooded his head. What he remembered were bits and pieces of a day that would come to change life as he knew it.

Five years ago

It was 2 p.m. The traffic and crowds were moderate. Gas prices were a little lower than usual, at fifteen dollars a gallon.

The two candidates running for mayor, D. Bag and Scammed U., were having heated debates. Billboards lined the street covered in false promises and convincing propaganda.

"Another wonderful day in Harshtown," Jason scoffed to himself. "At least the pizza's decent here." He lifted his sleeve to check his watch and thought to himself, *Looks like I can still get the lunch special if I hurry.*

Once the light turned green, Jason began to cross the street. He was almost halfway across when he was met with a loud screech, and he heard a thud to his left side. He bounced off the hood of the car, was launched into the intersection, and fell to the ground, unconscious.

———

The offending car came to a sharp stop in the intersection. An obviously shaken woman emerged from the driver seat, ran to the front of her car, and stared in shock. A group of witnesses rushed to the scene.

"Holy hell!" yelled the woman. "What have I done?!"

One of the witnesses, similarly in shock, said, "Yeah! Look at that dent in your car." A few witnesses agreed, nodding, while others gave their own skewed input.

"Damn! Now I'll have to pay some mechanic to re-pair this crap. And look! Look at these blood stains. How the hell am I gonna get these out? Now I'm gonna be late, too! Dammit." She continued to mutter in aggravation as she walked toward the injured pedestrian on the ground. "I can't believe this! Just my luck."

The woman sighed as she looked down at the scoundrel's battered body. "Son of a bitch!" She spat on him, and then stomped away, as the witnesses laughed about the situation and carried on about their business. She got back into her car, and peeled out.

Jason lay on the ground in the middle of the street, his

busted body unresponsive, as cars passed.

A businessman scurried along the crosswalk, but stopped briefly to take a picture of him with his cell phone.

A teenager and his little brother rushed to the unconscious man's side. The smaller boy reached out to touch his shoulder, and looked around his body nervously. The boy made eye contact with his teenage brother, and then shook his head. With no further hesitation, he removed the man's watch. The teenager then reached into the man's pockets and took his wallet, before he finally kicked him in the back.

"Thanks for lunch, dumbass!" The boys made a break toward the pizzeria, just in time for the lunch special.

A well-dressed woman stopped mid-stride, near the unconscious man, who lay at her feet.

"Helene," she said snootily., "Come on. We can't be late." The woman's dog raised its leg, pissed on the man's freshly cut hair, and continued to paw around alongside her. She continued on, marching merrily along, and crossed the street.

The day continued to carry on as though nothing had ever happened along the busy street. Just another day in Harshtown.

An hour after the incident, a police officer arrived at the scene. He stepped out from his car, looked around, and sighed. The female driver from the accident emerged then from a nearby salon. She pointed at the scoundrel, shouting, "That's him, officer! He's the one who vandalized my car! I have witnesses!"

A few people nodded in approval, and one said, "She's telling the truth. I saw it with my own eyes."

The officer walked over to the unconscious body, softly kicked him, and waited for a response.

Nothing.

The officer exhaled, disappointed, as he handcuffed the man and lugged him into the police car, set for jail. The officer approached the lady with admiration in his eyes.

"Thank you for reporting this, ma'am. Please remember to stay safe. There are a lot of thugs out here. After all, this world can be very harsh at times."

"I will." She smiles. "Thank you, officer."

The cop nodded as he got back into his car, and then drove away. Due to the bumpy roads, and the fact that the officer did not buckle up the lawbreaker, the unconscious criminal's body was repeatedly bounced about the back seat. The woman grumbled to herself, and then to one of the witnesses, about suing the scoundrel once she finds out who he is. She returned to her perch in the salon, highly disgruntled.

—

Present day

Jason sat bitterly in the maximum-security sector of Harshtown Prison. Tales of the incident continued to swarm about the prison, and the inmates sidestepped him in fear. He had never once said a word to any of them, and yet no one uttered a peep whenever he passed.

Over time his expression has become angrier and darker, as he waited out the last of his wrongful sentence. Jason had always been a man who had followed the rules, worked hard, and done very well in school. Despite that, this was how his community had treated his dedication and diligence. Each day, he came closer to reclaiming his freedom and righting the wrongs done to him.

—

Jamaal, like Jason, was a hardworking man who came from a middle-class family. Jamaal and his family both valued competition and a job well done. He was present that day during Jason's "criminal act." Originally, he had been on his way to a corporate building that had a job opening. He had stood in disbelief watching how a group of ignorant people could show such little empathy for an injured college-aged kid. After the incident he testified in court to defend Jason, however, the opposition was too strong.

As for Jamaal, his parents had always told him that if he worked hard enough, his dreams *would* come true. This principle stuck with him throughout life. In grade school, he got straight A's, and always made the honor roll. Not only was he good in school, but others considered him a good person. He was respectful to his peers, as well as his elders. Helping those in need, while staying humble, was not much of an issue for him.

While attending middle school, the trend continued, and he did well in school, and was respectful to everyone. His elders constantly reassured him that he could be anything or anyone he wanted, when he put his mind to it. Eventually he landed himself in community college, majoring in what he loved doing most of all: underwater basket weaving. Getting a job in that field had always been his dream, especially since it was a very rare profession, which made it high in demand. With support from his family and friends, Jamaal was even more motivated to pursue his dreams, particularly since underwater basket weavers are paid a generous salary.

Jamaal applied for the job online shortly after finishing his associate's degree. To his dismay, he wasn't receiving any calls about his application, which prompted him to visit the office, and investigate. He was even further dismayed, upon his arrival, when the receptionist informed him that he needed a bachelor's degree to qualify for the position. He fussed with the young woman, but he primarily achieved showing everyone how irate he could become. Defeated, Jamaal sucked it up, and transferred to a different college.

It was not difficult at all for him to obtain a bachelor's degree. However, he was disappointed that not all of his credits transferred. This caused him to finish in three years instead of two. That fact baffled him, because he already knew the material, and had to do a hell of a lot of repeating when it came to taking classes in his major. Shortly after receiving his bachelor's degree at age twenty-four, Jamaal happily applied for the job again. At first, he remained nonchalant about the lack of calls, yet time passed on with no results. He went back to the office, and asked if they were hiring, but to his dismay, again, the receptionist said that he needed to get his master's degree in order to qualify. Jamaal clenched his fists tightly, sucked it up, and went back to school.

After four more years of monotony, he received his master's degree. His graduation was delayed for a year due to his dead-end job he had to have in order to fully support his dying grandmother. He was required to take more classes than usual due to the intensive nature of his major. He stared at his certificate, and sighed.

"Here I am, twenty-eight years old, and finally able to fulfill my dream."

Without hesitation, he applied for the job again, but still not a single call.

"I'm sorry. You don't qualify, sir. You need a PhD for this position."

Jamaal banged the receptionist's desk furiously with his fists.

"What do you mean I need a PhD?! Last time all I needed

was a master's, and before that, a bachelor's!"

The receptionist spoke in a monotone voice, which pissed him off even further.

"Sorry, sir. Times change, and the economy is bad. Corporations have really had to step their game up when it comes to hiring people."

Jamaal stormed out of the personnel building, and headed back to the school campus.

Jamaal worked extra hard, and got his PhD. It took him five years to finish. His scholarship expired after he finished his master's, so he had to take some time off to save up money to pay his way. At age thirty-three, he finally had his PhD. He applied for the job again shortly after graduation. To his surprise, he still wasn't getting any calls! Keeping his composure at this point was such a tough thing for him. All he wanted to do was fulfill his purpose, and do is his life's work. Why did things have to be like this?

It was as if the receptionist expected him. Before he could get a word in, she said, "I'm sorry, you don't qualify, sir. You will need some military training for this job. At least four years to qualify."

Jamaal paced furiously. "Why the hell do I need military experience? Ugh! Never mind."

He stormed off, and headed to the air force recruiter's office to enlist. He remained in service for five years, and was honorably discharged after being shot in the leg. Rather than just staying the four years, he remained enlisted in to be sure that there were no further qualifications. He absolutely refused to accept that he needed to do something else. The injured leg took about a year to heal completely. At age thirty-eight, Jamaal had completed the requirements to become an underwater basket weaver. Shortly after, he returned to the office.

"I'm sorry, sir, but it seems you are over qualified for the job."

His mouth dropped, and Jamaal was dumbfounded. "Over qualified? What the fuck?!"

The receptionist nodded nonchalantly. "Yes, sir. I do apologize. You served in the military for five years instead of the required four. We do, however, have an opening for a custodial position that doesn't have any qualification requirements."

———

Cecil crossed his arms and looked at the cynical former college student. He had decided to visit the coffee shop before heading over to his new job at the retail toy store. While in the building he noticed a troubled guy that appeared to be around the same age as him, so he decided to talk to him since people were avoiding him. The two talked together for a little while, but the conversation was awkward. The former college student has basically told Cecil his whole life story. Cecil found this odd, because they were complete strangers an hour ago, however, he understood that this man is going through a hard time, and sometimes people need to vent their frustrations. Based on his understanding, this man has been working towards his dream job, but would constantly get turned down.

Cecil asked, "What is your name again?"

"Jamaal Johnson."

"Jamaal, I really hate to be that guy, but you can always quit when you can. So far, nothing good has come out of working toward becoming an underwater basket weaver. Maybe it is a sign from God that you need to do something else in your life. Everything happens for a reason."

"First, I see some innocent guy get run over. Rather than

finish my business right away, I tried to get the guy the help that he needed, but people were uncooperative, and by the time that I returned he'd already been handcuffed and taken away by the officer. Then I'm told that I *still* don't qualify for the job, and now you are trying to lecture me while I'm trying to have a nice cup of coffee. You don't understand! A lot has happened in one day, and I always wanted to be an underwater basket weaver— ever since I was little! I refuse to give up right now, especially after coming so far. I'm going to enlist in the air force. Thanks for the pep talk, man, but I'm the type of person that does what he has to do. See ya!"

Jamaal stormed away from Cecil. Cecil observed the former college student, and thought to himself, *We're both thirty-three years old. The difference between me and him is that I learned to accept the cards that were dealt to me. I seriously hope that things work out for him. Who knows? Maybe he will become a vice president of a corporation—or maybe even a CEO someday.*

Cecil waved at Jamaal. "Take care, and good luck with your career!" He then headed for the toy store. He'd recently been hired as assistant manager, and today was his first day.

An hour later, Cecil had gotten to the toy store:

The toy store manager, named Tim, has stated, "Do you see that guy over there?"

He nudged Cecil and pointed angrily at a worker who was very diligently straightening the shelves. What caught Cecil's attention the most was that the employee was muscular, had tattoos of daggers on his arms, and was bald. Just as angrily as he'd said before, Tim stated, "We are going to fire him."

Cecil looked at Tim with a confused and curious expression. "Fire him? Why?"

"He's lazy, doesn't know how to do his job, and he comes to work late all the time."

The confused Cecil reflected on this deeply, but in the end, it did make sense, especially since the mysterious person appeared to be a thug. "Hmmm. Makes sense Tim. Gotta have a competent worker."

As Cecil began to gather his belongings to leave, Tim cautioned him, "You are the new supervisor, and he is going to work under you tomorrow, so it's just a warning."

Cecil thanked his manager for all of his insight about the shady man.

The next day, to Cecil's surprise, Hector, the man that Tim had ranted about the day before, entered the building on time. Hector greeted him warmly, and welcomed him to the store as a new coworker. Cecil returned the favor as he kept in mind what Tim had told him ("He's lazy, doesn't know how to do his job, and comes to work late all the time.") While Hector was heading over to his assigned department, Cecil gave him a wary stare. "So much for being late, but I still have my eye on you, slacker."

Later in the evening, he approached Hector calmly.

"Hey, Hector. This is what I want you to do. You see the clothing zone over there? I want you to help those customers, and keep that area cleaned."

Hector did as instructed, with no objections and without presenting any problems. About thirty minutes later, the customers that Hector had assisted approached Cecil. They complimented Hector on his nice behavior, and his knowledge of the store. They said to Cecil that they recommended the company to hire more people like Hector, since the service he'd given them was outstanding. He thanked the customers, but this confused him even more after the store manager had told him in so many ways that Hector was a terrible worker. Perhaps he was just trying to be a good person around Cecil.

Cecil muttered warily, "Hector must have some dirt on him. Everyone is guilty of something."

Cecil took a walk around the store and saw that most of the departments were dirty. This wasn't surprising since Christmas was around the corner, and his store was the best toy store in Harshtown. While doing his store-wide cleaning evaluation, he walked over to Hector's area. What he saw shocked him. The area was spotless, yet the so-called slacker was still finding things to do, even though there was clearly practically nothing else left. Still convinced that Hector was a bad worker, Cecil continued to search for something that was in line with what he'd heard the store manager say. He talked to a few workers about Hector, but the main thing he heard was positive feedback. To him, it was like listening to a broken record in which the same lyrics kept on repeating.

"He is easy to work with, very hard working, is a nice guy, funny, always on time, would make a good supervisor. Hell, he could run the whole damn store!"

Cecil decided to talk to some of the supervisors. Half of them said positive things, while the other half, who had not interacted with Hector, simply agreed with Tim for the hell of it.

Cecil reflected on what a supervisor told him. *Well, if the boss says he is a bad guy, then he must be. Just look at him! He's a gangster. I hope he gets locked up."*

"No point talking about him," Cecil said to himself. "Might as well go up to him, and talk to him in person." Cecil didn't see the point in trying to be subtle anymore.

Five minutes later, he approached Hector.

"Hey, Hector. You seem like a very hard-working guy, and very chill."

Hector nodded, and replied calmly, "Yes. I value hard work a lot, regardless of how I get treated."

Cecil crossed his arms and narrowed his eyes. "Why is it that I hear that you aren't a hard worker? I was told that you were a trouble maker."

"Because Tim doesn't like me! He talked down to me once, and I talked back to him because I didn't appreciate it. I told him that I think the Crazytown Crazies suck as a football team. That right there *definitely* did it. Since then he pretty much has me work one or two days a week, but I'm fine with that because I have two other jobs, and I attend college part-time." Hector scoffed, "I guess this is how society treats hardworking and honest people."

Cecil completely believed Hector, and he sympathized with him. "That's messed up, man. I'll talk to Tim about this, and try to work something out."

The next day, Cecil was about to clock in, but he paused, eavesdropping on an argument that was taking place in Tim's office.

"You're fired! Now get the fuck out of my store!"

Cecil listened as Hector argued back. He then watched Hector storm past him. Cecil entered the office feeling very confused.

"What was that all about?"

Tim scowled. "Hector was late again—ten seconds late—again! I told him that he needs to stop being late all the time. Lazy fuck."

Cecil thought he must have lost brain cells or something, because this all sounded completely ridiculous to him. "He was always ten seconds late and you fired him for that?"

Tim nods proudly as he crossed his arms. "Yes. The nerve! And it gets worse. He said the Crazies suck! Don't give a fuck if he is going to college, working two other jobs, and trying to support his family. That fucker has gotta go because of that!"

Cecil would have resigned then and there, but he really needed this job in order to survive.

———

Five years later, present day

Cecil hopped out of his car. As he walked down the street, he gave some change to a homeless man. For some odd reason, people were either completely ignoring the transient, or talking about him behind his back. Cecil shook his head at them, disgusted over their actions. He approached the toy store, and reflected for a moment. He almost didn't recognize the building in which he'd once worked. He saw that the parking lot was moderately crowded—something he had not seen much of when he'd worked there.

Maybe things have changed a bit here? He pondered for a moment. He also wondered if that guy that he'd talked to five years ago had finally become an underwater basket weaver. Cecil would guess that by this time the disgruntled guy was probably done with the air force.

Either way, his kids' birthdays were coming up soon, and this place had the best toy selection in all of Harshtown. Better sooner than later, he figured.

Cecil shopped for his items, and couldn't help but notice the unfamiliar faces in uniform. He didn't recognize any of the current workers. *Maybe that's a good thing. It seems things have changed a bit here.*

He strolled happily toward the cashier to pay for the gifts. He heard a nearby argument, and slowed down near the customer service desk. From behind the office door he heard clearly, "What?! You don't like the Crazytown Crazies?! You're fired!" The worker stormed past Cecil and out of the store without another word.

Cecil saw Tim through the opening of the door. He remained in place, and watched Tim rise from his chair, and then reach for the door. He smiled awkwardly at Tim, and noticed Tim's trademark scowl in response. Tim slammed the door, knocking papers off the customer service desk.

"Nope," Cecil muttered as he paid for his purchases. "Nothing has changed at all."

———

Laura walked down the sidewalk toward her job. The streets were empty for the most part. She accidentally bumped into a man, dropping her purse. She slowly knelt down to pick up her belongings, but the man beat her to it.

"I apologize, ma'am." He picked up the purse, and handed it to her. Laura took a good look at him, and then shrieked. She was terrified! Despite his kind mannerisms, the man in front of her had a shaved head and what appeared to be prison tattoos on his arms.

"Help! I'm getting mugged! Someone! Anyone! Save me!" yelled Laura.

The man held out his hands. "Woah! Calm down, lady! Stop causing a scene! I'm trying to return your belongings to you. I'm just trying to go to my job, so please calm down."

Laura looked at the man, astonished. He was still offering her the purse. She nodded at him, and retrieved it. "Thank you, and I apologize about that, sir. What is your name?"

"My name is Hector. Don't sweat it, ma'am. It ain't the first time that someone judged me based on my appearance. At least you had the audacity to hear me out. Take care." Hector nodded at Laura, and began to walk away.

"You too."

Laura also walks away, checking her purse to make sure that all of the contents were still inside. Fortunately, nothing had been stolen by Hector, the thug who had obviously been pretending to be a good guy—at least from her perspective.

Thirty minutes later, Laura continued to walk toward her job, but was stopped by another man.

"Can I have some cash, ma'am?" he asked.

Laura felt frustrated. She was hoping to be able to walk past the homeless man that was waiting patiently near the toy store—without being asked for change this time. She turned to him, smiled warily, and shook her head.

"I'm sorry, sir, but I don't have any money to spare."

This was very true since Laura worked for minimum wage, and could barely keep up with her bills. After she'd paid her rent, she had practically no money left in her bank account. To say that she had no money to spare was right.

The man then replied, a hint of sorrow in his raspy voice, "God bless you, ma'am." He cried in despair as he ran away.

The next day, the same man sat on the same corner. With pure indifference in his voice this time, he said to her, "Can I have some cash, ma'am?"

Laura again refused, but shortly after a man walks over to the homeless man. The man handed the broken man a five-dollar bill, and walked past Laura, projecting a look of contempt in her direction.

The following day, the scenario was the same. "Can I have some cash, ma'am?"

She simply shook her head, and watched a family walk up to the man. The littlest girl reached into a coin purse, and said,

"Here, mister, you can have my dollar. Mommy said it was for candy, but you can have it." The mother teared up with pride, and ushered them away.

As they passed by Laura, one of the older kids looked at her venomously, and yelled, "Stingy-ass loser!"

"Son!" the mother snapped. "That's no way to talk to strangers. Let the cheap insensitive asshole —errr, woman—be on her way."

Laura sighed as she walked off, pretending she'd heard nothing.

The next day, the homeless man had the same indifferent attitude. "Ma'am..." The man just held out his palm.

Laura sighed, and said no. Crowds of people now surrounded the two of them. Laura turned around, uneasy and scared.

A man yelled angrily, "What the hell is your problem, ma'am?! Don't you see that this guy is suffering? Do you not give a shit about him?"

Laura felt very alarmed. The crowd had formed so quickly, and they all gave her a bad vibe.

"No! You don't understand. I would give him money if I had it to spare. I work in a fast-food restaurant, and I barely can pay my bills as it is now. I'm behind on my payments *again*. I'm facing eviction! Don't you see? I may get kicked out of my house, too, and become homeless myself."

A woman in the crowd said sarcastically, "Typical. The only person you care about is yourself. Let's go, people! Leave this selfish whore to her greed.

Laura arrived home from work. She changed out of her greasy clothes, and then went to look for a snack. There wasn't much available, since payday was days away. She grabbed a few carrots from her nearly bare fridge, and reminded herself to get some food before work tomorrow. She plopped onto her threadbare couch, turned on the TV, settled on the news channel, and listened in amusement to the news reporter.

"Yes, that is a new record! We congratulate ten-year-old Tony for the most boogers picked in a minute! And now to our top story tonight, it was reported that Laura Spokovich has yet again refused to give the homeless guy some money."

The field reporter interviewed the crowd—the same crowd that had surrounded Laura earlier. A woman in the crowd said, "Yeah, I saw it all! That whore didn't give this guy a damn thing. Not even a penny! Hell, I at least gave the guy a breadcrumb."

The reporter said in disgust, "Well there you have it, folks, Selfish Whore Laura Spokovich"—her picture appeared on the screen, defaced with her name in horror-movie-style font—"doesn't give a damn about the homeless. In other news, we will continue to embarrass Laura even more by featuring this story tonight, tomorrow, and—"

Laura had had enough, and she zapped off the TV. Crying herself to sleep seemed to be the best way to release her frustration and sorrow.

The next day was by far the toughest walk to work she had ever had, and people were constantly glaring and sneering at her.

A man spat on her face, followed by a woman who slapped her. "Selfish whore!" Kids sang songs, teasing her. The rest of the neighborhood joined in on the songs as she hung her head dejectedly and walked by.

With very little emotion, the man rasped, "Ma'am,..can I have some money?"

Laura gave him the same response, knowing fully that things would continue to escalate. "No, I do apologize, sir."

The homeless man nodded since he hadn't expected another answer. One person in the background yelled, "Of course the answer is no! She is a selfish whore! Die, you selfish whore! You suck!" The whole neighborhood began to chant this as Laura continued to head to work.

Once her day was over, she sprinted home, hoping to escape the criticism. As soon as she arrived home, she flipped on the television, but *every* program on was dedicated to bashing her. One program on the International Channel showed children at a birthday party, beating a piñata that looked like Laura, and was wearing a t-shirt that said "Selfish Whore Laura."

The next day she rushed past the teasing kids and the angry crowds. She ignored all of the insults as she walked toward the destitute man. "Sir? Here, you can have this." She reached into her purse and gave the man twenty dollars. "I'm giving you this, not because of all the bad things that have been happening around me, but because I sincerely wish you the best."

The man shed tears, and was extremely grateful. "God bless you, ma'am! Thank you!"

Laura then walked off to work in silence. No crowds, songs, or insults. Though all the feedback from the crowd had paused, she was fully aware that the people still wanted to say something negative. She shook the feeling away. She had done her good deed for the month.

The homeless man walked to the alley while nobody was looking. He ripped off his moldy clothing to reveal a three-piece suit underneath. He reached down and picked up his briefcase that was hidden nearby. The man chuckled to himself as he went to get into his limo. The driver then set off toward the so-called homeless man's mansion.

Three weeks later, Laura was homeless because she could not pay her rent, nor keep up with her bills that month. She appealed to her landlord's sense of generosity, and asked him to allow her to pay the following week, but she'd had no such luck.

Laura's belongings were promptly discarded to the sidewalk as the apartment was emptied. Her eviction was followed by getting mugged that night for the little money she had. She remained in the spot near the toy store where the homeless man had been, and to her surprise, he wasn't there anymore.

Laura surveyed the passersby, and asked in the same tone the homeless man had used, "Change, sir?" She was met with spit in her face. "You're the selfish whore who didn't give the homeless guy money all those times. Karma's a bitch, isn't it!"

Nobody stopped to give her money, and she avoided everyone because she was constantly bullied. Since then, the teasing had resumed, and she was again known by the world as "the selfish whore." Eventually, the manager of the nearby toy store that Laura used to frequently visit approached her. He furiously told Laura to stay away from the property because her very existence was detracting customers.

———

Tony, a ten-year-old grade-school student, entered the classroom nervously. He had to sneak past a group of bullies who were messing with and making fun of some random homeless lady. He did not bother to help save the lady, because his mom always told him not to talk to nor associate with strangers—especially if they were adults. Even though this was the case, he could not help but feel sorry for the homeless lady. She got bullied on a consistent basis by literally *everyone* in town. Being bullied was something he could relate to, especially since Tony was bullied so horribly last year. As of now, things seemed to be working out for him since the bullying had stopped. People were indifferent to him, and nobody made any negative comments to him or gave him disgusted looks. Over time, the other classmates came inside the classroom. Tony witnessed a new kid in class getting heckled by the usual gang of bullies. Tony thought to himself, *I used to be that kid a year ago. Those were the days.* He began to reflect on what he had gone through recently.

One year ago, Tony stood in the hallway in front of his locker.

"Hey, kid!" Tony stopped in his tracks when he heard the voice that he dreaded most. He turned around, and spotted a crowd of kids his age all gawking at him.

With anger and confusion, their leader said, "What the hell do you think you're doing?" Tony had to think about it for a moment like it was rocket science as he scratched his head. "Going to class?"

The leader eyed him up and down. "Your clothes are out of date! You know what we do to people like you?" Tony shrugged nervously as he tried to figure out what was going to happen. The whole group grabbed their victim, shoved him into the locker, and locked the door. Unfortunately for Tony it took a couple of hours for someone to realize that he was in there.

Later that day, Tony had gone to a department store.

"I hope this works. All I want to do is fit in." He observed the new clothes that he'd bought for himself. He felt very grateful he could remember the details of what the other children had been wearing earlier.

The next day when he went to school, Tony received the same reception as he had before, followed by another visit from the same group of bullies. The leader looked at Tony, and shook his head at him, motioning for the rest of the gang to grab Tony and take him to the bathroom. They gave Tony a swirly, and left him with his head in the toilet, covered in brown and yellow stains.

"Your shoes suck! Do something about them, idiot!" Regardless of this terrible treatment, Tony was going to fit in this time. He had made it his goal from the beginning of the school year.

The next day he bought the most popular shoes. He was thankful that he'd made enough money over the summer selling lemonade. He went to school again, but he still got the same treatment. Girls in the hall stared at him as though he was covered in putrid slime. Shortly thereafter, the same group of goons approached him. The leader sighed, and said angrily, "Dumbass!" They grabbed Tony, and dragged him outside where he was violently thrown in the dumpster. "Do something about your hair, kid!"

Tony got a buzz cut, just like many of the boys there. He went back to school and so far things seemed to be going well. Everyone was indifferent to him now, which told him that this time he'd gotten it right. He sighed in relief because he could finally relax, but over time the indifference began to get to him. It was one thing to be the bullied, but another for people to ignore him. Nobody acknowledged him except for the faculty. Tony walked up to his locker and saw that someone had left a note for him. The note said, "Dumbass! You wear glasses! Get contacts! Also, we're calling today 'Ignore the Dumbasses Day,' and that's you! Dumbass!

Tony was feeling rather depressed because he was still unpopular, and almost out of money. He'd worked so hard for it all summer. Tony puts contacts in before school. He went to school the next day, and what he saw shocked him altogether. Everyone was wearing nerdy-looking clothes. What had not changed was that people were still gawking at him. The group approached him with their leader, who spat on Tony's shirt and gave him a noogie.

"What the hell are you wearing, dumbass?! The fad has changed."

For the rest of the school year, Tony still got bullied and ridiculed. His attempts at fitting in were all done in vain, and he would have to wait until the next school year to give it another go.

Presently, Tony sat down in his desk.

He murmured to himself, "That was all in the past." He smiled innocently, and said confidently and optimistically, "This is a new year and everyone has matured, so things will be *much better.*" Tony's positive outlook was shattered as someone grabbed his head violently, and then bashed it against the desk repeatedly. The bully snickered. "What the fuck are you doing, dumbass? Talking to your imaginary friend, since you don't have any real ones? Things will *never* get better for you, dumbass!" All of the children started laughing at the situation. Even the teacher gave a little chuckle before she started class.

Ten years ago, in Harshtown High

A teacher paced back and forth in the classroom. He looked at his students, and said, "Does anyone disagree with what was said about conformity? Do you all agree that it is best for individuals to conform to what society wants, as well as to what individuals want?"

Rachel raised her hand. The teacher looked at her, and nodded approvingly.

"Teacher, the situation is not as black and white as it sounds. It really depends on the situation. I will use this as an example: Let's say that we have a grade-school kid who's being bullied on a consistent basis. For explanation's sake, let's name this kid Tony. Tony tries to conform to the the popular kids, but that does not work out no matter what he does. At that point, Tony should have just quit trying, and done things that made him happy instead."

Another girl, Milena, raised her hand. The teacher nodded. Milena cleared her throat.

"If the kid does that, then he will be unhappy. Tony will get bullied even more for being an individual. Since this is the case, he might as well just conform to everyone, and hope for the best. He will at least be able to make friends, and fit in with society."

"That is not always true. Just because a person conforms to the norm, this does not guarantee happiness. Studies have proven that a good ninety percent of people live regretful lives due to the fact they haven't been true to their own interests. Even if the kid continues to get bullied after refusing to conform, statistically he will be much happier than the ninety percent who simply go with what is expected of them."

"But, that's not..." said Milena.

The teacher interrupted the two students, and said, "Okay, you two made very good points; however, we must move on with the lecture."

Rachel was the new girl in school, but this was a situation she knew well, and even enjoyed. She'd grown up in a lower-income family who had always relied on their wits to survive. She'd always spent a lot of time traveling from place to place. No matter the situation, her family always adapted to change, and made it through.

Milena, on the other hand, had lived in Harshtown for a very long time, and was renowned for being quite spoiled. She was the kind of girl who always got what she wanted—by whatever means necessary. She had no problems with bullying people in order to get her way. Milena's personal philosophy was that the strong have the right to do whatever they want to the weak. Her family was wealthy and influential, so she never found that she had to do much more than demand.

The two girls, as well as three other students, were assigned a project to do together, which eventually had to be presented in the auditorium and in class. For the project, the group had to decide how they were going to make the world a better place. They were allowed to be creative.

The group gathered together in order to discuss what they were going to do for their project. Their team consisted of Rachel, Milena, and three boys. Milena, with confidence, started the conversation.

"First, we need to come up with an outline, and then we need to come up with a skit. After the skit, we need to come up with a visual presentation, and then we need to sing a song. After the song, we should show our cartoon."

The boys nodded in agreement as they took notes; however, Rachel had conflicting views. This did not stop her from being calm and polite.

"Wouldn't that be too excessive? I mean, we only have thirty minutes to present this. All of this would go way over our time limit, and it would detract from our grade."

Milena gave Rachel a fake smile, pretending to be polite, and retorted with uncertainty, "Yeah, yeah, I was thinking that, but I think we should time ourselves just to be sure that it stays within the time limit. My organizational skills are awesome, too, so don't worry about it." Rachel nodded at her, but inside she was still having some doubts, and she easily sensed that Milena was being phony.

The group had until the end of the semester to wrap things

up, and a couple of weeks had passed. They met up again, Milena began by happily giving them more of her input. She retained her slight wariness of Rachel as she spoke calmly.

"Okay, so my mother agreed to help us on the project. She said that she would dance with us, and her friends will join in on the dance! I think it's an excellent idea, and the more help, the merrier. Let's get the whole town to join in on our project."

Rachel sighed in disbelief, and shook her head. Was this girl serious? It was becoming increasingly difficult for her to hold her composure, and it was beginning to show in her voice as she attempted to remain polite. "It's just a school project, not a performance. That's too...excessive."

Milena went blank for a moment, and thought to herself, *Did she really just reject my idea?!* In a somewhat snarky voice, she replied, "But it *will* make the project better! We will not only be number one, but we will all get A's. Can't you see that?!"

Rachel lowered her head, and sighed. "Fine." The boys in the group nodded, and they presented what they had done so far. They were simply trying to do what they could to get by.

A few weeks later, they were close to wrapping it all up, and it was time for them to present their presentation in class. Rachel and Milena's group were the first ones called upon.

"Okay," said the teacher. "Show us what your group is presenting."

Rachel was about to start, but Milena butted in rudely.

"Okay, since I'm the leader of our group, I'm going to speak. Our project is going to have a bunch of visual effects in it. I decided that it was best that we trash everything we did. It just wasn't working. I figured that since my family is rich, we'd hire some celebrities to help me. I mean 'us.' First, we are going to have a circus performance, then—"

"Milena!" Rachel screamed angrily. "That wasn't part of

the plan!"

Milena glared at Rachel, and sneered, "It will help out a lot, and I have this covered! Leave it all up to me."

Rachel stepped to Milena. "This is a group project! This isn't all about what Milena wants."

The teacher broke them up. "Okay, girls. Calm down. We will get to your group another time."

Later that night, Milena was standing in her bathroom looking in the mirror. She brushed her hair.

"You are a pretty girl," she said to herself. "Everyone loves you. You are the best. Nobody is as smart as you are. All the boys like you. Your family is perfect. Everything about you is perfect. You are god-like"—she stopped abruptly as a hallucination of Rachel appeared in the mirror—"and *you* are an obstacle." Milena clenched her fist so tightly that it caused her palms to bleed.

A day later, it was now time to present in the auditorium. Milena and Rachel's group were the first to go, but there was dissension among the cohorts in the backroom.

Rachel spoke up first. "We decided to do the project as planned."

"What the hell?!" Milena stomped angrily toward Rachel. "All of the performers and celebrities are here! We are *not* doing this shit the original way. I said we were going to do it *my* way, so get that into your numbskull head!"

The door was opened by an upper-class female student who entered the room. All attention turned to her, which brought the argument to a halt. She looked at them nervously, feeling the tension in the air. "Oh! I apologize for interrupting! Have either of you seen a mace? And I'm not talking about the spray can mace. The mace that I'm talking about is a metal club like weapon that was used in the medieval times. It was a prop that was supposed to be used by the drama club for the upcoming play, but it has been missing all day. Have any of you seen it?"

The boys and girls shook their heads no.

"Ah, you haven't? Okay, well I apologize for interrupting. If any of you see it, then please return it to us." She closed the door.

Rachel said calmly, "As I was stating, we are doing it the original way. We did all the work for it and there isn't anything you can do about it Milena. Come and present with us. It will go very well."

Milena crossed her arms furiously. What was upsetting her even more was the fact that Rachel was so calm about the situation, as if this was nothing. It was apparent to her that her classmate was not taking her very seriously.

"Fuck you, Rachel."

Rachel let loose a sigh. "I understand that you are pissed off, but trust us. This will work out."

Rachel's last statement played in Milena's head on repeat. Her mind tuned everyone out, and she got to the point where she went blank, and she was motionless for a moment, like she was a mannequin. Rachel, uneasy, waved her hand back and forth, attempting to get Milena's attention.

The voice in Milena's head said, *"You are smarter than her. She doesn't know what she is doing. They don't understand! Your family is richer! Who the hell is she to you? She's a nobody. You are a goddess. Have your way because you are perfect."*

Finally, without any emotion, Milena said, an odd grin on her face, "Sure. Let's do this...partner."

The dissonant group began their presentation, and so far all was going well. Milena was the one who was supposed to present the visual portion of the presentation, but when her turn came, she didn't bother to turn on the overhead.

The group looked at each other, confused, as everyone else

in the auditorium sat in confusion. Milena gave an eerie, blank stare. Rachel started to move toward the podium to get her attention, but inched away when she noticed Milena twitching slightly as she was reaching for something inside the podium.

The boys in the group tried to get Milena's attention, but she just stood there for a minute. First, as a mumble, but progressively louder, she began to chant. "I...I...me...me...my...my... not yours...mine!" From inside the podium she pulled out the missing metallic mace. Rachel's eyes widened in confusion. The audience was just as confused, too. There was nothing but silence in the auditorium.

Most of the spectators thought this was a part of the presentation, and they sat and observed in anticipation.

"Milena, what are you doing?" asked Rachel. "Isn't that the missing prop? Put that away! That's dangerous! You could hurt yourself!"

Milena turned to Rachel. Her lips curled up into a sinister grin. She then rushed at Rachel, and attempted to bash her with the mace as hard as she could. To Rachel, it was as if everything was moving in slow motion. Her mind refused to comprehend the current situation. At the last second, Rachel dodged sideways, but her shoulder sleeve got ripped apart in the process. Milena barely missed, and bashed the wooden floor so hard that she created a hole where the mace came down. She immediately began to try once again to bludgeon Rachel, but she barely missed each time.

Rachel was moving by pure instinct now. She could not believe that this was happening, and did not understand why. A few people in the crowd applauded the performance that was happening in front of them. Once her mind had accepted the current situation, Rachel yelled frantically, "Help me! Someone! Anyone! She's gone mad!"

Her "acting" earned her more applause from the crowd, as well as whistles and more anticipation. After more frantic ducking, rolling, and dodging, Rachel jumped away from the stage, and ran outside of the auditorium since she was obviously on her own, despite having that many nearby witnesses. The boys in the group were fully aware of how dire the situation was, and they sprinted away from the stage in order to find the nearest security guard.

Milena gleefully chased Rachel while the sound of applause could be heard from behind. Unfortunately for Rachel, the hallways were empty, and most of the classroom doors were locked because it was after school hours. She attempted to look for a place to hide until help came, but she couldn't think straight due to the stress of the situation. She heard the sound of glass shattering.

Milena was breaking every window she passed by with the mace as she continued to hunt for Rachel.

"I...I...me...me....I...kill you...break every bone in your body! Not yours...mine! Get back here! How do your insides look? Let me see!"

Rachel finally found a classroom that was unlocked. She hastily opened the door, closed it behind her and locked it, and went to hide under the teacher's desk. She began to cry, and she prayed that God would come through to save her from this demon. The sound of broken class got louder and louder until it stopped near the room Rachel was in. For a moment, there was nothing but silence. Rachel continued to pray. She held the cross that was tied to her neck as she trembled. A moment later, the glass to the classroom door shattered, and Milena reached inside to grasp the door handle to unlock the door. She opened it, and gently closed it behind her—like the well-behaved student that she was. She held the mace against her right shoulder, and slowly paced around.

"Rachel, I know that you're here. I can feel you."

Rachel remained silent and motionless.

"Rachel? Where are you, my dear friend? We have a little disagreement. You said that the plan wouldn't work out. Let's talk like usual."

Silence. Disappointed, Milena slowly left the classroom. After a couple minutes, and after she'd regained her courage, Rachel crawled out from under the desk. To her dismay, however, she saw a pair of sneakers in front of her. She looked up to see Milena, grinning gleefully, holding the mace.

"There you are," said Milena.

"Milena! Please don't do this! We can do the presentation your way. It's not too late. You can still have your way," Rachel pleaded.

Milena slowly raised the mace. "I'm sorry, dear friend. We are way past the bargaining stage now. All that is left is acceptance. After all, that is the last stage of death, just like we learned in class." Milena raised the club like weapon to deliver the mortal blow.

Rachel cringed, shielding herself, and screamed, "Noooooooooooo!"

Several seconds later, a huge thud could be heard. Rachel slowly opened her eyes, and saw that the security guard had come through. Milena had been restrained and was on the ground, unarmed. She attempted to break free to lash out at Rachel like a rabid dog, but the guard's hold was too strong. The boys in their group rushed inside of the classroom. Soon afterwards they escorted Rachel, who was shaken up, out of the classroom.

Ten years later, in the present, in the Harshtown Correctional Asylum, Milena stared blankly at the ceiling, tugging thoughtlessly at the straps of her jacket. Her room was quiet, bright, and warm. She smiled, as she imagined that the light shining down from the ceiling was a spotlight. She heard a roaring noise from outside her door, and believed it to be the cheers of adoration from her millions of fans.

"I...I...me...me...my...my...I'm beautiful...I'm smart...I'm the best...I know everything...everyone loves me...I'm rich..." This replayed in her head day in and day out.

———

Jamaal listened intently to the music coming through his headphones, and sang along. He danced as he waxed the battered hall floor. It was a good thing he'd found this temporary opening at the Harshtown Correctional Asylum as a custodian. Money was getting tight, and things had been looking a little bleak after all the money he'd spent on schooling.

"Whew!" He slumped in a nearby waiting-room chair. "Finally done."

He saw her in her room from behind the door, and he asked the other worker, "What's up with her? What does she have?"

"She has IeyeMemee Syndrome. People get it when they let their egos get the best of them. It used to be a rare disorder back in the day, but nowadays it is becoming much more common."

CHAPTER TWO

MICHAEL SAT ACROSS FROM HIS COLLEAGUE, Jerome, in the break room of the Harshtown Counseling Office. They were both counselors. Michael held his forehead, and shook his head.

"I don't know if I can get to her, Jerome."

Jerome gave him a curious look. "Who? Are you talking about Milena?"

Michael nodded. "Yeah. During our counseling sessions she constantly lashes out at me for no reason. I always need a guard to help ensure that the sessions proceed safely. When she's in her cell, she has these psychotic delusions of grandeur and fame. Out of the ten years that I have been a counselor, I have never had a patient that has been as troubling as her. I seriously do hope that Milena has a speedy recovery, but I feel as though I need counseling myself just from working with her."

There was a brief silence between the two men. Feeling conflicted, Jerome stirred his coffee with a slim, red straw, and pondered over his colleague for a moment. He desperately wanted to warn him about something, but he did not want to add to the stress that Michael was already feeling.

Michael flipped through a few notepads in preparation for his upcoming session. Jerome had had this feeling for a while about a young man, who was the most recent arrival. It was only fair that Jerome, being the veteran of the facility, give Michael fair warning.

"Man, I know we are professionals, and we aren't supposed to say this type of stuff—and I know that you are having problems—but that new patient that you are watching is crazy! And just when you thought Milena was bad. This one is the icing on the cake! I'm sorry for bringing this, man."

Michael took a sip of his coffee, and was very intrigued to hear the story, but was also very reluctant because Milena was enough as it was. "Oh? Tell me, how so? I seriously need to know."

"He used to be one of my clients, and he was an ex-con. He's gotta be on some type of shit, man, only"—he sighed— "he never mentioned anything remotely reminiscent of a history with drugs. He keeps mentioning crazy stuff about police and society. It doesn't even make sense. None of it does! I'm just glad he's in the insane asylum right now."

Michael stared at Jerome, who was obviously shaken. There was an awkward cloud of silence that lingered, as Jerome gazed into his steamy drink.

"Well," Michael urged, "Out with it. Seems about as heavy as the cream in your coffee. Maybe I can help. Just because I'm having a hard time doesn't mean that I'm giving up on the job. Get on with it."

"All right." Jerome cleared his throat. "It started three months ago."

Three months ago, in Jerome's office, Jerome sat behind his desk while listening to his patient's story.

"That's what happened, sir—or at least what I can remember. It keeps coming to me like a bad nightmare."

Even though Jerome was a counselor, and was supposed to

remain neutral, he could not help but feel that this man was nuts. He attempted to keep a straight face, but failed. This whole time he'd been looking incredulously at his patient, Jason, as he jotted the details of his unbelievable story down.

Jerome said confused, "So, Jason, you're saying that in this nightmare, that some woman ran you over in her car, got out, and was worried about the damage that had been done to her car."

He continued, barely able to conceal a chuckle. "And that there were witnesses who were also concerned about the car damage, and they left you there in the intersection for an hour. You were robbed, urinated on, and you heard a camera click."

Jerome shook his head in disbelief as he continued down the list of complaints. "After all of this, you were arrested by an 'Officer Lives' on the claim that you vandalized the woman's car. You were sent to prison on false accusations and locked up for five years for no reason?"

Jason sighed. *Finally*, he thought. *This guy finally gets it!* Jason wiped a tear away from his eye. "Yes, that's what happened—at least that's what seemed like happened."

Jerome saw that their time was up. "A good intro session," he said to Jason, "but we will have to schedule a follow-up for next week."

A week later, during the second session, Jerome said,

"That isn't how the reports go, Jason. The report says you vandalized the woman's car, and traumatized her. There were witnesses present corroborating her claims." Jerome tapped his pen against his plastic clipboard.

"What are you trying to say? Say what you mean!" Jason scooted forward in his chair, anxious and visibly irritated.

"Meaning that, Jason, you aren't remembering this clearly." Jerome straightened up in his chair, and cautiously set his paperwork in his lap. "It is very possible that the scenario is just an illusion in your head that you created as a coping mechanism over the guilt that you feel about your crime."

"Are you fucking saying that I'm crazy?!" Jason banged his fist on the desk furiously. "Because I'm not, man! I have that same dream every night, over and over again. I know that is how it happened, and nobody gives a damn!"

Jerome faked a smile, and nodded, despite his increasing nervousness as Jason continued on with his rant. He eyed the door, hoping for an intervention.

"You seem just like the rest!"

"I'm here to help you, Jason." Jerome stood, and extended his hand that was slightly trembling. "I apologize that I offended you."

Jason scoffed at him, refused to shake the counselor's hand, and left the office, slamming the door behind him.

Jerome jotted down in his notes afterward that his patient had anger management problems, was very unstable mentally, and probably shouldn't be around the general public.

A week later, during the third session, Jerome has stated, "Jason, I apologize again for the last session."

Jason's eyes remained focused on the floor, and he shrugged a slight acceptance of the apology.

Jerome took out some cards, and held them up. "Here in my hands are some random cards. I want you to tell me the first thing that comes to your mind when I show them to you."

Jason looked at Jerome, and nodded.

Jerome presented the first card, which had on it a picture of a speeding car. Jason twitched, and quietly muttered, "Car."

The next card that was shown had a picture of a police officer on it. Jason rolled his eyes, and grunted, "Corrupt officer."

Jerome then showed him a final card, which was a picture of

a green, glowing traffic light. Jason, having grown increasingly irritated, didn't respond.

"Jason, what word comes to—"

"This is stupid, man!" Jason knocked the cards out of Jerome's hands. "The only thing that this is doing is reminding me of that day! You're supposed to help me, and all you're doing is making it worse for me, dammit!"

Jason stormed out of the office, enraged, spewing profanities as he left. Jerome walked out into the office corridor, and explained to everyone that his patient was having a psychotic episode. The workers nodded their understanding, and then diligently went back to their work.

A week later, during the fourth session, Jason sat angrily glaring at Jerome.

There was an uneasy silence between the two of them. Jason decided to speak up first.

"You're lucky that I decided to actually come back after what happened last session."

"Exactly what happened, Jason?" asked Jerome. He was attempting to use reverse psychology, and he was determined to make this work. The main thing this attempt earned him was an angry stare.

With just a thread of composure left, Jason said, "You know what the hell happened!"

Jerome remained calm. "What I did, Jason, was show you some cards, and then you had another psychotic outburst. Do you remember?"

There was silence again. Jason continued to glare at Jerome.

"Perhaps my methods weren't so effective. I've thought of another exercise we could try. This time we will work with random audio that I've pieced together. You can tell me what you think after hearing it."

Jerome puts a CD in a small stereo, and shortly after he pushed the play button. The first sound that popped up was the sound of a car coming to a screeching stop, and then hitting something—or someone.

That was enough for Jason, who rapidly got up and pounced on Jerome. He punched Jerome in the face as hard as he could. Jerome pushed the button behind his desk to call for security. The security guards rushed inside the room, and they immediately pried Jason off of Jerome, who was terrified, and then knocked Jason out with a club. The guards asked for an explanation.

"That dude is crazy, man!" said Jerome. "I tried to help him out but he just attacked me for no reason." Jerome showed the guards his notes on Jason.

Present day

Jason was in a cell that happened to be next to Milena's. He could hear her constantly chanting, "I...I...I....me...me...I'm pretty... everyone likes me...I'm rich...I'm the best...everyone likes me, including the guy next to my cell!" Jason yelled angrily, "Shut the fuck up!" Once it had died down, he just stared blankly into space. He had been there ever since the incident with Jerome, and was strapped to a chair, unable to move.

Michael approached Jason's cell door. He opened the door with his key, then he briefly reflected on what Jerome told him. He looked at Jason, and simply shook his head, making a note to transfer Jason to the block with the highest security. If it was true that this guy was worse than Milena, then putting him there would be best for everyone's sake.

Dear Jason,

I do not know of your circumstances, but I wish you the best. I will pray for you every day, and I sincerely hope that you have a speedy recovery. I understand that we live in troubled times, but if you persevere, then I believe that everything will work out for you. Enclosed are some items that I hope you appreciate. They consist of a few books that you may find entertaining and enlightening.

Sincerely your friend,
Cecil

Cecil placed the letter inside of the box that contained many books he used to read. They were primarily self-help books and fantasy novels. He closed the box, taped it up, and then dropped it off at the post office. Cecil cared deeply about helping out the world. It was not uncommon for him to do volunteer work, as well as help out those in need. He found an outreach program in which he could help out the mentally unstable. The patient Cecil had been partnered with was a young man named Jason. Even though Cecil sent him letters and gifts, he had yet to receive a response from Jason.

After Cecil quit his job at the toy store, he signed up to be a guinea pig for scientists because he was desperate for money. After a week of enduring experimentation, he found a much better job because of his skills dealing with the general public, as well as his education. Even though this was the case, Cecil attended a lot of counseling sessions due to the built-up stress that retail work—and Tim—had induced. The first counselor that Cecil had confided in had given him a bad feeling. Even though Cecil had been explaining to him about his hardships, Cecil always got the vibe that his very own counselor thought he was crazy. It didn't take him long to end the sessions, and find a more competent professional.

Cecil and his friends were currently all coworkers for a non-profit organization that specialized in helping out the needy in whatever way possible. They had all been working together for a couple of years now. Every night he had a reoccurring dream, but dismissed it as a mere coincidence. Over time, Cecil began to feel that his dream was a message from God. It always started out with him on some type of mountain top, seeing visions of poverty-stricken people, and himself, along with a bunch of others, helping them out. They were doing this in some type of recreational building, but how he had attained the resources to build this place was beyond him. Most recently during his vision, a feminine voice had given him directions on how to manifest his dream into reality. Due to his drive, the visions resonated with his core beliefs.

The next day he and his friends were assigned to work together on a project. They were required to figure out new ways to help the needy, as well as what demographic to focus on. This was perfect for him, and he saw this as his call to finally act.

After the meeting, Cecil was thinking to himself. "It all makes perfect sense now," he muttered.

A couple hours later, he and his friends gathered together to talk about ideas for what needed to be done. For now, Cecil just listened to their input. Most of the ideas that they had were dismissed by Andrew, who simply laid back in the recliner while eating potato chips. The only thing he said was, "Nope, that wouldn't work." *The slacker usually doesn't contribute to any work efforts*, thought Cecil. Honestly, if it weren't for his friends, he wouldn't even have a job right now. Cecil decided that it was best that he waited a little longer. So far they had all been going around in circles trying to think of ideas—except for Andrew, who just sat there.

A day later, they gathered together again to actually make some progress for a change. Andrew was back in his usual position, except this time he was eating candy. Cecil stayed silent as he lets his friends continue to debate, but it still didn't go anywhere. After they ran out of ideas, he decided to finally make his move. First, he talked about the recreational center while repeating everything that had been in his dreams. Everyone simply listened in silence, including Andrew. Cecil told them that he had seen this in a vision that had come to him every night. Everyone was silent, in awe, until Andrew decided to put in his two cents at last.

"This vision that you have sounds like b.s., and this plan that you're talking about wouldn't work anyway, but I guess it is worth a try. It's the best idea that we've thought of so far. When it fails, I'll laugh in your face."

A week later, it was time to present the info to their boss. Since it was Cecil's idea, he decided that he would do the talking. They all met up in the conference room, where the boss glowered at them dubiously.

"Okay, tell me what you got. And this better be good, or else you're all fired!"

Andrew rudely interrupted Cecil before he could speak. "Okay, so this is what I came up with..."

Cecil didn't have a big problem with Andrew speaking until he'd started telling the boss Cecil's vision was his, and not giving any credit to Cecil. In addition to the boss's rudeness, Andrew's actions were also causing tension in the room.

"Brilliant! Absolutely brilliant, Andrew! How did you come up with this idea?"

"This may sound strange, but I had this vision every night for the past couple years. At first I didn't believe it, but due to current events, it started to make sense. I am just doing my duty to the community, and I am doing God's work, sir."

There was still silence as Cecil's friends looked at Cecil, expecting him to say something, but he stayed silent. He was shocked about this, and thought to himself, *What am I supposed to do? Why aren't you talking? Is this part of plan?* He received no divine guidance.

"Do we need a lot of people to help with this?"

"Nah, the lackeys that we have here will be useful for a change." *Nothing? Nothing?!,* thought Cecil. His friends all started to make excuses to leave the room. They didn't appreciate being considered as worthless lackeys. Cecil was the last one to stay, because he was still expecting for the voice to guide him. But there was nothing. He was left in silence, even after everyone had left. *Why didn't you give me the words?! Did you give me all of those visions just to see me crushed in the end?*

Later that night, Cecil received constant phone calls from his friends—except from Andrew. They were all having their doubts about following through with the project, and many of them wanted to quit their job. He didn't blame them, because he felt similarly. Andrew had been on Cecil's mind all day, so he decided it was best to just call him and get it over with.

Seeing it was Cecil calling him, Andrew reluctantly picked up the phone knowing that this could get nasty. "Hello?"

"You betrayed me! Why did you do it?" Cecil began to sob. "That was my vision—not yours! You took all of the credit for yourself, you fat bastard! You fat, lazy, good-for-nothing bastard!"

Sarcastically, Andrew retorted, "But I *did* come up with the idea! You told your story! I thought about taking credit for it because I know for a fact that I can do better than your stupid vision. And now it's going to work out my way!" He laughed, and then hung up on Cecil.

The next day, Cecil approached his boss, and explained that he could not be a part of the project, and put in his two-week's notice. The boss tried to talk him out of it, but failed. Cecil explained the whole situation about Andrew, including him stealing Cecil's vision, but the boss chose to remain neutral.

"You have been a good and loyal coworker, but I honestly don't care about that. All I care about is helping the needy so that we can profit off of them some day. That's how many non-profit organizations function. We appear to look good, gain popularity, take money from giving bastards, then keep ninety-eight percent of it for ourselves. This is a job, and you need to keep personal issues personal. I don't fully agree with Andrew's methods, but I'm not going to punish the guy for what he may or may not have done."

Over the next two weeks, Cecil didn't say much to anyone. He simply observed everyone in the background while Andrew did his thing. Cecil's friends also quit their jobs and moved on. Andrew didn't seem to care—he mainly cared about what was to come.

A month later, it was rumored that Andrew hadn't been able to pull off the project, and not only had he lost all of his assets, but he'd also lost all of the company's. He was fired, and nobody would hire him. Andrew would end up standing next to the rich homeless guy, asking for some change, but unfortunately for Andrew, people always showed the imposter more charity.

———

Tony opened the front door. He spotted a girl who was wearing some type of scouting uniform and was holding a box of cookies. She appeared to be the same age as him; however, they were clearly in different classes. The girl smiled innocently at him.

"Hello, sir. Would you like to buy this box of cookies and donate to the Little Charitable Seekers?"

Tony scratched his head, and shook his head no. "No, thanks. Mom told me to never donate to charity organizations since only two percent of the money ever actually helps out the needy. She said that if I really want to help someone, then I'm better off giving to the needy in person or doing volunteer work."

The girl looked at him, and pleaded, "What? But we *are* helping out the needy! I don't know what you're talking —" Tony instantly and shamelessly closed the door on her without giving her a chance to finish.

"Now, to business," he said to himself.

The boy then headed upstairs toward his room to watch movies. Some time later, Tony had finished watching the movie *Bully Tactics*, and afterward he watched a similar movie. Once that was done, he continued to watch more and more movies related to bullying, including videos about kids who had been victims of bullying. He learned about cyber bullying, physical bullying, and emotional bullying. Despite the fact that what he had in mind may not have had to do with cyber bullying, Tony felt that it was important to gain as much knowledge as possible. Last year, Tony had been a victim of bullying, because he hadn't been able to fit in no matter how hard he had tried.

His mother peered at him as she walked past the room. "Tony, I noticed that you have been watching a lot of movies related to bullying."

He smiled, and nodded. "Just learning about bullying, Mom."

"That's good. Being a bully is wrong, and no matter what happens, bad karma comes back to them. It is very good that you are very much against it, my boy."

Tony nodded again, but the truth was, the reason why he was watching these videos was because he wanted to become what he feared. He wanted to become the best bully who had ever existed, since just fitting in hadn't worked. Running his peers and the school would be a new experience for him, and he expected it to be very rewarding. In addition to the videos, for the past few weeks, Tony had been practicing bullying tactics like he'd been practicing martial arts.

"I wish there was a bullying sensei." Tony grinned to himself. "Maybe I can become a grandmaster of bullying and start my own dojo!"

The next day, he went back to school with a new attitude and outfit. He wore a leather jacket that had a picture of a skull on it, and to advertise the grandmaster look, he wore a fake black belt.

"Nobody can mess with me! I own this joint! I'm the best around! Nobody's gonna ever keep me down!"

He felt like he was invincible as he cooly walked with a very mean look on his face. The leader of the gang of kids who'd bullied Tony in the past, a guy named Lee, approached him. He was confused as to why Tony was trying to look like a tough guy.

"Hey, dumbass. What the fuck is up with you? You better get rid of that mean streak before I kick your ass again!"

Tony thought for a moment of what to say, as the movies came to mind. "Suck it"—he thought of the movies again—"bitch!"

"You're gonna get it dumbass!" Lee scowled, and swung at Tony, who quickly dodged the punch. He countered by grabbing Lee's arm, and then locking it. Afterwards, Tony gave him a super noogie. The rest of the kids observed in awe as Tony bullied Lee, and shoved Lee into the locker like he was trash.

"Amateur!" He paused for a moment, and thought to

himself, *I'm the real deal!* Pretty much everyone left him alone after they saw and heard about the event.

After school, Tony was about to board the bus, but was stopped by Lee and his gang.

"You caught me by surprise that time, but this time I'm ready, and I got my friends!" They all attempt to jump Tony. One guy swung at the bully *grandmaster*, but Tony dodged, grabbed him by the back of the head, and shoved his face into the dirt.

"How does it taste, bitch?!"

Lee angrily tackled Tony, but the bully-in-training reversed it, and screamed. "Wet willy time!" Tony then licked his own index finger, held Lee's head down on the ground, and began to shove his wet finger in Lee's ear. A third guy grabbed Tony, and pulled him off of Lee. He tried to choke him, but Tony elbowed him in the gut, which caused the guy to loosen his grip. Tony quickly gave the guy an atomic wedgie, and shoved his face into the dirt. The final guy tried to kick Tony, but Tony grabbed his foot and tripped the guy. He gave the guy an atomic wedgie as his reward, and then dragged him into the bathroom, and gave him a swirly.

"I run this joint! There is a new bully in town, and his name is Butch! Remember my name, and respect it, bitches!" yelled Tony.

The next day in class, to Tony's surprise, he was considered a hero, even though he'd tried to become a bully. People applauded him as he walked through the doors. He was approached by Lee and his gang a minute later.

"Hey, Tony. You probably think we want revenge." Lee looked defeated and looked away from Tony in shame. "But the truth is...we respect you. You said that you were the best bully, but you haven't bullied anyone yet. We would like to teach you how."

Tony thought about this for a moment, and then finally agreed. Lee and his gang taught Tony how to become an even more vicious bully. For a month, he had gleefully been verbally and physically abusing people. He became feared pretty fast after not showing mercy to anyone, and bulling whenever he wanted. Even Lee and his gang were afraid of him, and they were his friends now.

A week later, a new kid joined the class. He was very small, and appeared to be feeble. Tony had even heard that this kid had some type of disease. The weirdo also wore glasses, had diabetes and asthma, and his name was Kenny. He was a very shy boy, which made him a very ideal candidate to Tony. But to Tony's surprise, he was the one person to ever consider bullying him. Even Lee and his gang didn't touch the kid, because they really pitied him. Tony approached his fellow delinquents casually.

"Hey, Lee, this is the plan. We'll jump Kenny at lunch, then take him into the bathroom. We'll then give him a noogie, an atomic wedgie, a swirly...and then we will take his inhaler away from him!"

The thought of this caused the whole group to cringe. "Dude, we pass, man. We are gonna take a little break from bullying."

This disappointed Tony. "Suit yourselves, wusses."

In the hallway, Tony watched his prey as he put stuff in his locker. He quickly approached the kid, and grabbed him while covering his mouth so he wouldn't scream. Once he'd forced him into the bathroom, Tony gave Kenny a mischievous look. Kenny looked at him in confusion.

"You are the new kid. Let me introduce myself. My name is Tony, but everyone calls me Butch, and I run this joint! I am the toughest and meanest kid there is. You are fresh meat, so it's time to get your initiation beating!"

Kenny continued to look at him, befuddled, as if what was being told to him was in another language. Tony grabbed him, and was about to force his head in the toilet, but to Tony's surprise, he was overpowered by Kenny, who effortlessly resisted getting his face plunged into the turd-infested bowl. He then gave a confused Tony one very hard elbow to the stomach, which caused Tony to double over and loosen his grip.

The roles were reversed as Kenny gave Tony, the bully, a swirly. The smaller boy states gleefully and proudly, "And they call ME the bully killer!" Kenny lifted Tony's head out of the toilet bowl, and then punched him very hard in the stomach, later accompanied by a noogie.

Tony was then given an atomic wedgie, and afterwards, he was thrown out of the bathroom and into the empty hallway. Kenny punched Tony in the face repeatedly, causing the bully to back away. Tony was in a daze. The primary thing that his broken mind could comprehend was the fact that he was in pain and desperately needed help. However, the help did not come. Eventually, Tony was thrown out of the front door. He began to cry. However, this was just the beginning, as Kenny rushed outside with a baseball bat in hand. Kenny slammed Tony into a nearby garbage can, closed the lid, bounced the garbage can as if it were a basketball, and then threw it up in the air with amazingly strange strength. Kenny clenched the bat with both hands as he looked up at the airborne garbage can. Once the timing was perfect, he hit a home run with as much strength as he could.

"Bat 'er up!"

Several hours later, the rest of the events that happened seemed like a dream to Tony. He couldn't remember all of the details, but the beatings went on for about an hour after the home-run hit. He lay in the hospital bed in bandages, crying in despair. Clearly his plan to become a bully hadn't worked out. The doctors and nurses chuckled at him since they'd had to nurse many patients that had come in as a result of his bullying. They gave the bandaged and broken Tony very poor treatment. His mother sat on Tony's other side shaking her head in shame.

"My son, where did I go wrong raising you?" She sobbed.

———

In a retail store that sold clothes and sporting goods, Hector stood behind the cash register. He spotted a small boy in front of him who appeared to be of grade-school age. The boy shyly approached the register, and asked Hector curiously, "Umm, sir, umm....umm....do you sell bats here?" The boy held up a bat that was splintered and broken in two. Hector assumed that this kid must be one heck of a baseball player. "I broke this yesterday at, err, baseball practice."

Hector chuckled. "You got quite the batting arm there. What's your name, kid?" The boy smiled, and swayed back his hair, "My name is Kenny, and I do have quite the batting arm, indeed." Kenny's expression darkened slightly.

"Well, Kenny, we have all types of bats. I'll show you if you like." Hector showed Kenny to the bat section. Kenny browsed through the merchandise until he spotted a silver bat. He picked up the object, gazed at it in awe, and then gave it a few test swings, batting the air a few times as hard as he could. Hector could feel the wind from the swings.

"Woah, kid! Pardon my language, but you are one hell of a bat swinger! You could probably go pro!"

Kenny smiled, looked at Hector, and nodded. "Thank you, sir. I would like to purchase this."

Hector escorted the kid to the cash register, and finalized

the transaction. Kenny paid for the bat, and observed it again with wonder.

"Sir, do you have a marker that I can use?"

"Sure, kid." Hector handed Kenny a marker from behind the counter. Kenny took it, and began to write on his bat. When he'd finished, it had the words "B. Slayer" on it. He handed the marker back to Hector. Kenny looked at Hector one last time, then told him thank you.

Kenny left, holding his new silver bat. A few seconds later, Hector was approached by his supervisor, who was named Marpha. She yelled angrily at him, "I saw that transaction! You sold a weapon to a minor!"

Hector sighed, and said, "Marpha, it was a baseball bat! The kid was going to use it for baseball practice, not to assault anyone!"

"Well, whatever! I'll let it slide this time. Be more mindful of your transactions."

Not too many people enjoyed working with Marpha because she was so worrisome all the time. Coworkers always complained about her, and it wasn't purely because she seemed to be addicted to stress, but also because she was very incompetent. Many of the staff were baffled over how she was able to become a department supervisor in the first place. Hector was the only person in the store who could tolerate her, and he remained open-minded, understanding that nobody was perfect. He saw the good in her whenever he recalled the times they had had serious and casual conversations.

Several days after Hector had assisted Kenny, Marpha quickly approached him, a concerned look on her face. Hector sighed, wondering what he'd done wrong this time.

"I heard that you got fired from your last job."

"Yes, I did get fired, Marpha. I even explained this issue to

Rachel, who hired me." Hector continued to work diligently. This wasn't the first time that he'd been through this, and it certainly wouldn't be the last. "Based on the conditions and what happened, she decided to hire me regardless, and she placed me on a thirty-day trial. I exceeded her expectations, and she decided to keep me full time. I have been working here, and with you, for five years now. Five years! This conversation is completely asinine."

"Well, you should have told me this before." Marpha paced back and forth, still unconvinced. "How can I trust you as a worker? What else did you lie to me about?"

"I didn't lie about anything, and I have been very dependable and reliable. You are blowing this *way* out of proportion."

"I'm going to keep an eye on you just in case you act up." She headed back to her office.

The next day, Hector was approached by Marpha, and he was already getting the same vibe off of her as he had yesterday.

"Hector, you were supposed to empty all of the crates."

This confused him, as he recalled emptying every single one of them.

"I did empty all of the crates," he said.

She immediately grabbed one, and opened it.

"Look at this! You see all of this dust inside? What if the dust got carried into the air and caused Josh to choke? You know that he has asthma! What if the dust builds up, and goes into the ventilation?" Unbeknownst to Marpha, she had attracted a small crowd behind her as a few customers observed the whole incident like they were watching a dramatic play.

"What if the door to the stockroom were open and a customer saw this? For that matter, what if quality assurance saw this?! Then we would all be without a job. What then? If that happens, what would I do? What if I lost my home, and what if

I lost my whole life's work?"

Hector stopped paying attention after the first two "what ifs." He continued diligently working, since he'd learned how to selectively block her out a while ago. It took a lot of time and patience, but he'd eventually mastered it. The whole process was as simple as choosing "select all," and then pressing "delete." She stormed out, continuing to complain about the whole situation since it was clear that Hector could care less.

A few days later, Marpha had gone on her vacation, much to Hector's relief. However, he'd been called into the main office by a supervisor, and was somewhat unnerved. Since she was gone, the day had been peaceful in the store up until now. He walked into the office to see the irritated looking supervisor who was handing him the phone. Hector was curious as to who would call him on a busy day like this, thirty minutes before the store closed.

"Hello?"

He heard a loud voice in his hear, saying, "I hear that you called out sick two days ago right after my shift!"

What the hell? She was supposed to be on vacation! "Yeah, I had a cold. I didn't call out sick, though, I just came in an hour late because I was at the doctor's."

"Why couldn't you do it on your day off? What if Craig had needed your help?"

"I have never been sick before until now. I didn't know what was happening to me until it happened."

"Now I see why you got fired from your last job! Also, why didn't you tell me that you had to come in late? I need to be fully aware of what is going on, Hector! I am the boss, and any slip-ups could mean a major disaster." Hector hung up the phone, as Marpha continued on, oblivious.

Days later, in the parking lot of the store,

Marpha's vacation is finished as she walks through the parking lot ready to start her shift. The woman panics as she sees rocks on the ground.

"Oh, no! Someone could trip over these and hurt themselves, and then sue the company!"

Marpha quickly picked them up and tossed them into the grass. Afterward, the supervisor walked up to the door, and noticed that the sign was missing a letter.

"False advertising! Better hurry up and put an 'O' up there!"

She swiftly rushed inside, complaining to the ones working at the front desk that the sign was messed up, and instructed them to fix it. Marpha went to her department. The first thing she saw was her most loyal worker assembling a display. She rushed to him, seeing a hammer in his hand.

"Stop, Hector! You could hurt yourself, and then you could get worker's compensation."

He rolled his eyes at her, and went to find something else to do. *Here she goes again! God, it's too early for this.*

Marpha saw something else that caught her attention, and she rushed to a display near the elevator exit.

"What if someone stumbles on that?"

Marpha quickly sets it away in a fit. Hector stopped what he was doing, and approached Marpha. His annoyance was replaced with major concern. He wondered why he hadn't thought to say what he was about to say when he'd first met her.

"Marpha, you need help. I don't mean that in a disrespectful way, but—"

She rudely cut him off as she tended to another issue.

"What if those kids break the display! I need to fix that fountain before someone passes out from dehydration! Do we have enough money to do that? What if the company goes bankrupt?! Then I will have to find another job! But the economy...

it's messed up! What if I can't find a job? Then I will have to sell my things! But what if I don't make enough money? That would mean that I would have to move in with my parents! But what if they don't want me there?"

A week later, Marpha sat in Jerome's counseling office as he wrote down notes while counseling her. He noted that she was very sane, and fit to be around the public. He also felt that the one who recommended she get help was probably the one who needed counseling.

"Marpha, you seem like a very intelligent woman that has it together. You don't have any mental disorders."

This caused her to smile, and thank him. She shook his hand, and he returned the favor, then resumed writing his notes.

"Marpha, a suggestion I have for you is to fire the guy who got you here. It's obvious that he doesn't know what he's talking about, and should be the one seeking counseling."

Marpha kept Jerome's advice in mind, and fired Hector the next day.

———

In a convenience store, Hector said happily to the clerk, "Oh, wow. Even though I got fired, it looks like everything worked out in the end. It looks like I came in third place in the lottery! I can start my own business now, and not even worry about being fired over crappy football teams or counselor recommendations. Thank the gods! Time to cash in this winning ticket!"

"Congrats, man," said the convenience store clerk. "Maybe I'll work for you. I feel like I'm being underpaid."

A nearby business woman looked at Hector with an expression of disgust, "It must feel nice to *not* have to work hard for what you have, and receive government handouts instead"

"Excuse me?" asked Hector.

"You heard me, you dirty thug. You have no right to complain, especially since my tax money is paying for your livelihood Must feel good to live off of government cheese while us real citizens have to work for a living. How many kids do you got? Five? Seven? Eight? All from different mothers?"

"I have a college degree, ma'am. I have no children, I'm single, and my GPA was a 3.5. I majored in business management. My family consists of a bunch of hard workers."

The woman chuckled.

"Right, like I'm gonna believe you. You have a problem with what I'm saying? You gonna call your homies? You don't intimidate me, punk!"

The woman rudely bumped Hector out of her way like he was nothing, set her goods on the counter, and gave the clerk a condescending stare. "This will be all, sir. I don't want to be here any longer than I have to be."

The clerk looked at Hector, who simply shook his head. Hector decided to just let it go. The clerk rang up the woman's merchandise, and bagged it. "Thanks for shopping with us, ma'am."

The woman took her belongings, and walked away. As she left, Hector and the clerk glared at her.

"Wow, what a bitch," said the clerk. "She went off on you for no reason."

"Tell me about it. I'm just gonna let it go."

The business woman's name was Marisol, and she was the CEO of a company known as Mirrors Service, Inc. She had had a few bad days at work because of a newly hired executive who had been slacking off.

An hour later, In the CEO's office of Mirrors Service Inc, Marisol ranted to her receptionist named Rachel.

"She doesn't do any work. Every time I see her, she'd either sitting around, or is doing something else."

Marisol paced back and forth, ticked off. The corporation was in shambles, and she had finally found out why.

"I took this woman under my wing because I had only heard good things about her. She does average work, and I could get an Average Joe anywhere I want. I don't need an Average Joe, I need a key player!"

Rachel twiddled her fingers, sighing as she thought of an explanation.

"There must be some type of logical explanation for this. How about you give it more time? She hasn't been here for very long, and perhaps she is just adjusting."

"All right." Marisol stopped pacing. "Maybe you're right. It has been a couple weeks after all." Marisol turned to Rachel. "On a side note, you seem to be down. What's the matter, if you don't mind me asking? Still having PTSD over Milena?"

Rachel looked away. "At my other job, a friend of mine got fired for practically no reason. He gave the supervisor some advice, and in return she fired him for it. Her excuse for firing him was that he'd sold a minor a weapon. The truth was that our store doesn't sell weapons, and my friend simply sold a baseball bat."

Marisol reflected on this. "I see, well feel free to take the rest of the day off. I can't have my receptionist mentally exhausted."

The new executive they'd taken on was named Fatima. Rachel recommended that Marisol take her on, but so far, it appeared that things weren't working out. Mirrors Service Inc. was in heavy competition with similar companies. They all agreed that whichever company came out number one in sales stayed in business, while the others would just quit altogether, thus creating a monopoly for the winner. So far they were in second place out of the four companies, but it wasn't good enough, because they still had a year until the competition finished.

Marisol noticed that the only thing that changed was that all of the executives, except for Fatima, had been doing more and better work. Fatima pissed Marisol off because she couldn't just fire Fatima since she technically hadn't done anything wrong. She decided to go check on Fatima, who was sitting back, reading a magazine. Marisol clenched her fists in anger, but was able to hide it just in time.

"Fatima, how are things here?"

"Production is going splendidly, and we aren't too far behind first place." She turned a page in her magazine. "Just a little bit more sales, and we are good to go."

This behavior told Marisol that without a doubt, without this underachiever, the company would be in first place. This was good to know. If she couldn't fire her yet, then she needed to force Fatima to quit her job.

Marisol started by lowering her hours down by two every week. She heard no complaints from Fatima, because Fatima was fine with it since it meant more time to spend with her family. Marisol was determined, so she checked out the production, only to notice that they had been slipping toward third place now from first. She'd anticipated this because of laziness, so Marisol picked up the slack. Eventually, Jamaal the full-time janitor, approached her one day with words of wisdom.

"Hey, boss. Why is it that Fatima isn't working as much as she used to? I miss her company, and now she is thinking about working for one of our competitors."

Marisol barely hid her smile at this information.

"She doesn't do too much work. Honestly, we are better off without her. If I hired anyone else, we would be in first place right now."

"Based on what I've seen, boss, I don't know about that. You may want to make her happy. Don't you see the pattern? The unhappier that Fatima is, the more that the company sinks to the bottom. It started when her hours were lowered."

"What the hell would you know?" Marisol chuckled arrogantly. "You're just a janitor! If you actually went to school, and worked hard, you wouldn't be in this situation. I'm not going to take advice from some underachieving loser."

Jamaal threw his broom at her, which caused Marisol to stagger backward. "What the fuck would you know about hard work?" he yelled. "You know what? Fuck you and fuck this job!"

He stormed off, pissed over his stupid boss and his unfair life in general. Marisol was in shock, but at the same time, she could care less, because saw him as an uneducated and underachieving janitor. She could hire another one just like that.

A few days later, Marisol walked into Fatima's office to see her playing a golf game on her computer. Marisol didn't care at this point, because Fatima had already put in her two-week's notice, and was going to work for the company that was in last place. Fatima would be out of a job, as well as one of their competitors. Marisol was going on vacation tomorrow. Fatima nodded as she continued to play on her computer, carefree.

A week later Marisol returned from vacation to find out that her company was now in last place—ever since Fatima had left. Marisol had a conference meeting with her remaining executives to find out what had happened. She was thrown off guard, so she listened silently to their input.

"Ever since Fatima quit the job, everything has gone downhill. She was the major key player. She kept the morale of the company up, ensured that everyone got their work done, helped everyone out, and even helped out that janitor who quit, Jamaal."

"Yep, she told us so much about the competition, and she was a very hard worker. What the fuck were you thinking when you made her quit?"

The executives waited for a response from Marisol, eyeing her like vultures. Just hearing them confused her even more, because she'd always seen Fatima doing other things. Everyone in the conference agreed that lowering Fatima's hours, as well as forcing her to quit and join the competition, was by far the worst move that Marisol had ever made. Along with that, they agreed that Marisol was not fit to manage the company, since she could never see the full picture of any situation.

There was one month until the competition was over. Marisol worked very hard to pick up the slack, but it just wasn't working out at all. Everyone was unhappy, and the company just constantly kept sinking deeper and deeper into the hole. Meanwhile, she found out that the company that Fatima was working for was in first place. When she got home that day, she watched the news and saw Fatima was now the CEO for her new company.

Marisol was in complete shock over this, and to add to this, Jamaal, the janitor that used to work for her, was Fatima's vice president. She found out that he had a Phd, as well as military experience. *My janitor is more educated and talented than I am?* she thought to herself.

Six months passed and Mirrors Service Inc. was now out of business. Fatima bought the building and renovated it. She then hired Marisol as the janitor. Based on what Fatima had seen and researched, as well as her interactions with Marisol, she thought that would be the best career fit for her. Fatima was aware that Jamaal was very talented, and since Marisol could only see what was in front of her, Fatima knew Marisol was terrible at recognizing talent—even when it was right there. With all of this factored in, without a doubt Fatima was convinced that Marisol's career should have been as a custodian from the start.

———

"Do you see that lady over there, Carmen?" Carmen's mother motioned to a female janitor. The janitor appeared miserable as she diligently did her work. A business man, who Carmen recognized as the vice president, approached the female janitor. He stated calmly, "If you had actually gone to school, worked hard, and done something meaningful with your life, then you wouldn't be in your current situation."

The female janitor scowled at the vice president without saying a word. The vice president left in a fit of laughter.

"Everything he says is true," said Carmen's mother. "Fortunately, you won't ever be in her situation, because unlike her you take your life seriously. There is something else that concerns me that I'll talk about when we get home."

Carmen sighed, because she knew exactly where this was going. The two left the building after finishing their errands.

Later, at home in the living room, her mother said to her, "You need to make some friends, Carmen! You are ten years old now, and you still haven't made a single friend yet. You need to get your act together! If your father were still alive, then he would feel ashamed of you. You are disgracing our family by not integrating yourself within society!" Carmen's mother glared down at her daughter. She was sick of hearing the same excuses over and over again.

"I'm trying, Mom, but it isn't easy! Nothing is ever easy for me! You never understand me—just like everyone else!"

Carmen had always been the black sheep in pretty much

everything she did. She had problems relating to people in general, which caused her to feel like she should have been born on another planet, or in another century. She tried so hard to become friends with her peers, but either they bored her, or they thought she was crazy. Not many understood where she was coming from.

After her argument with her mother, Carmen went to the park. She played by herself since she had already tried to become friends with everyone that was present. *These kids are a bunch of morons*, she thought to herself. After boredom set in, Carmen sat down on the bench, and sighed. She spotted a boy who she'd always considered a nimrod, sitting on a bench.

The boy's name was Tony, and the two were in the same class. He was covered in bandages, and he looked extremely depressed. Carmen chuckled to herself, and muttered, "Bullied the wrong kid, eh? Serves you right, nimrod!"

A few minutes later, to her surprise, another girl who was wearing a Little Charitable Seekers uniform, approached her, and offered to sit next to her. Carmen agreed, and the two began to talk for a very long time. The girl's name was Eliza, and she and Carmen had a lot in common. She was a very smart and gifted girl, just like Carmen. The two had had the same problems, and they had the same interests and hobbies. To Carmen, it was like meeting a long-lost sister.

Over time, they started to spend a lot of time together. Carmen's mother was proud that her daughter had finally found a friend, and was no longer a disgrace to the family. Carmen couldn't have cared less about how her annoying and stupid mother felt. The primary thing she cared about at this point was her own feelings. She became so obsessed with Eliza that Carmen came to have lots of pictures of Eliza in her room. She even created a shrine and dedicated it to Eliza.

Several weeks later, in Carmen's room, Carmen had been talking to Eliza on the phone for several minutes. She tried to talk Eliza into allowing her to visit her house, however, the conversation was not going well. Eliza stated, "No, I'm sorry Carmen, but my cousins are coming over, and only family members are invited." Eliza hung up the phone after saying goodbye.

Hearing this news shattered Carmen, because she'd always been welcomed to visit her best friend.

"I don't care! Does she consider me family? I might as well be her sister! I'm going."

Carmen needed to be around her friend, so she headed over to Eliza's house. She rang the bell, and shortly after Eliza's father opened the door.

"Carmen, what a surprise! How can I help you?"

Without any hesitation, she said, "Eliza invited me over, so now I'm here."

Eliza's dad asked Carmen to wait while he talked things over with the rest of the family. In the background, there was a debate whether to allow Carmen in or not, and eventually, they agreed to allow her inside. The visit wasn't what she expected, since Eliza wasn't giving Carmen her full attention. Instead, she was playing with her cousins, but this didn't deter Carmen. She kept making her presence known. Even though it was acknowledged, her best friend would go back to playing with her family, which caused Carmen to become pissed off. She left the house, and became even more pissed off when she thought about the fact that, for the past few days, her friend hadn't been calling her like she normally did, and it was beginning to drive Carmen insane.

A few days later, after school, in the gym, Carmen called out to Eliza, "Eliza! Hey! I haven't heard from you in a little bit, so I figured we should hang out." Carmen gave Eliza a hug, accompanied by a smile.

"Carmen, I didn't expect to see you here." Eliza returned the hug nervously.

"You decided to play in the gym, and you didn't invite me over? Oh well, we can hang out right now."

"Carmen, I felt that we needed some time apart. We have been spending a lot of time together, and I need some *me* time."

"'Me' time?" Carmen looked around as she observed the other children. "Looks like you are playing with other kids. Well, whatever. I'll be right here when you want to chat."

Eliza nodded, and went back to what she was doing. What irk Carmen was that the kids who Eliza were playing with were the ones who wouldn't give Carmen the time of day. The situation had been like this for a week. Carmen would make herself part of Eliza's world whether Eliza wanted a companion or not.

A couple weeks later, Eliza's birthday was approaching, and Carmen was invited to the party, much to her relief. She spent Eliza's entire birthday party around her, no matter what. Even when the birthday girl's other friends had wanted to interact with her. Carmen had made it clear to them that this was *her* friend. Later on that day, Eliza finally decided to confront Carmen about her behavior.

"Carmen, I appreciate you as a friend, but you really need to back off. I need my space, and you being like this is really killing me."

Carmen twitched for a moment, but decided that it was best to remain cool. "I'm sorry if I did anything to offend you, and I'll do as you advise."

To everyone's surprise, Carmen left like nothing had happened, even though many of them had heard what had gone on. That night, Carmen said a prayer to Eliza's shrine.

"I will do what it took to make it all work out. I shall do this for your best interest. I shall do this for my best interest. In the name of Eliza, Amen."

Sometime later, Eliza had been missing for a week, and the police had looked everywhere, but there wasn't a single trace of her. Eliza's parents were devastated, as well as her friends. Surprisingly, Carmen was taking the news well, because according to Carmen, she and Eliza weren't friends anymore, and Eliza hadn't wanted anything to do with her.

She calmly spoke to an officer at her front door.

"Officer, she was my best friend, but she was too clingy for my tastes. She may have played it off like I was the clingy one, but she was always in my face." Carmen began to sob. "Everywhere I went, she was there, too. It was all right at first, but I just needed some alone-time, and she would never give it to me."

The officer tried to comfort her. "Yeah, I can't stand people like that. Usually those types of people have never had friends, and are probably better off locked in the crazy house. I apologize that you experienced something so terrible, but look at it as a learning experience."

Carmen nodded, and shortly after, the officer left. She closed the front door, and made her way to her room. Carmen took one of her dolls from her toy box, and then said a brief prayer to her shrine. She then left her house, went to the forest, and into a cave. Eliza was there, where Carmen had tied her to a chair. She was crying, her mouth had been gagged, and she was emaciated. Carmen placed the doll on Eliza's lap.

"It is best this way. We can be friends forever and ever, and I will always know where you are. Also, you don't have any say in this, do you?"

CHAPTER THREE

JEROME WAS WALKING HOME, feeling very proud of himself. He had helped out another client and had done another good deed. He recalled Marpha's advice. On the way home, he spotted a missing-person poster. Curiously, Jerome observed it, seeing a picture of what appeared to be a young girl wearing a Little Charitable Seekers uniform. Jerome mentally read the words.

The girl's name is Eliza Jones. She is an eleven-year-old that is also a fifth grader that has been missing for weeks now.

Jerome sighed, and shook his head. He wiped a tear from his eye, and slowly walked away from the poster.

"What a shame," he muttered to himself. "A little girl getting kidnapped like that..." *I will stay on the lookout. There are so many problems in this society, and many people can be so crooked and evil. Thank goodness I chose to be a counselor*, he thought. This reminder at his profession lightened his mood. *God, I love my job. Thank goodness being a counselor pays well, too. Not only do I get to help people get their lives set, but I also get a hefty paycheck.*

His plans for the rest of the day were to get back home and spend time with his wife and children. He had been spending a lot of time at work ever since he'd been dealing with Jason's case. To Jerome's relief, that scoundrel was in the Harshtown

Correctional Asylum where he belonged.

Unfortunately, Jerome's car was down, but it wasn't a big deal to him, since his job wasn't that far away from home. He didn't even need to drive there since it was a ten-minute walk. Jerome stopped at the nearby convenience store. He talked to the lackadaisical clerk before retrieving some things to take home. Jerome didn't pay too much attention to his surroundings, and he wasn't aware of the shady people who had just entered the store. Suddenly, one of them pulled out a gun on the whole store.

"This is a robbery! Stay calm, give us all of your belongings, and all will go well!"

Jerome swiftly rushed to hide behind one of the aisles. One of the robbers approached, pointing a gun at him.

"Give me your wallet! Now!"

Jerome knelt before the shady man, trembling. "Please don't rob me, sir! I have a wife and I have children at home! Rob them instead! I'll give you my address! I even have a hell of a lot of money at home! Just leave me alone! Do whatever you want with them! Sell them into slavery, rob them—just don't hurt me!"

For a moment, the robber was silent in disbelief over what he had just heard. Then he burst out laughing. "You're pathetic! You would sell out your own family just to save your own hide? Hey, gang! Get over here! You won't believe this!"

He grabbed Jerome and threw him down on the ground where the other robbers were.

"Please! Spare me! Don't hurt me!" Jerome began to sob. "Like I said, I have a wife and I have children who you could rob instead! My mother also lives nearby, and she has some valuable things you could steal!"

Jerome was a pathetic, laughing stock to the robbers. The

customers were confused, wondering who the true villain in the situation was. The leader didn't care very much. He asked Jerome directions to his home address, as well as to Jerome's mother's house. Jerome quickly told him the information without hesitation. To Jerome's relief, the robbers decided to spare him, but they robbed everyone else and left.

"Thank god!" Jerome sighed in relief.

The police arrived shortly after the robbery to question everyone. Jerome explained everything that had happened, except for the part regarding his family. He didn't feel ashamed of what he'd done, but covered it up based on self-preservation. Since his life was pretty much ruined thanks to the robbers, it was time for him to move out of the country to start over.

Rather than head home right away, Jerome waited to see what happened. He waited patiently for a phone call, but there wasn't one, so he decided to suck it up and just head there. When he arrived, everything was intact like nothing had happened. His wife and children wondered where he had been. After he spoke with them, he visited his mother's house. It was the same—her house was intact. She was happy to see him since he didn't visit her very often. Jerome returned home, and proudly explained the robbery situation.

"We were robbed at the convenience store. They didn't rob me, because I saved the day. As a counselor, I talked them out of robbing everyone, and I talked them into changing their lives."t

The children began to cheer, calling their father a hero. His wife was impressed as well, and she was glad to have married Jerome. Over time, everything seemed normal, except for the fact that Jerome had given a different testimony from the other witnesses. It wasn't too big of a deal to the cops, and as weeks passed, even this became increasingly minor over time. The cops couldn't find any leads, and the robbers had left no evidence of their arrival or departure. There wasn't even a fingerprint—it was like it had never happened.

Two months later, Jerome headed home from work. When he arrived, what he saw shocked him. His home and his mother's house were not even there anymore. The spaces where the homes used to be were empty. There were a bunch of cops trying to figure out what had happened. Unfortunately, it had happened so quickly and so efficiently, nobody saw the act or who had done it. Jerome wasn't sure what had happened at first, and then it hit him later on—it was the robbers from before. His wife, children, and mother were missing. Maybe the robbers had decided to keep them as slaves or something—or worse. Jerome whistled.

"Oh well, it happens. I'm still alive, and that's what counts."

He quit his job two weeks later, and then prepared to move out of the country to start over. This time he wouldn't make the same mistake again, which was to leave some of his money in the house.

———

In a classroom, at Harshtown Elementary School, Kenny approached his friend Marcus.

"Hey, Marcus. I think we should do our project on that recent story."

Marcus gave Kenny a curious look. "Huh? Which one?"

"You know, the one about the guy whose family disappeared."

"You mean the same guy who was caught up in that robbery at the 96-69 that's a few blocks from here? Jerome…I forgot his last name, but I know who you're talking about."

Kenny nodded. "Yeah, that guy."

"Sounds like a good idea. I heard that one of his kids went to our school, but now he's missing, just like that Eliza girl. We probably should cover that story, too. A lot of strange things have been happening in town," said Marcus.

Kenny and Marcus had been friends ever since Kenny had enrolled in Harshtown Elementary School. They always sat with each other during lunch time, and on the bus. The best friends would talk and walk with each other in the hallways between classes. Kenny always wanted to visit Marcus outside of school. Kenny would always allow him to visit, but it would never happen the other way around. Every time Kenny would try to talk Marcus into allowing Kenny to visit his home, Marcus would find some way to change the conversation. One day, however, Marcus' parents asked to have Kenny over. Kenny thought it was about time, and was glad he would finally get the chance to spend time with his best friend at his house. He was very excited about this, and he definitely wanted to make a great first impression.

Kenny gets dressed, and packed up all of his games. He was going to spend the whole weekend at Marcus's house. An hour later, he rang their doorbell. A tall and strong-looking man with a crewcut opened the door, and greeted Kenny with a wary stare. Despite this, Kenny remained kind and excited.

"Hello there! My name is Kenny. I am Marcus's best friend! Are you his dad? Is your name Mr. Tank?"

The man narrowed his eyes as he nodded at Kenny. In a very deep voice, he said, "Yes, I'm his dad. So you are Kenny? I expected you to be more...well behaved than this, but I'll give you another chance. Can't judge a book by its cover."

Kenny was confused as he thought to himself, *So much for the first impression. What did I do wrong? I greeted him kindly, just like my mother always told me to.*

They walked into the hallway and up the stairs. Kenny saw a lot of military-related things in the house, like plates with flags on them and model combat planes.

"How did you meet my son?"

Kenny was filled with confidence and pride. "I saved him from a group of bullies! They call me the 'bully killer' at school, and I wasn't going to let him get pushed around, Mr. Tank!

The only thing that this earned Kenny was a sigh from the big man, who continued to narrow his eyes. His dad seemed to be having a hard time maintaining his composure. "We will need to have a talk tomorrow morning. It is late, otherwise I would do it now."

Marcus's father knocked on his son's door. Marcus opened it, and he was wearing a chicken suit. Kenny began to laugh at his best friend, because he looked so ridiculous in it.

"Marcus! Why the heck are you wearing that?! You look stupid!"

Marcus gave Kenny a covert look, trying to signal to him to stop laughing, but Kenny couldn't help it. The whole situation was hilarious to him. Marcus's father closed the door, grumbling about terrible youth in society who hadn't been raised.

Marcus sighed in relief. "Phew! You got off easy!"

Kenny's laughter was replaced with confusion. "What did I do wrong? And why are you wearing that?"

"I was bad today. I accidentally misplaced one of the plates in the kitchen on the table by half an inch."

Kenny gasped. "You got in trouble for that?! And you have to wear a chicken suit because of it?"

They weren't able to continue their conversation, because Kenny was suddenly called downstairs.

Marcus's father had his arms crossed, looking down at Kenny. He had a serious expression on his face.

"Kenny, I understand that you come from a different family that has a different value system, but so far the only thing that you've shown me is utter disrespect."

"What did I do wrong, Mr. Tank?"

"For one, since I am your elder, you need to address me as 'sir.' Not doing so is very disrespectful. Second, you need to ask me permission to speak. You can't speak to me whenever you want to! That is also disrespectful. You need to say, 'Sir, may I have permission to speak? If you can't say 'sir,' then say 'master,' 'führer,' or even 'czar.' Also, once you are done saying what you need to, say, 'I am finished, my superior elder.'"

Kenny was completely dumbfounded, and was having a hard time believing what was happening.

Dinner was terrifying. Kenny constantly had to ask for permission to take a bite of food, and had to do this before every scoop of food. Not only that, but he also had to chew his food quietly, and at the same time as Marcus and his father, in perfect rhythm. Due to his disrespect earlier, Kenny had to wear a pink chicken suit for the rest of the night. Marcus seemed pretty calm about the whole situation since he had been living it his whole life. It was no wonder to Kenny why his best friend always wanted to spend the night over at Kenny's house.

Nervously, Kenny asked, "Sir, may I have permission to speak?"

"Yes, you may, cretin."

"When do I meet your wife? I am finished my superior elder."

"She will be here tomorrow morning. You will get the pleasure of meeting her. Right now she is locked in the basement where she belongs. Once I leash her and let her out for a walk, and then to make breakfast, you will see her."

Before the disappearance of Jerome's family, Jerome was having a conversation with Michael in his office about parenting. Jerome asked, "Michael, do you think that there is a such thing as being too strict?"

Michael looked at his colleague. "In what sense?"

"Let's say that I know someone who's overly strict with his children, in my opinion. Do you think that being strict can be detrimental?"

Michael pondered this for a moment. "I don't have any kids. However, a system in which the children do not have a voice can be very detrimental, in my opinion." He then chuckled. "But of course I'm talking about text-book definitions. Like I said, I do not have any children, so I do not have any personal experiences. It really would depend on the family, because not all families have the same value system. What works for one family may not necessarily work for another, and vice versa. Alternatively, there are many functional-dysfunctional families if that makes sense."

Jerome reflected on this. "Thank you, Michael."

"No problem."

Five minutes later, a group of mental health doctors in a counseling room were ready to witness the impossible. Michael had worked extremely hard with Milena ever since she had become a patient. He was the last one who hadn't lost hope with her, even while everyone told him to just give up. At times, it felt like no progress had been made—until he finally got her to crack.

In a professional and confident voice, Michael said, "All right, Milena, tell them what you told me." Milena lay in the recliner, looking at everyone. She took a deep breath.

"The world...doesn't revolve around me. I may come from

a rich family, but I'm no better than anyone else. Trying to kill Rachel at the school was a horrible way to handle the situation, and she had every right to question me about the project. I'm... sorry," Milena said nervously.

There was silence in the conference room for a while. Everyone was in complete shock over this breakthrough. The silence was then replaced by applause, which caused Milena to smile. She didn't let this go to her head, however, because she had been completely humbled by her experience.

A week passed, and Milena was no longer a patient in the asylum. She had been released, and was allowed to go back to her home to start things over.

———

Presently, in the break room of CJ Pickles, four female coworkers were gossiping with one another.

"I hear that she actually lied about being cured, and is plotting to kill everyone who got her locked up in the first place!"

"Yeah! I hear that at home she needs to be locked in a cage, or else she'll shank people!"

"Rachel better watch her back! She's waiting for the perfect moment to strike! She better protect her family, too."

"Yep, shit is going down soon."

Rachel walked into the break room. Normally, she didn't like to eat her lunch there because of all the gossip, but the last few sentences she'd heard caught her attention. At first she was upset over the fact that she was being talked about, but she tried to keep her cool.

"What are you all talking about?" Rachel asked.

It was Marpha who had been talking this time, which was no surprise to Rachel since Marpha worried about everything.

Except maybe this time what Marpha was worried about was actually relevant. Rachel heard that Marpha had received counseling, but it must have been a shitty counselor if Marpha had been told that she was perfectly fine, and was told to fire Hector—the best employee in the store.

Marpha turned to Rachel, and her nervousness gradually became more apparent. "You didn't hear? Milena isn't locked up anymore...and she is coming for you!"

Rachel, curious, paused as the memories of what happened to her in high school resurfaced.

"M—M—Milena...is out?" Rachel asked.

"Yes! She pretended to be normal, but she lied. She is plotting to get revenge on you! I'm surprised you didn't even know this. She has been out for a little over two months now. Probably got herself reestablished at this point. Her parents died while she was locked up, so she inherited all of their money. She doesn't even have to work...like the rest of us."

Rachel wasn't convinced about this. *They are just being morons again. Might as well carry on*, she thought to herself.

At home, however, she decided to conduct some research on Milena. She began to see that Marpha and the other buffoons may have been right. The psycho had been out of the asylum for a couple months now, but Rachel had no idea where Milena lived. Suddenly, out of the blue, Rachel began to worry for her family. Not only was she in possible danger, but her family could also be.

"What if they are right? Then that means I will have to protect myself—and them! I'm not going to take any chances."

She attempted to warn her family, but they weren't convinced of the danger since there was no physical proof.

A few days later in the break room, Marpha approached Rachel.

"Rachel, I found out where Milena is living. You remember that abandoned haunted mansion in the creepy woods near the hazardous mountain? That's where she is!"

"Why the hell would she stay there? That place is supposedly cursed."

It took a moment for Marpha to come up with a logical reason. "Think about it! It is far away from people, there is a lot of room inside to plot whatever is she is plotting, and nobody would dare to go there."

Rachel had to see this for herself. After work, she nervously drove to the mansion. She didn't get too close to avoid being spotted. Rachel approached the place quietly, and fortunately for her, it was night time, so Milena wouldn't be able to spot her very easily. Rachel snuck toward a window that had a source of light coming from it. Based on what she could see from the outside, the room must have been a kitchen. She heard Milena speak to someone. Rachel didn't hear another person speak to Milena in response, so either Milena was having a psychotic break down, or she was talking on a phone.

"The score will finally be settled between me and Rachel. Her family is going to get it, too. That's good! I want the packages sent to her whole family! I want them to all know that I'm very serious about this, and I don't want to leave any stones unturned, The children will understand, too! Don't forget about all the people who were present that day when I tried to kill her. They are going to get theirs, too."

Rachel was alarmed at this point, and she realized this was all the proof that she needed. Rachel left hastily after having heard enough. Rachel told her family what she had heard, and fortunately some of them were convinced. The majority of them just went on with their lives, and they dismissed the whole thing. Rachel went to the police to explain the situation, but because she didn't have any physical proof, they weren't able to do anything about it. A cop did watch over her for a couple of weeks, but since nothing happened he stopped. Rachel would have to take matters into her own hands. She took a class in how to use a gun, and now kept a gun with her at all times. She thought to herself,

You may have missed bashing my skull in all those times back then, but I won't give you a chance to correct the situation. Also, I won't let you hurt my family.

Weeks have passed, and yet nothing had happened. This hadn't stopped Rachel from staying on guard, as she continued to remember the conversation she'd heard Milena having, as well as what Marpha and the others had been saying for some time now.

One day, as Rachel was walking home from work, she paused when she saw a familiar figure. It was Milena, dressed very professionally.

Milena just stood there looking at Rachel with a very serious and determined look.

"This is the day when that tragic incident happened. You still remember, correct? I tried to kill you, but you kept dodgin' and dodgin'."

Rachel glared at her. "Of course I remember! How could I forget? You haunted my dreams every night for a year! And here you are again! Coming to finish the job?"

Milena grinned. "Indeed, this incident has been a thorn in the side for all of us—now it's time for me to do what I should have done from the start!"

Milena reached into her pocket. Rachel swiftly pulled out her gun, and shot Milena once in the chest. Milena, a shocked look on her face, slowly collapsed.

The last thing she said before she lost consciousness was,

"I...I...I'm...s—sorry Rachel"

Milena dropped what she had had in her hand. There were witnesses who observed the whole thing in shock. Many of them pointed at Rachel so there was no confusion as to who shot the unconscious woman on the ground. Rachel saw a box, which was accompanied by a letter that had dropped from Milena's hand. Rachel opened the letter, and reads:

> *I'm sorry, Rachel. I didn't know any better when I was younger. I was spoiled rotten, and I only did what I was raised to do. If I could go back in time, I would have stopped myself. I sent this letter to your whole family, as well as this necklace. I hope that we can be friends someday, but if you don't want to be, then I understand.*

From triumphant to emotionally devastated, Rachel opened the tiny box, and saw that inside was a heart-shaped necklace made out of pure gold. It must have been worth a lot. Rachel was in complete shock, and she sank to her knees.

"This isn't happening! I went home today, put all of my stuff away, and went to sleep. I woke up the next day and I went back to work. Milena never got out of the asylum. Nothing unusual happened." She chanted this over and over again out loud and in her head, even while the police sirens gradually became louder.

Fortunately, Milena was able to recover from the shot since it wasn't fatal. Rachel was placed in jail, but the police felt that it was more fitting to leave her in the insane asylum. Rachel was now in the cell that Milena had once occupied. The fantasy world that she lived in carried on as if the incident had never happened.

—

A day after Milena's release from the Harshtown Correctional Asylum, Jason sat, feeling bitter, in the hallway, his head low.

"So...she finally decided to get out," Jason said to one of the other patients.

The patient nodded. "Yeah. I think she was feigning insanity for five years now. Don't know why she chose to remain here. Probably the guilt of her crime made her feel like she deserved to remain locked up. I guess she finally decided to forgive herself and tell the truth."

"She was the sanest person in this joint. Even saner than all of the people who work here."

"Yeah, tell me about it. Milena will be missed. Whatever ego trip that she had, has been long gone. Lately she has been such a peaceful, compassionate, and self-sacrificing woman. This place won't be as bright without her. Her encouraging words have helped me pull through."

Jason looked up at the clock, and then stood up. "Well, it looks like it's time. I'll see you later, dude. Unlike Milena, I have been trying to convince people that I'm sane, but nobody believes me, except for you and Malik. Speaking of which, our meeting is soon. He said he has some really important things to say to me."

Ten minutes later, in the recreational room, Jason paced back and forth as he spoke to his friend. Jason has said, "I didn't do it. People keep on saying that I'm crazy, that I got what I deserved, but I know for a fact that I didn't do it. I tried so hard to convince myself that they are right, but deep down inside, it just doesn't feel right."

Jason sat on the ground with his back against the wall. He was with a different patient, who had become his best friend. They had been talking for a while, but this was the first time that they had ever talked about this. His friend, Malik, was here due to similar circumstances. The difference was that Malik used to be a true criminal. He told Jason that he was the best thief to have ever existed, and could get out of any tight situation—including this asylum. As a matter of fact, he said, escaping the crazy house would be easy for him. When Jason questioned him about escaping, Malik had previously said that the reason he chose not to was because he had no desire to leave and start over just yet. Malik said he was in prison because he was betrayed by his cohorts who wanted all of the loot for themselves. He was put in prison because he preferred this scenery, and he pretended to be insane. His plan worked perfectly since the cops in Harshtown were so quick to transfer their inmates to the asylum.

"I believe you. Jason. We have been friends for months now, and we are the only sane people here. Oh yeah, Milena is sane, too, but since she finally revealed that she is, she was released yesterday. I feel ready to leave this place, and I want you to come with me. I can teach you the trade, and we can both start over and become richer than in our wildest dreams. In this world you have to take what you want, but there is a code you must follow."

Jason felt like he'd just won the jackpot.

"How can I turn this down? You are my best friend, and you can count me in! If the world wants to believe that I'm a crook, then I might as well live up to the name."

An hour later, Michael was in the counseling office. He had worked very hard with Jason ever since he had come to the asylum.

"Jason, what have you learned during your time here?"

Jason didn't bother looking at him. To some degree, Michael reminded him of Jerome, except that his methods were actually effective at times. If it weren't for the fact that Michael sided with Jerome, the douche bag, then they could have been friends. Jason laughed at the question.

"What have I learned?! I learned that society is bullshit! The only thing you hacks care about is making money and going home. You are all a bunch of yes-men who, deep down inside, don't give a shit about anyone but yourselves. I'm not gonna bother telling you what happened to me, because you already made a conscious decision about my situation. I'm also sick of pretending to be insane just so I can get back to my cell! I hope you remember this, because this is the last session that we will ever have, motherfucker."

Jason wasn't worried about Michael figuring out what he and Malik had planned, since Michael would probably just think Jason was having another psychological outburst. This time, however, Jason's words did actually move Michael a little. He hadn't written anything down in his notebook. He just sat in his seat, in awe.

Over time, Malik taught Jason the art of stealth and thievery. He even taught him his code of honor, which was not to kill, and to only hurt out of self-defense, if possible. Eventually, the time to escape came upon them. Midnight approached, and Malik managed to steal the keys from one of the security guards. When there was nothing but silence, he opened his cell door, and then snuck over to Jason's and opened his. The two snuck quietly to the basement area. Malik had used anti-camera spray on himself and his cohort. He was able to smuggle the spray, and trick the guards into thinking that it was just hair spray. The spray allowed the two to appear invisible to the camera.

Jason wondered how it was possible for a spray to cause someone to appear invisible to cameras, but Malik wasn't going to tell him all of his secrets just yet. The only thing that Malik had told him was that a scientist had given it to him for a price. This was just too easy for the two of them, and Jason thought how foolish it was of him to think it would be difficult. The security guards were either asleep, or were focused on something else, but things didn't get tricky until the two finally arrived at the basement.

There was a sewer lid in the room. Jason knelt down to it, and placed his hand on top of it in an attempt to open it. He instantly shrieked in pain.

"What the hell?! It's burning hot! How the hell do we expect to escape into the sewers if we can't even open the lid?! We're fucked!"

Malik was calm about the situation. He didn't respond right away.

"Man, I should have known this was a bad idea," Jason said. "We did not anticipate this at all."

Malik told Jason to hush. He'd heard someone else heading to the basement. It was the maintenance man, who walked over to where the sewer lid was because he'd been scheduled to make sure that it wasn't loose. The man was about to take out one of his tools in order to open the lid, but he wasn't aware of the two men hiding behind the shadows. Malik tackled him, and put him in a choke hold until the maintenance man was unconscious.

Malik dropped the man's body, and grinned. "Right on time. All right, let's open this, and escape."

Malik used the man's tools to open the lid, and then the two escaped into the sewers. Nobody noticed that they were gone until the next morning. It was just like Malik had said, escaping the joint was nothing but child's play. Michael was even more shocked about his last session with Jason, because he was warned that this would be the case. Every day, Michael wondered if what Jason had told him was true—had Jason been convicted of a crime he hadn't committed? If this was the case, then Michael would have to live with the fact that he'd failed to help someone who was innocent.

A week passed after they'd made their great escape from the asylum. Jason, Malik, and a few others were trying to find the perfect store to rob as a practice run. Jason saw a familiar figure cross the street and enter a convenience store. It was Jerome, and as the memories began to surface, Jason wanted to beat the guy to a bloody pulp for being part of what ruined his life—but Jason took Malik's code seriously. He must get revenge on Jerome in some way, however, because he couldn't just let it slide. Jason pointed at the convenience store.

"All right, let's rob that place."

They all agreed with him. They parked, and then entered the store. The gang had all decided to let Malik do all of the talking.

"This is a robbery! Stay calm, give us all of your belongings, and all will go well!"

Jason saw Jerome rush to hide behind one of the aisles. Jason approached him, and pointed his gun at him.

"Give me your wallet! Now!"

Jerome knelt before Jason, trembling. "Please don't rob me, sir! I have a wife, and I have children at home! Go and rob them instead! I'll give you my address! I even have a hell of a lot of money at home! Just leave me alone! Do whatever you want with them! Sell them into slavery, rob them—just don't hurt me!"

Jason was speechless. He couldn't believe what he had just heard, and he thought to himself, *And this is the guy that* diagnosed me *as crazy?!*

—————

Lee headed over to Tony's house. On his way over he spotted a wanted poster on a billboard. Curious, Lee had a glance, and saw that it read:

Wanted: Jason Smith

Description: He is a male in his mid-20s with short, black hair and fair skin.

Crime: Jason has vandalized a poor woman's car years ago for no reason. The woman was traumatized due to the event. He was sent to jail for five years, but was released after serving his time. Once out, he did not learn anything from his mistake. He proceeded to threaten his counselor, and then assaulted him for no reason. Jason is highly dangerous. He was last seen in the Harshtown Correctional Asylum, but he has escaped as of a couple months ago. If you spot him, please contact via the information below. He is highly dangerous. Feel free to shoot on-site, and turn in his head. Happy hunting.

Contact: Officer Lives

Phone number: (666) 666-6666

Reward: $1

Lee laughed. "One dollar?! What type of fool do they take me for?"

Lee continued on toward his destination. He had been pissed off for the past few days. From what he could tell, Tony had been avoiding him and the rest of his gang, and this had been going on for a while. In school, the twerp hadn't said more than hello and goodbye to them. After Tony had gotten his ass kicked by Kenny, he had been silent, which was understandable. Who wouldn't be silent after a situation like that? As of now, Tony seemed to have recovered physically and emotionally from his ass-kicking. Tony was even talking to Kenny a little, despite their past history.

He still hadn't interacted much with Lee and the gang. Even in class he seemed to have shut just about everyone out completely. Tony didn't seem to care about fitting in or bullying people. His mind seemed to be focused on other things, but Lee had no idea what. One day, he decided to visit Tony's house to see what the deal was. He knocked on the door. Tony's mother opened it, and told Lee that Tony was in the backyard playing with his dog. This news was shocking to Lee.

"Dog?! He has a dog, and he didn't tell me?"

"Yep!" Tony's mother smiled proudly. "He is so happy now, and this is just what he needed after getting beat up in school. His spirits are lifted, and the dog is teaching him about discipline and responsibility."

Lee walked to the backyard.

"Hey, turd! Why didn't you tell me that you have a dog?"

Tony didn't respond right away, because he was in his own world, as usual. Tony didn't even notice Lee enter the vicinity. Tony continued to play with the dog, a mesmerized look on his face. The animal responded by barking happily. Based on what Lee could tell, the dog was a puppy, and a Siberian Husky.

"Hey, turd! I'm talking to you! Quit courting your girlfriend for a moment, you jackass."

This caught Tony's attention. He attempted to hide the irritation in his voice, and said, "Hey! My bad, man. I didn't even know you were here—and this isn't my girlfriend. He's my pet dog, named Ace!"

The puppy ran into the dog house as Lee approached him,

which made him laugh.

"What a scared, wimpy dog! Look at it whimper! He kinda reminds me of you when you were all lame and shit. Looks like you're lame again, because you aren't spending any time with us cool kids anymore. You obviously have been spending your time with some stupid mutt!"

Tony glared at Lee.

"What's your problem? You're starting to sound like Carmen! I need some alone-time, and I'll be back with you guys when this is out of my system. And don't you dare talk badly about Ace. I'll give you a black eye if you do!"

"Don't even worry about hanging out with us again, because we aren't friends anymore, scrub! Also, don't compare me to that...freak...Carmen! I'll see you in school, loser!"

Tony didn't care, and went back to tending to his dog, which pissed Lee off even more. He couldn't understand what Tony's problem was, and why he was choosing some inferior mutt over him. He was the most popular kid in school, and his gang was feared by everyone except for Kenny.

The next day at school, Lee was in the hallway, and approached Tony.

"Hey, dumbass! You got your ass handed to you by a kid smaller than you!"

To Lee's no avail, there was no response from Tony. He tried again, and yelled down the hallway, "Hey, dumbass, your cloths are outdated! What's the problem?! Why did you go back to wearing geeky clothes, you dumbass!"

There was still no response—not even a look of sadness or fear from Tony. The others, with Lee, laughed at first, but their laughter died down, because it soon became lame to them. Lee and the gang all approached Tony, who just looked at them and waved.

"Since you aren't a cool kid anymore, and since you aren't our friends anymore, we get to pick on you again."

Nonchalantly, Tony replied, "That's nice, guys."

He closed his locker, and headed for class. All day, Lee and his gang attempted to do different things in order to make Tony feel badly. They threw paper balls at him, but Tony just shook them off. The teacher caught one of them in the act, and sent him to detention. The gang decided to go the subtler route, and they drew defamatory pictures of Tony, and wrote rumors about him. He was known to the school as the "Dog Lover." Even though Tony was laughed at by his peers, he didn't care. Lee wasn't satisfied one bit, because he wanted to hit Tony where it hurt.

During after school hours, in the hallway, Lee pointed at Tony and yelled:

"Here's the Dog Lover!"

Everyone in the hallway laughed at Tony, who just simply waved at them, smiling. He walked toward the bus outside after school was over. Lee grabbed Tony by the shoulder, which stopped him in his tracks.

"Hey! What the fuck is your problem!? You need to cut the indifference act right now before we all pound you to the ground!"

Lee's lackeys egged him on. "Yeah! You tell him boss! You tell him!"

Tony sighed, and gave Lee a very serious look.

"I have been through a lot of phases in my short life. I cared so much about fitting in—hell, running the whole damn school—but now I don't give a fuck anymore, because it is all bullshit. The reason why I tried to fit in is because I lacked self-confidence. The reason I bullied people is because I hated myself, so I wanted to elevate myself by making other people feel bad. That is what a bully does, after all. You would know, because you are one. It's all bullshit, and the main thing that should matter is how I feel, not what some ass-wipes feel about me. You all may be in my world, but you all are temporary. This is grade school, and then I move on to middle school, then high school, then college, then work. The chances that you all will stay in my world are slim to none! Even if you are still there—even then—what the hell should it matter how you feel about me? You all are a bunch of ego-driven, self-centered, esteem-lacking, douche bags, and I may have been one of you, but you won't be seeing me on my death bed regretting my life the way the rest of you will be—all because you do what other people want you to do. I'm finished!"

There was dead silence as Tony entered the bus. Even the witnesses were silent, except for Kenny, who clapped and wiped a tear from his eye.

"That...was...beautiful!" he said.

A few days later, Lee was thinking about how he didn't understand a word that Tony had told him that day, but what he did understand was that Tony was a completely different person now. What he was curious about was if he would continue to be this way if his dog were to be taken away from him. Tony *had* become this way ever since the dog incident, after all. Lee walked through the neighborhood toward Tony's house. On the way over he walked past some guy who was in a heated argument with another guy. It was over a pair of shoes, or some other nonsense like that. Similarly to Tony, Lee had blocked out the outside world, and was purely focused on achieving his goal.

Lee arrived at Tony's house, and snuck into his former friend's backyard. He was planning on stealing the dog in order to see if Tony was full of shit. The dog was asleep. Hastily, Lee grabbed the mutt and threw him into a sack he'd carried.

Fortunately, Lee was able to hide most of the whimpering sounds that the pup is making. Lee began to sneak out of the yard, but suddenly, his sack was ripped open, and the puppy was outside of it. Lee looked down at the creature, which snarled at him. He laughed, knowing that he could kick a field goal with the pup if he needed to.

The dog charged at Lee. He tried to kick it, but he missed, and was met with a bite, which caused him to scream. The puppy clamped down on Lee's leg, and swung Lee from one side of the ground very hard and then to the other. He could not believe what was happening to him. It reminded him of what had happened to Tony when he'd attacked Kenny. The swinging happened at least twenty times until the puppy swung Lee around in a circle, and launched him into the air.

An hour later, Lee was unconscious in the hospital, and covered in bandages.

The doctor asked the nurse curiously, "What happened to this one?"

The nurse sighed.

"This kid was foolish enough to mess with a Computer Siberian Husky. He probably confused it with a Siberian Husky. Siberian Huskies can be used for sledding. Computer Siberian Huskies, however are the toughest, fiercest, and strongest dogs to ever exist. They may appear friendly, but if you upset one, then you better run for your life. Fortunately, this kid got it good, because I have seen far worse cases."

———

A boy named Lee walked past Cecil, and Cecil pondered for a moment why a kid would be outside and in this neighborhood at this time. The only reason why he guessed that the kid's name was Lee was because it was written on the back of his shirt. He decided he was best off focusing on his current situation. He was feeling extremely confused. The only thing that he had done was walk past the man in front of him, and bump into him accidentally. He was aware that this was a bad neighborhood, and this wasn't the usual way he would walk home, but he hadn't expected for things to escalate to this level. He apologized to the man, but that seemed to have made things worse.

"What the fuck is your problem, man?" As the man talked, he spat in Cecil's face. "And I don't fucking like the tone you're using with me!"

"I....I...apologize for offending you, sir. I didn't mean for it to be this way. All I'm trying to do is go home."

"Apologize, my ass! And why the hell are you yelling at me?! Better yet, why the hell are you being all apologetic and shit?!"

Arrogantly, the irate man eyed Cecil up and down. "You think that I'm some helpless child? You think that you need to baby me?"

He pushed Cecil, who didn't even bother to push back. Cecil just accepted the push, and apologized again. This somehow made things even worse.

"What?! You think you're too good to fight me back, bitch?!"

The situation continued to escalate. Now there was a crowd of people who were gleefully observing the whole thing. They egged the man on while Cecil tried so hard to explain the misunderstanding.

"Punch him! Beat the crap out of him! You're gonna let him be nice to you like that?! Kick his ass!"

It was like a sports stadium filled with people cheering for their favorite team. This went on and on until a police officer came to the scene, and parked his car. He opened the door, got out, and walked over to the crowd.

"Can anyone tell me what the hell is going on here?" the officer asked.

The irate man started in, "This motherfucker is pissing me off! He keeps on yelling at me, and treating me like a baby! He's treating me like trash, and he acts like he's too good for me!"

The spectators shouted in agreement. The officer crossed his arms, and slowly looked over at Cecil, who felt very nervous now. Things seemed to be getting worse and worse.

"Officer! This is ridiculous! This is what happened."

Cecil tried to calm himself down before he continued with his speech, but before he could say anything else, the man interrupted, taking a swing at him, and punching him in the face as hard as he could, knocking Cecil to the ground. A cheer erupted from the crowd—like their favorite football team had just scored a touchdown. Instead of holding the aggressor back, the officer rushed to Cecil, and swiftly restrained him.

"Calm down now! No need to get violent unless you want a charge for assault! Now tell me what happened! Now!"

It took Cecil some time to come back to his senses after the punch. All he could see were stars, until his vision slowly returned.

"I walked past this guy, and accidentally bumped into him. He was about to hit me, but I apologized to him and shook his hand. He threw down my hand, and started cussing me out—when I was trying to be polite to him. He kept on accusing me of being rude, but I was trying to set things right. Then these people show up, and try to get him to attack me. I don't want any trouble! I'm a peaceful man, and I just want to go home!"

The officer thought about all of this for a moment, weighing both Cecil and the irate man's stories. This baffled Cecil, because he clearly hadn't done anything wrong.

"I'll be back. I'm gonna need backup for this," the officer said.

"Backup?! For what?! I didn't do anything!"

"Watch your tongue, sir, and shut the fuck up. Or else I'll have to handcuff you!"

Cecil went silent, and the officer got into his police car. While the officer was distracted calling for backup, the irate man quickly punched Cecil in the face a few more times. He then kneed Cecil in the gut, kicking him with joy as Cecil lay on the ground. The crowd cheered, deciding to join in on the beating. The sound of new sirens caused everyone to halt. More cops arrived at the scene, and they all began to question why Cecil was being beaten up.

"We had to defend ourselves from him, Officer! He went crazy, and tried to attack us!"

The rest of the crowd agreed, except for Fatima. She had observed the whole incident from her car while she waited for the perfect time to lend her support. She knew instinctively that it was too dangerous for her to jump in prior to that, especially since there is a crowd of them. Now that the cops are here, things should be much safer.

"No officer, that isn't how the incident went! This man was being a gentleman, but the whole time, this other guy was being a dick."

Fatima's words cause the crowd to become silent, because she was being defiant, and they found this very intimidating. The officers analyzed the whole situation while Cecil lay there unconscious. He eventually awakened from his coma, but he was very much in pain. Fortunately, Fatima was attempting to tend to his wounds, and she seemed to be the only one who cared about him.

"I'll get you out of this. Don't worry," she whispered.

The first officer returned to Cecil, a gun in his hand pointed at Cecil.

"We decided to arrest you for now. It is obvious that you are causing a disturbance here. You are dangerous, and you caused this whole crowd to have to defend themselves. Try some crazy shit, and I'll shoot you down. We have snipers on the roof tops, so you better not dare."

There was no resistance from Cecil, who now felt hopeless and depressed as he was handcuffed and lugged into the police car. Fatima tried to protest, but it was to no avail. Instead, she was met by another officer who handcuffed her.

"You are under arrest, ma'am, for being his cohort, and helping him cause the disturbance."

"What?! I didn't do anything!"

It was too late, and she was placed in another police car headed toward jail. Cecil sat in the police car. On the way to the jail, they passed a decrepit-looking nursing home, among other things. Cecil didn't take notice of the events outside the car, and wept silently in despair.

CHAPTER FOUR

Two CARETAKERS ESCORTED AN ELDERLY MAN to the shower area. On the way over, one of the caretakers said, "Hey! Did you hear about the fight that happened a couple weeks ago?!"

"Yeah, I saw it from a distance. That was some terrible stuff, man. What's up with society?"

"What do you mean?"

"The guy was just trying to walk home, and some asshole kept on messing with him. Beat his ass, and the whole neighborhood got in on the action. And you won't believe it! Once the cops arrived, they arrested the victim! What the hell, man?!"

The first caretaker shook his head in disbelief.

"What a shame. People nowadays are losing their morals and their minds. I really fear for this society's future. We need someone to guide us in the right direction. Issues like this need to stop; otherwise the human race won't make it."

The second caretaker nodded. "I hear you, man. I don't even want to have kids, because I don't want them to grow up in a society that is this messed up and corrupt. You definitely can't trust the police nowadays."

The elderly man that was being escorted, named Carl, agreed with these two. However, he felt that it was best not to voice his opinion to the caretakers.

A few minutes later, the three arrived at their destination inside the shower room.

Once inside, the atmosphere changed. The friendly bickering caretakers frowned furiously, and then they ripped off Carl's clothes, and violently threw him toward one of the showers. Carl was late, because he was having problems eating his food. Ever since the elderly man had lost all of his teeth, eating just hadn't been the same for him. This type of treatment was the norm for everyone in the Typical. After he was thrown face-first into the wall, the caretakers slammed the door on him.

"Take your fucking shower NOW! Or else we will have to come in there and beat your old ass to a bloody pulp!"

Carl simply nodded obediently as he began to wash himself in the shower. The only thing that was left for him was cold water. The elderly man muttered to himself sarcastically, "Just another day in the Typical."

Five minutes later, a few of the caretakers entered the shower room as Carl continued to clean himself. While he had his guard down, they grabbed him quickly.

"What the fuck is taking you so long, old-timer? You've gone over your limit by a nanosecond. You know damn well that now is your nap time, so you will have to be punished for this."

"I'm sorry, sir. I'm eighty years old. My mind isn't how it used to be. Please show a senior citizen some mercy. You all have parents my age and—"

They didn't allow him to finish, and dragged the poor man to his cell, throwing him against the wall as hard as they could. He had nothing to sleep on, and only a blanket. Carl hit the wall face-first, lost his last remaining tooth in an instant, and then landed on his back. Carl held his last tooth in the palm of his hand, and sighed. He was expected to take a nap at this time.

Carl lay on the dirty floor, pulled the infant-sized blanket over him, and attempted to force himself to fall asleep.

It was very tough for Carl to sleep, mainly because he wasn't sleepy. Every minute and every day was scheduled like this, whether he liked it or not. A couple hours later, his cell door was opened, accompanied by a loudspeaker announcement.

"Wake up, you annoying old people! Time for some recreation time to get those decaying brains functioning!"

This was one of the best times of the day for Carl. He got to interact with his friends, so he stepped outside of his cell to head for the recreation area. He eventually spotted his best friend, sat at his table, and spoke to him.

"Whatever happened to Carla? I haven't seen her lately."

"The hacks got sick of dealing with her, so they put her away. She's dead now, and nobody cares except for us inmates of the Typical. They killed her, man. They killed her!"

"What?! Yeah, right! Their job is to take care of us, not hurt us. The only reason why we are treated like this is because of protocol, not because they absolutely hate us."

"Not because they hate us?! Open your eyes, man! The warmest that the showers ever get are thirty degrees. We always get insulted, and yet half of these people were kids in our neighborhoods before we became this old. They throw us around, treat us like shit, and they enjoy it!"

The two were interrupted by the loudspeaker.

"Recreation time is up, old fucks! Get back to your cells for more nap time!"

Gabe, Carl's best friend, sighed.

"See? We had our recreation time for two minutes, and it's *already* over! These guys don't care about us, and if you ask me, things have become stricter over time."

Five minutes later, in Carl's Cell, Carl simply sat down,

looking at the wall.

He wasn't sleepy at all, and he waited patiently for lunch time. His cell door was opened, and an angry nurse entered. The hack shrieked.

"What the heck?! You're supposed to be asleep! It's nap time, and you need your diaper changed."

"I wasn't sleepy, sir."

The hack sighed, and shook his head. "This is no good. We need to knock him out." He turned to his cohort. "Mallet?" The other nurse handed him the mallet.

Carl's eyes widened, and he began to plead and beg, "Can you *please* show mercy on an old man?"

The nurse, weilding the mallet, didn't allow another word out of Carl, and bashed him in the head, instantly knocking Carl unconscious. This put Carl to sleep for a while, and caused him to miss lunch and his second recreation time. He did wake up in time for dinner, and to a rude loudspeaker announcement.

"Geezers! Wake the hell up! It's dinner time!"

These loud and harsh announcements caused his ears to become worse and worse over time. Carl gently bonked his head in an attempt to get rid of the ringing in his ears. In the past he attempted to tell this to the hacks, but none of them cared. Usually his complaints were met with him being tied up and thrown into solitary for a week as punishment.

In the lunchroom, in front of the waiting line, a caretaker slammed a tray of food on a table in front of Carl.

"Here is your dinner! Now get the hell out of my face!"

Carl looked down at the food that had been served to him, and saw that it was mashed potatoes filled with maggots.

"Miss? This has bugs in it. Can I have something else?"

The cook scowled at him.

"I spent a lot of time preparing this food for you geezers,

and yet you still complain! Eat your goddamn food and shut the hell up!"

"But ma'am...this has maggots...it's not edible!"

"Edible, my ass! You geezers have no idea of all of the trouble that we go through to watch your worthless asses! Now eat your food, or else I'll call a guard and he will shove it down your throat!"

Carl argued no further, and simply took his tray and sat with Gabe. Gabe just looked at his maggot-filled potatoes, and sighed. The two did not bother eating their dinner.

A couple hours after dinner ends, Carl listened to the loudspeaker announcement.

"Final recreation time, hags!"

Carl was able to get some candy from the vending machine in order to make up for missing dinner, even though he wasn't supposed to eat sweets. He searched for Gabe, but didn't see him anywhere. Carl headed for his best friend's cell, and he saw a crowd of people. Carl was able to spot his friend, who lay on the ground, motionless. Everyone in the crowd was talking.

"He was alive during dinner time."

"Doctors said that it was lack of nutrients that got him, and some others said that he was an old hag, and would have died soon anyway."

"I heard it was because they changed him into dirty diapers constantly."

Carl heard rumor after rumor, but the only thing he could focus on was that his best friend Gabe was dead.

Ten minutes later, another announcement came over the loudspeaker. "Recreation time is over, assholes! Get back to your cells!"

Carl was late returning to his cell because he was mourning over his deceased best friend. A hack caught him walking slowly, so he grabbed Carl and threw him into his cell. It was now night time according to their standards, but Carl was not sleepy since it was just four in the afternoon. Later on that night, Carl was greeted by a hack who had gotten sick of his crying, so he bashed Carl in the head with a mallet to put him to sleep. To Carl, it was just another day in the Typical Nursing Home.

———

Laura stood in front of the Typical Nursing Home. She had never considered using this spot to ask for change. She thought she could hear screams in terror coming from the building, which she found unsettling. Laura scratched her head, and guessed that it must be her imagination. There was no possible way that terror could happen in a nursing home. After all, the elders were supposed to be taken care of properly. As people began to walk past her, Laura held out her mug, and got to work.

"Change, sir? I'm hungry, and I haven't eaten for days now. Can you at least give me ten cents?"

Laura was met with spit in her face as the business man walked by.

"Change, ma'am?" She tightened the grip on her mug.

The woman slapped Laura in the face, and then continued on her way.

"Change, sirs?"

The group of teenage boys laughed at Laura. One of them snatched her mug away, and then shattered it on the ground. The other boys pushed her around as they sang "selfish whore" over and over.

"Check out the trash right here!"

"Selfish whore!"

"This is what you deserve!"

The pushing went on for about an hour as people nonchalantly walk by. Some of them stopped to observe the show until they got bored, while others simply laughed and joined in on the song.

Laura shook the dirt off, and the boys left just as another man walked toward her. She asked him optimistically, smiling, "Change, sir?"

"Why should I give you money?" he hissed at her. "You are the selfish whore!"

The disgruntled man picked her up, and dumped her into the trash.

"In you go! Now you have a home!"

He laughed as he walked to wherever his destination was, showing no remorse toward how he'd just treated the helpless homeless woman.

Laura climbed out of the trash. She had been living on the streets for at least three months now, and yet people were still treating her the same way ever since the incident had first occurred. It was as if the world never wanted to forget about her being unable to give change to the homeless man. Due to this horrible treatment, she had lost her faith in humanity. Suddenly, her curiosity was piqued by a flier that was in the trash. Laura read the flier, and saw that a new church was opening nearby, and that these church people were helping out the homeless.

An hour later, in front of the church, Laura spoke to a cheerful, young female volunteer,

"I hear that your organization is helping out the homeless. I have been homeless for a while now. Can you help me?"

"Sure, ma'am. We are offering temporary jobs to the homeless. It is only for one day, but you will be paid two hundred dollars for your work."

Laura pondered this for a moment, because it sounded

shady—too good to be true. It didn't make sense to her that a homeless person would have work, but beggars couldn't be choosers, and it was better than nothing. She did the work for the whole day, doing some cleaning and repairs for the church.

The workers were being observed by an odd-looking, middle-aged woman who was wearing what appears to be a lab coat. Afterward, Laura was paid the two hundred dollars, and for the first time in a long time, she had more than ten dollars in her pockets. This money could last her for months if she was careful. Hell, she could even rent a room and stay there for a day, just to have the temporary feeling of being more than homeless again. Laura decided to go to the church's Sunday service, since she was beginning to regain her faith. Perhaps this was why things had never worked out for her. She was an Atheist, after all. She guessed that it couldn't hurt to have faith, but she was raised to not believe in a higher power.

Two days later, there were already a lot of people inside of the church. Laura took her seat to listen to the service. She noticed that everyone seemed to be enjoying themselves as the service went on. The priest gave his sermon, and he preached like he was singing,

"I know it's holiday time! I know you all have the money! God knows you have the money! I understand you all want to give gifts to each other, but if you donate sixty dollars right now, then that money will multiply! That is what is said in the Good Book! This is what God wants!"

The audience cheered the priest, who was named Abraham, as he gave his sermon. Many of them were crying in joy, while others were running through the aisles and swinging along the chandeliers.

"Donate sixty dollars now, in the name of God! You will be blessed in the kingdom of heaven tenfold if you just donate in the box! It doesn't matter if you are poor and you are about to be—or are—homeless! Donate what you have! It will all go for the higher cause. If you don't donate, then God knows this, and you will be put in the lake of fire. You don't want that, do you?!"

A poverty-stricken woman in the crowd approached Abraham. It was one of the workers that had worked with Laura. The audience began to cheer as she reached into her wallet to take out the two hundred dollars she had made.

"Logically, I shouldn't do this, because this is all that I have left, but I believe in you, preacher," she said, wiping away a tear.

She gave all that she had to Abraham, who took it and blessed her. Shortly after, more people began to donate their money to him, but most of the ones who donated were many of the homeless workers. This didn't make sense to Laura at first, but she took a deep breath as she thought it through. Normally she would not agree with the man, especially since giving the twenty dollars to the homeless man years ago had caused so many problems.

If what he says is true, then I will get a lot more money back. If it's a lie, then what difference does it make? I'll end up spending it all, and then I will continue to be where I'm at. What do I have to lose? she thought to herself.

Laura, the former Atheist, sighed as she put the two hundred dollars in the basket. Once service had finished, the preacher told his audience that the money was going to help out the needy, and God would repay them all back tenfold. Service was concluded an hour later. The audience and the staff left the church. Abraham entered his office with his donation money clutched close to him. Instead of putting the money back in the donation box, however, he put it in his wallet, and debated over which new car he was going to buy—or maybe he would use some of it to visit Jerome, his younger brother.

Days passed, and then weeks, but Laura was still homeless, and was being treated the same way as before. She returned to the church to see if she could get any additional help, but she was told that the donation money had already been used to help out the needy. She nevertheless retained her faith, as the words of the preacher had really touched her heart.

———

"Hey, kid! Not so fast!"

Tony quickly stopped in his tracks. He was in a rush to get to school, however, he simply could not ignore an adult who was addressing him. He immediately turned to see a professionally-dressed man.

"Yes? I kinda am in a hurry, sir."

The man smiled. "This will be quick. I am a part of a church that was opened by the wonderful Abraham. Would you like to donate to us? A dollar, if you like."

"No, thanks. I don't donate to nonprofit organizations."

Tony turned to begin running to school, but he felt a hand grip his shoulder.

"Wait, kid. I insist that you donate. For your sake, it is for the best, because God—"

"Because what? Leave me alone, you creep!"

Tony brushed the man's hand away, and rushed to school. He shook his head, and thought to himself, *Normally I'm polite to adults, but that guy was a weirdo.*

Five minutes later, Tony ran inside the school into his class-room, and sat down at his desk. He quickly opened his book bag, pulled out a few papers, and began to work diligently on the work that he should have finished last night. He had been too distracted playing video games with his new best friend,

Kenny. Tony had forgiven Kenny over what had happened, and Kenny had done the same in return. Tony didn't pay attention to his classmates who had entered the room over time. He also didn't pay attention to the fact that a substitute teacher was scheduled to teach them, meaning that they could fool around. Previously, he would have joined the other kids when it came to causing trouble, but lately he couldn't care less about what they thought about him. Kenny was similar in this mindset, but he tended to fool around for the fun of it, rather than the popularity aspect that came with it. The last few substitute teachers had been a joke, and they hadn't lasted long. Most of them didn't stand a chance against Lee and his gang whenever they caused mischief.

The early bell rang, and their next substitute-teacher victim entered the room. There was a brief silence as a strongly built, tall man with a crewcut entered the classroom. Lee looked at the man, and then went back to fooling around without a care in the world. Kenny, however, was in complete shock, while Tony was indifferent, and continued the work that he should have finished the night before. The big man placed his belongings on the desk, and then wrote his name on the board. He turned to the class.

"Good morning, class. My name is Mr. Tank, but you may address me as master, führer, czar—whichever you prefer—as long as you ask for permission to speak."

There was a brief silence, until Lee started to laugh like he'd just been told the best joke ever.

"Mr. Tank? More like...Mr. Joke! You seriously expect us to talk to you like you're the boss of us?!"

Lee's gang began to laugh along with him, while the others remained silent. Even though these guys were scumbags, Kenny wished that he could warn these bullies. Because of his visit to

Marcus's house, Kenny knew that he needs to ask for permission to speak.

Mr. Tank took a deep breath as he approached Lee, giving him an emotionless stare.

"Ooooooooo!! I'm scared!" Lee said, sarcastically.

Mr. Tank furiously grabbed Lee's chair, and then slammed it on the ground with Lee still sitting in it. Lee's head banged very hard on the ground.

"Don't...FUCK...with...ME!" yelled Mr. Tank.

Lee was completely bewildered, and physically in pain. He was simply having a hard time processing what had just happened to him in the past few seconds. Thirty seconds later, the pain settled in. For the first time his classmates saw him cry like a baby. This didn't matter, though, because they had never heard a teacher use profanity, and they had never seen a teacher retaliate like *that*. The children were all only ten years old.

Kenny was very alarmed by Mr. Tank's behavior. Tony, however, was hiding under his desk, trembling and sobbing in terror. It looked like he wouldn't be finishing the work that he should have finished the night before. Everyone else was mirroring Tony's actions. Mr. Tank slowly observed the classroom as he began to calm down.

"All right, cretins, let's get started with the lesson."

Ten minutes later, Mr. Tank looked at his students sternly and asked, "Who was the first president of the United States, Inc.? Anyone? Hello?"

There was a lengthy and awkward silence, until Carmen raised her hand.

"May I have permission to speak, Master?"

Mr. Tank nodded at her in admiration. "Yes you may, cretin."

"The first president was George Washington, sir. I am finished speaking, my superior elder." Carmen bowed before she sat back down.

"Well done, Carmen. You got it right. Now for the rest of you, twenty push-ups—now!"

The rest of the children sighed, and then everyone got into position to do the push-ups.

Later, at a table, in the lunchroom, Lee yelled furiously, "That asshole! He had no right to do what he did! Teachers aren't supposed to touch their students! I'm gonna report him, and get his ass fired!" said Lee. He paced back and forth furiously. "And what the fuck is your problem?" He turned to Carmen. "Are you his little pet? You gonna lick his shoes after lunch is finished?!"

She rolled her eyes at him as she ate her lunch.

"You're a moron. I'm simply doing what I need to do in order to finish the day. Just follow his rules, and everything will be all right."

Tony simply nodded, and said, "Yeah. Also, technically, he didn't hit you. He slammed your chair down very hard. As for firing him? He is a substitute teacher, so he probably doesn't care either way."

Kenny nodded in agreement. Lee, disgruntled, grabbed his lunch tray.

"Why the hell did I chose to eat lunch with you losers anyhow? Mr. Tank isn't gonna get away with this!" Lee moved to an empty table.

Later, in the principal's office, Lee pointed at his head and said, "You see this big-ass bump on my head? Mr. Tank did it! He grabbed my chair, and then slammed it on the ground, and made me bump my head! Teachers aren't supposed to put their hands on their students."

The principal sighed, reflecting on this. He was trying in vain to take Lee, the bully, seriously.

"I see, but the thing is, technically, he didn't put his hands on you, and why should I trust your word? You are the most notorious bully in this school! Do you have any idea how many of my students come here to complain to me about you? Yet you think you have the right to complain about someone else who didn't put their hands on you?! Get out of my office! Better yet, talk to the school counselor, because you sure as hell could use it."

Lee tried to argue, but to no avail. He was kicked out of the office.

During the same time, in class, Tony panted exhaustedly. He then said, "Kenny, I can't take any more of this. What if Lee has the right idea?"

The class had been forced to do push-ups again since Carmen had been able to answer another question correctly. Tony could not endure this anymore.

"This isn't the first time that I've had to deal with him," Kenny whispered. "He is Marcus's dad, after all. We need to get out of here, dude, because I'm at my limit, too. My arms are gonna break! How about we talk to the newly hired school counselor?"

Tony nodded in agreement, finishing his last push-up.

Kenny raised his hand. "May I have permission to speak, Master?"

Mr. Tank looked at Kenny, and nodded. "Yes you may, cretin."

"Me and Tony need to go to the bathroom. May we go? I am finished, my superior elder."

Mr. Tank gave his approval, and the two boys instead headed to the counselor's office. When they got there, they noticed that Lee was in the waiting room. The three all waited together, and decided that it was best that all of them consult with the counselor at the same time. Once the group was allowed inside, they all took their seat. They all looked up at the newly hired school counselor, who took out his notepad to jot down what they were about to say.

"So you are saying that Mr. Tank tells you to ask for permission to speak, that he calls you all 'cretins,' makes you do push-ups, slammed your chair on the ground, used profanity, and orders you to call him 'master'?"

The three boys all simultaneously nodded their approval. Jerome, the newly hired school counselor, tried to keep his composure. He could not help but think that these three kids were crazy as he wrote down that they were all suffering from schizophrenia.

"Thank you, boys, for bringing this to my attention. I will bring this info to the principle, and action will be taken. It won't be today, but tomorrow. All I request is that you three endure the rest of the day."

The three nodded in approval, happy that action would be taken. They endured doing two hundred more push-ups, and generally being treated like nobodies. The next day, Tony, Kenny, and Lee were sent to the asylum on the condition that they complete treatment assigned before they could go back to school. In the meantime, the school board decided to keep Mr. Tank as a permanent teacher, and Jerome received an early raise.

———

Hector walked to his store. On his way over, he saw something that shocked him. There were three struggling boys, all in strait jackets, who were being hauled away to a van by nurses.

"You dumbasses!" one of the boys yelled. "We aren't crazy! Let us go! Dumbass Jerome! This is all your fault! We *will* get our revenge!"

Hector heard one of the workers state, "Looks like you already are experiencing a psychotic episode. Poor kid. Well… in you go!" The nurse tossed the boy inside the back of the van. The other two boys showed no resistance. They seem to be resigned to their fates as they looked down at the ground in despair. Hector recognized one of the boys as a kid he'd sold a baseball bat to about four months ago when Hector had worked at C.J. Pickles. Hector sighed, and wished the boys a speedy recovery from whatever mental breakdown that they were experiencing. Hector then reached into his pocket, took out his key, and opened the front door to his store. He entered, and began the preparations to open up shop. Fortunately for him, the $100,000 that he'd won from the lottery had really paid off.

An hour later, Hector whistled, bored out of his mind.

The store was dead until a female customer entered. Hector swore that he'd seen her somewhere before. He probably should have brought some headache medicine, and he regretted not having bought any.

The female customer, Marisol, hissed, "What do you mean I can't buy this?! It is sitting right on this shelf above the price! What type of store is this?" She paced back and forth.

"Ma'am, I do apologize, but that is a display holder."

"Display or not, you better sell this to me! Better yet, give me your supervisor! You obviously don't know what the hell you're talking about, and look at you!" Marisol eyed Hector up and down with a look of contempt, "Shaved head and prison tattoos. Does your store stoop down so low as to hire gang members? Give me your supervisor!"

Hector's frustration started to build up slowly, as it became apparent in his voice.

"For one, this is a display *holder*, not a display. This is used to hold up the plates, but the plates are sold out. Second, these aren't prison tattoos, rather pagan tattoos—ceremonial daggers. Third, I am the manager of this store, and I don't hire gang members. What I can do is search the stock room to see if there are any more plates."

Marisol crossed her arms. "I don't want any more damn plates!" She pointed at the display holder. "I want this!" She held it up in Hector's face like he had bad eyesight.

"We don't sell those, ma'am. They are very hard to obtain, and they aren't registered in our inventory. We do, however, have holders for sale that are similar to that."

She turned her back on Hector, and headed for the entrance. "You know what? Fuck you, and fuck your store!"

Hector, annoyed, shook his head at her, and, keeping a somewhat calm voice, said, "Have a nice day, ma'am."

An hour later, a child entered the store. Hector acknowledged him, and told the child he would be cleaning up if he needed him. The child nodded as he headed to the display holder. Shortly after, he handed it to Hector, and said, "I would like to buy this, sir."

Hector looked down at the child, and shook his head. "Sorry, kid, but that isn't for sale. That is a display holder, but we do sell items similar to it."

The child shrugged. "My mom told me to buy it. Can you please sell it to me somehow?" He pleaded with Hector unconvincingly. "I don't want her to beat me again like she does every night."

Hector gave him a curious look. "Who is your mother?"

"She is the lady that you talked to an hour ago. She said that since I'm a stupid brat that will lie about being abused, you would sympathize with me."

With a sigh, Hector placed his hand on his forehead. "Kid,

this isn't for sale. It isn't even in our system to sell, and it is hard for me to get access to these, so they stay."

The child looked down in shame. "Thank you, sir." He left the store in tears.

Thirty minutes later, Marisol entered the store once again. Hector eyed her warily, but he acknowledged her presence politely. She approached him with the display holder again.

"Can I buy this?"

Hector sighed once again. It seems like this day was full of disappointments.

"I apologize, ma'am, but as before, that isn't for sale." This earned him a confused look, and she shrugged her shoulders as if she didn't know what he was talking about.

"As before? This is the first time that I've been in here. Oh well, how about this?"

She presented him the item that he'd suggested to her earlier. Hector took the box, headed to the cash register, and rang it up.

"All right, ma'am. It costs five dollars."

Marisol was about to take out the money, but she paused at the last minute as something occurred to her. "The sign says that it is four dollars."

"Okay, I'll be right back to check." Hector headed over to where the box was, and saw that it did indeed say five dollars, and that it was the singles that cost four dollars. He headed back over to the annoying customer.

"I apologize, ma'am, but it is five dollars. What is four dollars, are the single packs."

"Can you give me a discount since I have been a good customer?"

Hector shook his head no. "Sorry, ma'am, the fact that the set is five dollars is already a discount considering that it usually is twenty dollars."

Marisol stepped up to him to get in his face. "It is only a dollar difference. Cutting off a dollar isn't a big deal at all. Come on! Hook a sista up! I have been such a great customer!"

"No negotiations, ma'am, and rules are rules. If you don't want to buy it, then it's fine. A lot of other people have been buying the set, and it isn't a big loss. This is the last hour of the sale before it goes back up to twenty dollars."

"Fine! No deal!" She immediately headed toward the entrance. "Shitty service, shitty store, shitty deal!"

A few minutes before closing time, Marisol entered the store again. She grabbed the display holder, and set it down on the counter. Hector looked at her, and instead of verbally saying no, he slowly shook his head. Disgruntled, she grabbed the box, and slammed it on the counter. Hector rang it up.

"That will be twenty dollars, ma'am."

Marisol's eyes bulged. "What the hell?! It was four dollars before!"

"It was five dollars, ma'am, and the sale lasted for an hour. For you, I could do this just this once, and ring it up for five dollars since you were here earlier and missed the sale."

She considered this for a moment. "Make it four dollars."

Hector gave her an angry stare. "Get out of my store!"

Marisol was very shocked about the outburst.

"I'm a customer, and I have every right to be here and receive—"

Before she could finish, Hector picked her up, took her outside, and then dumped her into the dumpster. He then went back into his store, slammed the door, locked it, and then put up the closed sign. Marisol was completely dumbstruck. Something moved around in the dumpster next to her, and a person emerged. It was Laura. She looked at Marisol curiously.

"You could always do what I do." Laura shrugged as she climbed out to continue begging for change.

Michael walked into his office carrying a box. He set it down on his desk, opened it, and removed the plate holders that were inside. The counselor whistled to himself. *Only five dollars for these! Thank goodness I made the sale*, he thought. He set them to the side, and neatly placed some decorative plates inside of them. He set the box aside, sat down at his desk, and began to prepare for his clients who had scheduled fifty-minute counseling sessions with him. His first session began at 10 a.m., which was fifteen minutes from now.

During the first session, at 10:45 a.m., Jamaal Johnson paced back and forth in Michael's office.

"Why does it have to be so complex?" Jamaal asked angrily. "First, they told me that I needed an associate's degree, then a bachelor's, then a master's, then a PhD., then military training, and then finally they told me that I'm overly qualified! For one, I have been doing underwater basket weaving ever since I was five! Why the hell do I need a piece of paper in order to prove to the world that I can do something that I've always known how to do?!"

Michael listened to his client's rant. *Why did he choose to do the military training for five years? Guess I'll ask him next session since he is pretty irate.*

"How about your job as a vice president?" asked Michael.

Jamaal shook his head no. "I make very good money, and it is way better than being a janitor, but it isn't what I want to do for a living. I don't have a problem with doing it on the side, though. The crazy thing is that I applied for the position again, and now they tell me that I need to be a CEO of a company in order to qualify!"

Michael tried to comfort his patient, and considered giving him advice, but he knew that it wasn't proper to give a patient advice. Instead, he wrote down that Jamaal was suffering from a lot of stress due to not having his dream come true after so much hard work. Michael signaled that the session was up, and then shook his patient's hand. Jamaal thanked him for being a good counselor, and Michael left the room.

During the second session, at 11:30 a.m., Tony, Lee, and Kenny were attempting to explain their situation to Michael.

Tony crossed his arms after finally explaining the situation to Michael.

"That's pretty much what happened, sir. We have a really mean teacher, and our school counselor said that we are crazy. He acted nice while he was talking to us, but you see the end result."

Michael thought about this for a moment as he looked through each of their files. He noticed that Lee was a delinquent, and that Tony had had his ups and downs, but was overall a good kid. There was nothing negative in Kenny's file at all, except for the fact that he was shy around strangers—which Michael didn't consider as a negative.

"And your counselor said that you all have schizophrenia? I don't see any history of mental illness in your files at all. Your immediate family members also seem to be fine mentally."

The other two kids had decided to leave all of the talking to Tony since he was the most well-spoken. They nodded their approval. Lee, however, decided to finally put in his two cents.

"It's that dumbass school counselor's fault! We told him the truth, and yet he called us crazy! Dumbass Jerome! I will have my revenge!" Lee crossed his arms, looked away, and scowled.

This caught Michael's attention the most, because he wondered if Lee was talking about the same Jerome that Michael knew—the same person that he thought had moved out of the country in despair over the loss of his family.

"What's his last name?"

Kenny thought about this for a moment. "Jerome...Incompetence, I think...Jerome Incompetence."

Michael sighed. "You kids can leave now. You obviously don't have any mental illnesses. I'll write a note to your school so you can go back. Your parents are going to pick you up."

They all sighed in relief as they left the office. Michael thought about Jerome for a little while, recalling how Jerome had been wrong about Jason, and how he'd told Michael that Jason was crazy. He even pondered the details behind Jerome's family's disappearance. Michael found it fishy that Jerome, who was supposed to be devastated over his family's loss, had suddenly changed his mind and decided to become a school counselor.

During the third session, at 2:15 p.m., Cecil Colombo cried, "I didn't do anything, sir! They kept on treating me like I was some type of common criminal! The only thing that I wanted to do was go home. My car was down, and I knew it was a bad neighborhood, but I figured that as long as I stayed polite, everything would go well."

After hearing Cecil's explanation and his pleas, Michael suddenly began to come down with a bad case of déjà vu. To him, this situation sounded a hell of a lot like the scenario that had happened to Jason.

"I'm a pacifist! I don't want to hurt anyone!" Cecil sobbed. "I have been a good citizen! Why did they have to treat me like that? Why does this world have to be so harsh? First, Andrew had to shatter my dreams, and now this!"

The counselor comforted his sobbing patient. Once the sobbing had stopped, Michael asked, "What was the name of the officer who arrested you?"

"His name is Fuxup Lives. Officer Fuxup Lives."

Michael asked Cecil to wait a moment while he looked through his files. Michael spotted Jason's file, and looked to see who had arrested him back then. He saw that it was the exact same person—Officer Fuxup Lives.

"They had snipers on the roof, and they were pointing their guns at me like I was a terrorist! God bless that woman for being able to get us both bailed out that night, but now I have a criminal record."

During the fourth session, at 3:00 p.m., Carl Ingram walked into Michael's office and bowed to him. The elderly man then asked politely, "Can I sit sir?"

Michael nodded at him, looking a little confused about why he'd asked to sit.

"Yes, you don't have to ask me for permission to sit. If anything, I should respect you for being a senior."

Carl's face lit up.

"R-r-respect me?! Wow. The last time I received respect was...." He thought for a moment. "Can't remember, but we certainly don't get it in the Typical Nursing Home."

Michael gave him a concerned look.

"That's the same place that my father went to. He died about a month ago, though. His name was Gabe...good guy."

This instantly caused an alarmed look from Carl. "Gabe Witkison?"

Michael nodded. "Yep, that was my father."

"Gabe was my best friend! He died because they treated him so poorly! Compared to prison inmates, we get horrible treatment! They slam us into walls, make us shower in subzero temperatures, bash us with mallets, give us maggot-filled food, *and* they insult us!"

Michael listened intently as he recalled how he was told that his father had simply died of old age—now there was a new possibility that his father had been killed due to horrible treatment. This caused Michael's blood to boil some, but he knew he mustn't let his anger get to him right now since he was counseling. Even though it didn't show on the outside, intense anger was building up inside him. He told himself not to make assumptions, and do the research first before acting. Otherwise, he would get chewed up and spit out by the court system—just like Jason.

"I can tell that you are a good guy—just like your father. Please help us. They are killing us in there, and nobody seems to care. Do something!"

Carl's nursing home caretaker yelled from outside of the door.

"Time's up, you old fuck! Get your ass out of there! Or maybe you just died of old age?"

Michael raised his eyebrow, as Carl got up out of his chair.

"See? Now you see firsthand how we are treated," Carl said, and he opened the door.

During the fifth session, at 6:17 p.m., Marpha Geewiz caused Michael to question Jerome's expertise as a counselor. Michael asked in disbelief, "And Jerome said that you don't have any disorders?"

Marpha nodded at her counselor. Michael placed his hand on his forehead, and sighed. This whole time, his patient was constantly worrying about things that weren't worth worrying over. It had taken about an hour just to get her to sit down because she was worried about getting dirt on her dress, which caused her to go into a tailspin of what-ifs. Michael didn't have a problem with it, though, because she was his last client today.

Marpha gave the counselor a confused look. "Did I do something wrong?"

Michael shook his head at her. "No, but I would like to schedule another counseling session with you, if that's all right. There are some tests that I highly recommend you get performed."

Marpha went through this in her head, and seemed very confused. "Are you saying that I have a problem? Because Jerome himself said that I'm fit for society, and that I have no problems." She stood up, and began to pace back and forth. "But what if he is wrong, and you are right? Then that would mean that I would have to pay for this service. But what if an unexpected bill comes up?"

Michael sighed. "Here we go again."

Marpha was in her own world, and didn't notice her counselor's comment.

"What if I don't have money to pay for that bill? Then I would have to borrow money, but my friends may not have it to loan. Then I would have to borrow from my family. I don't get along with my family. I won't have the money to pay the bill. That would jack up my credit score. I could lose my house! Then I won't be able to get another one with a jacked-up credit score! I'll become destitute. I will become like that selfish whore...Laura."

Thirty minutes later, Marpha turned to her counselor after her seemingly endless amount of pacing, and said, "How much is it going to be?"

Michael opened his eyes after having taken a little nap. "It won't cost anything for the testing," he said groggily. "Only if we find anything that needs to be treated, and you want it taken care of. Your insurance covers testing."

Marpha seeeemed very relieved. "Good."

Michael thought to himself, *And Jerome said that this woman is fit to function in society?! What the fuck?*

During afterhours, at 8:00 p.m., Michael walked down the empty sidewalk toward home. Today had been a very productive day for him. He had gained so much insight into all of the problems in town. For one, it was clear that Jerome needed to lose his job, because he had been diagnosing a lot of people who didn't have any problems, while allowing mentally ill people to roam the streets. Second, the cop, Fuxup Lives, was arresting innocent people, and there was no telling how many were in the jails right then. Third, the Typical Nursing Home needed to be shut down. Finally, people who were working hard to get their dream jobs were getting mediocre jobs, while incompetent people were being promoted left and right.

Michael was going to look into the issue of the nursing home some more, because the only thing he'd heard in person was the rude comment toward Carl. The Typical Nursing Home issue was a very personal issue for Michael as well. There was so much that needed to be done, and yet Michael was just one man and one counselor. Even though it was his job to help out a lot of people, it just wasn't enough.

Maybe I should run for mayor. It's going to be a lot of hard work, but I can do it, Michael thought to himself. As he walked home, he saw that the election was several months from then. He saw that Sell Out, D. Bag, and Jerome Incompetence were the three candidates so far. The last name listed sent a shiver down Michael's spine. *Now I really need to become mayor, or else Jerome will fuck things up even more.*

Mark was an eighteen-year-old boy who had his life together. He aspired to become a mayor someday so that he could fix all of the problems in Harshtown. There were so many of them, though, and he was just one young man—but he did feel that the job wasn't out of his league. He was the top student at his school, his family was very well respected, he was about to attend the top college in the country, and he was graduating from high school in a few months. His father was so proud of him because Mark had been nothing but a good child. To top things off, today was his eighteenth birthday, which was a new beginning for him, since that meant he was officially a grown-up now.

Mark got out of his bed with a yawn, knowing full well that it was the big day. He went to the bathroom to clean himself, and noticed that it was very quiet, which was odd, considering that it was nine in the morning. His father should be awake at least, but there were no sounds. Mark found this a little bit strange, but it wasn't a big deal, so he left the bathroom to get dressed.

As soon as he left his room, however, a prowler in the house snuck up on him, and held a gun behind him. Mark froze, feeling something pressed against his back. He raised his hands. There was an uneasy silence.

"Well, well, well...look at what we have here—a trespasser."

Mark instantly recognized the voice. "Father?"

"Shut the fuck up!" his father yelled angrily. "If you say another word, then I'll blow your fucking head off!"

Mark's father placed his hand on the trigger, and guided Mark downstairs, keeping him in his line of sight. His father, crazed, then called the cops as he glared at his son, who was completely confused. Mark wondered if this was some sick joke.

"What are you doing? Why did you do this?"

"You are trespassing, and usually I shoot trespassers on sight.

You're lucky that I don't blast you away right now."

Mark shook his head in confusion. "Is this some type of joke, father?! If it is, then it isn't funny!"

"You forgot, haven't you?"

Mark shrugged, trying to figure out how he possibly could have gone wrong. He had been nothing but a good son.

"Then let me remind you! I always told you that when you turn eighteen, you leave the house! And now you are eighteen, and trespassing on my property!"

"Father! I'm eighteen, but I still haven't finished school yet, and I'll be gone once I go to college! Just give me some more time!"

"I told you this way ahead of time. It ain't my fault that you didn't come up with a backup plan! Or maybe you thought I was joking when I said you needed to leave the house when you turned eighteen?"

The sounds of police sirens interrupted them. Mark, still confused, was handcuffed, then lugged into the police car that was set for jail. His father, Officer Fuxup Lives, waved at him, as his demeanor changed to one of admiration.

"Make me proud, my son! And feel free to visit! Don't be a stranger, and enjoy your high school graduation. Good luck in college! You got my support!"

Thirty minutes later, Mark was thrown violently into a jail cell. He tried to protest to the guards, but it was to no avail. Instead, they just laughed at him. He nervously looked at his cellmate, expecting to see some intimidating hulky guy covered in prison tattoos. To his surprise, his cellmate was his same age, and appeared normal.

"You just turned eighteen, too, didn't you?" his cellmate, who was named Joshua, asked. Mark nodded.

"I got the same treatment. Turned eighteen a week ago,

parents accused me of trespassing in the morning, then I get arrested. Fortunately, we won't be here very long. Doesn't matter, though, won't be able to finish high school due to my absences, and might as well kiss my dreams goodbye, because once I'm out, I won't have a place to stay."

Mark stepped up to his cellmate. "Come on! You gotta have more faith than that! You will get out of this just fine. We will have to work together! I'm pretty sure that one of our family members will let us stay with them."

Joshua slowly shook his head no. The two stuck with each other during their entire jail sentence, which was a month, until they were eventually released.

A week after their release, at C.J. Pickles, during an interview, the store manager said to Mark and Josh:

"So you are telling me...that you both are nothing but a bunch of bums who never held jobs? Because that is all that I'm seeing. Just a bunch of failures."

The store manager eyed his two interviewees. He chuckled at them, because they weren't even dressed professionally, and they smelled like garbage.

Mark decided that it was best that he did the speaking, since Joshua had very low self-esteem. "Well, we are working on the house thing. As for holding a job? We both have done very well in high school. I was the president of the Future Business Leaders of The United States, Inc., and Joshua, here, was the class president. Even though we haven't had jobs in the past, we are very hard workers."

The store manager shook his head. "Don't really give a damn about that, and this isn't high school. This is real life! I'm looking for experienced customer service reps, and all you give me is nothing. Hell, I can't even hire you two just because you don't have homes and phone numbers—that is the policy! Get the hell out of my store, you worthless bums...NOW! And don't you dare even consider stealing merchandise!"

Later that night, Mark and Josh stood in front of a house near the woods. Mark spoke to his uncle who is in front of the door. After he explained their situation to him for several minutes, Mark said, "So, Uncle Charles, can we stay? That is the situation. Our parents kicked us out of our homes because we turned eighteen."

Mark's uncle thought about it for a moment. "So you are telling me that all of this time, you never thought of a backup plan? Hell, your father told you that you would have to leave when you turned eighteen from the time you were seven years old! Sounds very irresponsible if you ask me!"

Joshua, with his head low, quietly said, "Yes, we were told this when we were young, but we didn't think that we would get kicked out as soon as we turned eighteen."

Mark nodded in agreement, while Uncle Charles shook his head at the two. "Excuses, excuses. Well, you can stay."

The two were relieved, and began to move their bags into their respective rooms. Once they were settled in, Uncle Charles called them downstairs.

"Okay, since you two are moved in, the rent is gonna be six hundred a month...so pay up—now." He waited patiently for the two to pay, but the two boys were confused, and nervous since they didn't have any cash.

Charles snorted. "The silence tells me that you two don't have the money, so that means you can't stay here, which means that you are trespassing. I'll give you two up to the count of ten to get the fuck out of my house, before I blast you both away with my shottie."

He started to count, and began to head for the back room to get his shotgun. The two boys hastily gathered whatever belongings they could take, and then rushed out.

A few blocks away from the house, Joshua sobbed, "Looks like we were destined to be bums from the start. It turns out that the real world isn't anything how they portrayed it in the media."

The two had missed far too many days of high school, which caused them to be unable to graduate, which meant they were unable to go to college. The only thing they could do was beg for change and dig for food out of trash cans.

A week later, Joshua committed suicide by jumping into a river. Mark was about to do the same thing, until he spotted a flier on the ground as he was walking toward the river, which said:

Did you just turn eighteen years old and get kicked out of your house? Well, you are in luck! We are a group of eighteen-year-olds who work together to build up our lives. All you have to be is a hard worker, and very cooperative.

Mark wiped a tear away from his eye in relief, and made his way to the place's address. Things were finally starting to look more positive. The building was located in one of the near-abandoned neighborhoods, and the home itself was broken down, but was being worked on by people his age. The workers welcomed him warmly, and they could easily sympathize with him. Mark sighed, wishing that Joshua hadn't lost all hope.

It was now time for Mark to build up his life from scratch. He was determined to lead a successful life—for his sake and for Joshua's. He would not allow his friend's suicide be in vain.

CHAPTER FIVE

MILENA LEFT THE BUILDING after a job well done volunteering. She had been volunteering a lot at the Shelter For Unprepared Eighteen-Year-Olds. Mark, a kid at the shelter. seemed to have a lot of potential for success. Milena felt that it was a shame that many parents simply kicked their children out of their homes, even if they weren't prepared to leave. She thought it was like giving them a death sentence. It was one thing if the kid was mooching off of the parent, but it was another if the kid was at least trying to be successful. Ever since she had left the Harshtown Correctional Asylum she had learned to cherish life, especially after getting shot by Rachel.

Milena began walking home. As soon as the crowd around her realized who she was, they screamed in terror and scrambled away. Some of them hid behind the bushes, while one of them ran into the street and was accidentally hit by a car. The rest of the neighborhood began to join in on the screaming, and then went inside their homes and locked their doors and windows. Even the stray animals were afraid of Milena, and all of the cats climbed up the trees while the dogs hid behind the bushes, their tails tucked between their legs, whimpering.

A police officer drove down the street, but as soon as Milena was spotted, he rapidly did a screeching U turn. All of the lights in the streets and in the houses turned off, and the whole area turned into a ghost town. The only sounds that Milena could hear were crickets as she continued to walk down the streets.

As soon as she arrived back to her mansion, she turned on the television. As she settled in, the news channel greeted her with, "We congratulate Lamar for his profit gain in the Typical Nursing Home. As for the political side, Jerome Incompetence offers his support to the nursing home, which earns him a lot of supporters for his vote for the upcoming election. In other news, there was a poll taken today to determine who is the most hated person in the country. So far, by a long shot, Laura Spokovich, the selfish whore who didn't give the homeless man money, is the winner. The second most hated person is Milena Purser, but she is the number one, most feared person since she is a psycho bitch that shouldn't have ever been released from the in-sane asylum in the first place. God bless Rachel for shooting the crazy woman, and it's a pity that she is still alive. That reminds me, The Milena Alert. She was last seen doing some volunteer work at the SFUEYO (Shelter For Unprepared Eighteen-year-olds) main building. One person was unfortunately hit by a car in a vain attempt to escape the psycho. Fortunately, the injuries were very minor. Milena is currently in her mansion, so be sure to stay clear of her."

Milena turned off the television with a chuckle, and thought to herself, *You assholes talk about me behind my back, but none of you have the balls to come to my face to say it.* She didn't care too much about what the world thought of her. She had already made her peace, and was doing what she felt was right in order to help the world—though sometimes she questioned why she even bothered in the first place.

Milena changed into something more casual, and went back

outside to head to the convenience store. She had forgotten to buy a candy bar there earlier, but it wasn't a big deal because she felt like going out for a walk. What irked her the most about this fear that people had of her was that sometimes she couldn't help those who needed help.

The next day, at a homeless shelter, the staff member of the shelter muttered nervously,

"M-M-Milena...how are you?"

Milena looked at the male receptionist in front of her, and then sighed, shaking her head.

"I came here to do some volunteer work for the homeless. I signed up a week ago, and here I am."

The terrified man gave her a fake smile, and said, "Sure."

Milena, slightly irritated, signed in, and headed toward where the homeless had gathered. What surprised her the most was that there were a hell of a lot of people there, to the point that a party could be thrown. As she got closer, Milena realized that these people weren't volunteering, but were picking on someone. This intrigued her even more, as she tried to figure out who the hell could possibly deserve this type of treatment. As soon as her presence was known, the crowd immediately screamed in terror, and scrambled away from whomever it was they had been harassing. Milena looked down at the victim, and easily recognized the woman.

"You are Laura Spokovich? The selfish whore? The most hated person in the country?"

Laura was completely filthy from the dirt the crowd had thrown on her. She coughed, shook herself, then slowly got up. She shielded herself as she saw Milena, approach. Strangely enough, Milena did not join in on the bullying, which shocked Laura.

"You aren't going to pick on me? The shelter is charging

people twenty dollars a minute to bully me. The people that you witnessed all agreed that it was one hell of a bargain, as well as an admirable thing for a homeless shelter to do—and yet you aren't harassing me. Who are you anyway?"

Milena introduced herself, and asked Laura how she'd gotten into such a mess. The story made Milena sick to her stomach. It was by far the most appalling story that she had ever heard.

"What a bunch of assholes! This society is fucked up!"

Laura smirked. "Tell me about it, but it's okay, because something good will happen to me eventually. I have faith in God now, and I've donated to the church."

Milena smiled slightly. "Something has...you can stay with me as long as you like."

Laura wanted to cheer, but she simply smiled happily so she wouldn't jinx things.

Laura got cleaned up for the first time in years, and afterward changed into some new and clean clothes. Milena was completely aware that Laura would have continued to stay in the situation that she had been in until someone intervened. It was very unlikely that Laura would have been able to build her life back up due to her horrible reputation. This was the best solution that Milena could think of. Everyone knew who Laura was, and she couldn't just apply for a job, and hope to have the same chances of attaining one as anyone else. Also, Milena had been very lonely, and needed companionship.

A week later, Milena was headed to another building to do some volunteer work when something caught her eye. She saw a crowd of people in front of a house that was on fire. There were firefighters who were working to put out the fire, but what caught her eye the most was the fact that there were people still inside the burning house. Milena approached, but as soon as someone realized she was there, the crowd scrambled away in terror, leaving her and the firefighters there alone.

"Okay, what we're going to do is rush in and save the married couple. Let's go now! Oh, shit! It's Milena!"

The rescue team instantly rushed away from the scene, screaming in terror. The ones holding the hoses did the exact same thing ten seconds later. Milena sighed, and thought, *For crying out loud! Could you dumbasses not be afraid of me for one minute! There are people in there who need your help!*

Left with no choice, she rushed inside the burning house. Navigating inside was a pain because of the smoke. She made it upstairs to where the couple was, who didn't pay much attention to how she looked. They blindly followed her as she signaled for them to come with her. She guided them through the house in just the perfect time, because soonafter the place collapsed. They panted for a moment as they observed the wreckage. The couple turned to Milena to thank her, and the husband spoke up.

"Thank you. You saved our lives. I'm not sure why those people and the firemen left, but if it wasn't for you we would be dead. Wait, I recognize you."

"Oh no! It's Milena!" the woman yelled. The two scrambled away in fear, screaming.

Milena screamed in frustration, "What the fuck?! I just saved your lives!"

Laura sat down on the couch to watch the news.

"Earlier today, a house near downtown caught on fire. For some odd reason, the crowd and the firemen ran away for their lives. After questioning a witness, we were told that Milena made a surprise appearance. Even though those two in the house could have died without help, it was more important to escape from the psycho bitch. The crowd did manage to get away from her, and nobody got hurt. The two in the house did manage to survive, but they are committed to the insane asylum after being too traumatized from an experience that happened shortly after they escaped."

Laura didn't get a chance to finish watching the news because Milena grabbed a mug and threw it as hard as she could at the television screen—breaking it.

———

"Mom! Why is it that you have to walk me to school like I'm a baby?" Tony complained. "I have been doing it myself all year and last year!"

"Son, I have been keeping up with the Milena Alert. It simply isn't safe to leave you unattended while that psycho is out on the streets! A woman like that needs to stay locked up! I hear that she lures children to her mansion that is made out of candy, throws them into a boiling caldron, and eats them!"

Tony hugged his mother, and then entered the school. The other parents were also taking their children's safety more seriously. The Milena Alert was a very beneficial asset to have in town. Who knew when a self-redeeming volunteer who wanted to help out the world in whatever way she could would prowl the streets and snatch away their children? It was better to be safe than sorry.

Fifteen minutes later, in class, Mr. Tank said, "All right, who was the pirate who discovered the Unites States, Inc.? Anyone?"

Tony raised his hand nervously, and reluctantly said, "May I have permission to speak, Master?"

Mr. Tank turned to his student, and nodded. "Yes you may, cretin."

"The person's name was Chris Colombia. I am finished, my

AND YOU THOUGHT YOUR WORLD WAS HARSH

superior elder."

The instructor slowly walked over to his student's desk as the boy looked up at him nervously. Mr. Tank, with a chuckle, said, "Chris Colombia..."

Tony chuckled along in uncertainty. Mr. Tank banged his fists on Tony's desk right away.

"WRONG! Sixty push-ups! NOW, CRETIN!"

Tony jumped up from his seat, and instantly did what he was told. This was why the students were afraid to answer the questions. Most preferred to just do the twenty push-ups for not answering.

"Anyone else want to take a crack at it?" There was silence until Carmen was about to raise her hand again, but this time, someone beat her to it. The new girl was called upon.

"May I have permission to speak, Master?"

Mr. Tank turned to the new girl, named Alik, and said, "Yes you may, fresh cretin."

She said articulately, "The name of the pirate who discovered the United States, Inc. is Chris Columbus. He discovered the continent in the year 1492 on October twelfth. The name of his ship was called the *Stowaway Express*, and his crew consisted of fifty-two people. I am finished, my superior elder."

There was dead silence in the class room. Everyone was in shock that there was someone who seemed to be as smart, if not smarter, than Carmen. Mr. Tank simply clapped.

"It turns out that I have more than one person who isn't below the line of retardation."

During lunch time, Carmen decided to sit with Alik. She wasn't jealous of her or upset that she answered the question so well. She was lonely, and felt they could become good friends. Although she would usually sit with Kenny and Tony, they were boys, and she didn't have too much in common with them, other than having common sense.

"Hello, my name is Carmen."

The new girl waved at Carmen. "I am Alik. I'm a transfer student, and I'm an orphan."

The two talked with each other for a while, and just as Carmen predicted, they had a lot in common, but the problem was that she wasn't all that interested in Alik. She didn't understand this, since they seemed compatible as friends. They did, however, spend time with each other outside of class, but it grew old for Carmen very fast. After the first week, Alik seemed to be obsessed over Carmen. Alik called every thirty minutes, visited every day, and constantly followed Carmen around.

Three weeks later during lunch, Carmen decided to sit with the boys. Tony and Kenny nodded their approval of her company. At first, they talked about the rumors about Mr. Tank, until Alik smiled at them, sitting down next to Carmen. There was an awkward silence, until Alik spoke up.

"It would have been nice of you to tell me you were sitting here. Oh well, it was easy to find you."

"Yeah, I haven't talked to Kenny and Tony too much lately, so I wanted to sit here."

Alik nodded at Carmen as she ate her food. The boys didn't say a thing, but they felt like they were walking on eggshells.

"You could have at least told me," said Alik. "We have been friends for a pretty long time now, and I don't like being mistreated by my best friend. It's rude and disrespectful."

Carmen rolled her eyes, and began to eat again, not responding to the comment.

"I see. I guess I'm not good enough for you. These stupid boys are much better than I am. Or maybe you are attracted to them? Aren't you a little too young to be attracted to boys?"

Tony spoke up hastily and defensively. "It isn't like that! We are just friends! Even if she is a little creepy. I mean, there are those strange rumors after all, but they can't be true, right?"

Carmen held up her hand to Tony in a gesture to tell him to stop talking. She then looked at Alik. "I just needed some personal space."

Alik chuckled at her somewhat creepily. "Well, whatever. Next time just let me know that you are sitting somewhere else."

Hours later, Alik was still stressing Carmen out. In order to avoid another scene similar to the lunch room, Carmen had told Alik that she would be at the park, but that she would be alone because she needed personal space. She played in solitude regardless of other people being present. She just needed time to recharge. A half hour later, a boy asked if he could play on the swing near her. Carmen complied, but resumed her solitude. A minute later, a familiar voice beckoned her rudely.

"What in the world?! You said that you needed some alone time, and here you are socializing, and letting this boy right here play with you!"

Carmen sighed. "He was just asking me if he could play on that swing near me. We aren't playing together, and I am just playing with these marbles alone!" Carmen glared at Alik, who gave her another sadistic laugh.

"You are trying to find a new best friend. I can see through you!" She paced back and forth. "Why can't you just tell me what I have done wrong?! Why did you make it so tough on me?!" Alik ran away in tears before Carmen could respond.

Three days later, Carmen was at her breaking point, and realized that she couldn't be too terribly nice to Alik anymore.

"My grandmother is dying," Carmen said to Alik on the phone. "This may be my last time to see her alive! The caretakers in the Typical Nursing Home told us that her mental state is deteriorating due to old age catching up to her. She was covered in bruises the last time I saw her."

"So your grandmother is higher up than your best friend?! First, the lunch room, then the park, and now this? We planned on going to the library to study together a week ago, and you better not back out of it—dying grandmother or not!"

"You need to chill out. I think you are a good person, but you need to give me some personal space, and work on your anger management and emotional swings!"

Alik cackled at her. "I need to chill out, and get my emotions in check?! My best friend chooses her grandmother over me!" She began to cry on the phone. "She chooses her grandmother over me."

"I'm sorry, Alik." Carmen hung up on her.

Three hours later, Carmen began to fix up her bed as she prepared to sleep for the night. She tried to tuck herself in, but while her guard was down, and since she was in the dark, someone else began to tuck her in after she laid down in her bed. Carmen, too sleepy and exhausted to think straight, simply allowed herself to be tucked in while thinking that it is her mother doing so. Two minutes later, realizing that her mother had gone to sleep before her, Carmen opened her eyes in alarm, and realized there was an intruder in her room.

"Hey, Carmen. Don't worry. It's me, Alik. I climbed up your window to tuck you in."

Carmen was very creeped out by this, but kept her composure, but her nervousness began to slightly show in her voice. "T-t-thank you, Alik...why did you come here?"

Alik chuckled. "I just wanted to apologize to you for overreacting about visiting your grandmother. I'll see you tomorrow. Sleep well. I won't make too much noise on the way out, and I'll lock the door since I took your keys a few days ago and made a copy from them."

Alik opened the door, then closed it silently behind her. That would explain why her keys had disappeared for one day, then had reappeared the next. The next day, Carmen tried to talk her mother into changing the locks, but it was to no avail. Her parent didn't see the point. Her mother didn't even believe her when she told her that Alik had a copy of the keys.

"Now you are just making up things. You are way too responsible to just let someone steal your keys, and pinning this on your new best friend is just dirty!"

A few days later, after school, Carmen purposefully missed the bus in order to avoid Alik. Alik, however, pretended to get on the bus to give her best friend the idea that she'd gotten on. In reality, Alik had gotten off the bus, and had started following Carmen home. Eventually, she caught up to Carmen, and caught her off guard.

"Hey, Carmen, for the past few days it seems like you have been avoiding me, so I wonder if there are any issues?"

"I told you before, over and over, that I need my personal space, but it doesn't seem to register in your head! Are you really as smart as you say you are?! Or maybe you are just some moron, just like most of the people in this world!"

Alik, with a saddened look, was about to reply, but Carmen cut her off.

"You aren't even that great of a friend. Hell, you may be a good person, but I'm not all that interested in you! We aren't best friends, we never were, and we never will be, so stay out of my life!"

Alik was in complete silence over this, and she began to cry in despair. Carmen felt somewhat badly, but had no choice but to do what she'd just done. Carmen resumed her walk home. Unfortunately, she was caught off guard again, as Alik hit her very hard in the back of the head with a board that she had hidden in her book bag.

"I didn't want it to come to this! You are my best friend, whether you like it or not!"

Carmen was knocked unconscious.

Two hours later, Carmen woke up to a putrid smell. She tried to yell, but her mouth was gagged, and she realized that she was tied to a chair, and was in some type of cave. She gradually began to recognize this was the place where she took Eliza, and all of the memories of how she'd handled her resurfaced. Her current situation mirrored the past, which had taught Carmen a valuable lesson. Carmen turned to the putrid smell to see that it was the skeleton of her former best friend, who had also been tied up and gagged. A minute later, Alik entered the cave with a smile.

"Hey, Carmen. I'm trying the best I can to be your friend, but because of how you are acting, this is the best way that things can be, and you have no say in this."

Carmen struggled to get loose, but it was futile. She did, however, notice that the knot on her right arm was loose, but it wasn't a good time to escape.

Alik sighed. "Unfortunately, I need to go back to the orphanage. It turns out that I'm finally going to be adopted. I'll be back tomorrow to tell you about it. Please don't die on me. I don't want to lose another best friend so soon."

Alik left shortly after. For the next hour, Carmen struggled to break free of the bonds. It turned out that the weak side was a little trickier than she'd expected, but eventually she was free. With her free arm, she moved the chair to a jagged rock on the ground, and then used the rock to break the rope on her legs and tied arm.

Carmen was able to escape the cave and the forest just before it turned dark. As she crossed the street, she saw a police officer park his car near her. The driver rolled down his window, and observed her for a moment.

"Are you Carmen?" he asked.

Nervous, she reluctantly nodded at the man.

"Your mother is worried about you. Get in the car, and I'll take you home."

Carmen got in the backseat, and soon fell asleep while the officer took her home. Her mother greeted her happily as soon as she made it back.

"Carmen, I was so worried about you! Where have you been?!"

She was about to speak, but realized she was too weak. She hadn't eaten anything since lunch, and escaping the cave had been very tiresome. Her mother tended to her.

Thirty minutes later, in the living room, Carmen's mother approached Carmen and said happily:

"Carmen, I have a surprise for you...you have a sister now!" This statement confused Carmen, because she didn't recall her mother ever having any significant other. Her mother left to go upstairs, and then returned a few minutes later.

"Here is your new sister! I adopted her today!" To Carmen's horror, Alik walked down the stairs. She looked at Carmen with a grin that was both joyful and sadistic.

"I saw you two spending so much time together, and she told me the story about how her parents died. She also said that she always wished she had a sister her age, so I figured why not?"

———

Hector began to wipe down the counter. He felt that it may be best to hire someone. Perhaps he should hire that clerk that cashed in his winning lottery ticket? He pondered this. He was indeed a hard worker; however, managing a store, cleaning it up, and performing maintenance was simply too much for one guy. A couple minutes later, a girl entered through the front door. He did not recognize her.

"Hey, if you need anything, then feel free to ask. I will be here."

The girl rushed at Hector, and clung to him, much to his surprise.

"You gotta help me, sir! You need to adopt me! I can't take being at home anymore! Alik won't leave me alone! She won't give me my personal space! Please, sir! I beg you!"

Immediately, a woman entered the door.

"Carmen! Get back here! Now! You are supposed to get your hair done! You know that this is the wrong building."

Hector had no idea how to act. He could tell that this was not a joke. There were no visible marks on the girl, so it did not appear that she was being abused at home. She gripped Hector.

"Please, sir! Save me! I can't take it anymore!"

It had been two weeks since Alik had been adopted into Carmen's family, and her tolerance and sanity had been chipping away.

The mother walked over to the two, and pried her daughter off of Hector. She started to drag Carmen away, who was screaming and crying.

"I'm sorry about her behavior, sir. I don't know what came over her."

Hector nodded. "No problem, ma'am. It happens...I guess."

Once the event was over, Hector reflected on what was to come. He was invited by his best friend, Jamaal, to attend a service of the newly built church. Hector normally did not get himself involved in religious affairs, however, his friend had invited him, he needed a break from work, and the two could have a good time together. The church service was tonight, and Hector felt like he might as well make the best of it.

Several hours later at church that evening, the preacher preached, "Come on! You have the money! God knows that you have the money! All you have to do in order to be saved is donate fifty dollars! Even if you need the money, even if it is all that you have, donate fifty dollars now for the higher cause and for eternal life, or you will be judged once you die, and God knows everything! God knows whether you will donate the fifty dollars or not! You could die in the next ten minutes, and the only reason you will be denied eternal life is because you didn't donate!"

Hector yawned in boredom as he looked at his watch. He wanted this to end. The main reason he'd come to this church was because his friend Jamaal had asked him to go. Hector respected everyone's beliefs, but what he didn't approve of was the fact that this church's service had lasted over two and a half hours. He also disliked the fact that Reverend Abraham was constantly begging for money, or at least this was how Hector saw it. Jamaal poked his friend to wake him up after he'd nodded off, but Hector shrugged him off and tried to go back to sleep.

"All right, thank you all for the money. It will go into my checking account—err—the donation box. Now for the next part of the service—who here is a first timer?"

Jamaal poked Hector again, and told him to raise his hand. Hector did so without realizing what he was raising his hand for, and he was called to the podium to stand near Abraham. The preacher shook Hector's hand, but then realized that Hector had tattoos of ceremonial daggers, and he paused for a moment. Abraham signaled for the music to stop, and then signaled for there to be silence. Jamaal observed, and wondered what was going on. Hector looked around, confused.

Abraham took the microphone, and said, "Looks like we have a heretic in the holy temple!"

The audience was confused as they listened silently. Abraham carelessly yanked Hector's arms, lifted up his sleeves, and then raised Hector's arms to reveal the tattoos.

"See this! He has ceremonial dagger tattoos! This man practices witchcraft! He is a witch!"

This caused an uproar from the crowd. Abraham ordered everyone to be silent again. This whole time, Hector was watching Jamaal to see if he would step up to defend him, but he was actually making fake protests with the rest of the crowd.

"Now even though he is a heretic, a demon channeler, and a witch, there is still hope for this man, as long as he chooses to be saved today!" Abraham turned to Hector. "So what will it be, heretic?"

Hector looked away from Jamaal in pure disgust, and then turned to Abraham. The so-called heretic swiftly snatched away the microphone.

"For one, I don't believe in demons! Second, I'm not a witch, and even if I was, witches are not how you portray them in the media! Third, I respect your religion and beliefs, and I don't think it's hard for you all to do the same with mine, but I do understand that not all people who practice your faith are like you all. And finally, no—I'm not interested in being converted!"

Hector dropped the microphone. There was nothing but dead silence in the church as he walked toward the front entrance. Jamaal stood up to follow him, but Hector pushed him down in his seat, and continued walking away until he'd left the church alone.

Hector tried to get into his car, but he was assaulted from behind by one of the church members. The attacker snatched Hector away from his car door, and punched him in the face as hard as he could, knocking him to the ground. Hector was about to get up and attack the guy who had hit him, but he was restrained, and held down by a few more members of the church.

"Tie his arms and legs up! Now!"

Hector struggled vainly to break free. The church members weren't successful at tying his arms and legs up, but one member of the crowd hit hector in the head with a club, which knocked him unconscious.

Thirty minutes later, Hector woke up, noticing that he had been stripped to his boxers. He was tied to what appeared to be some type of cross. His legs were tied to the bottom of it, and his arms were tied on the sides of it. There was some type of band on his head that felt bloody because he'd been hit hard there. The band itself felt a little bit prickly, like there were thorns or nails attached to it. Hector struggled vainly to break out, but the only thing this did was make his hands bleed some. He could hear crowds cheering, but he didn't see anyone because he was behind a curtain. A couple of minutes later, the curtain opened, and he realized he was still in the church. Jamaal just sat there looking up at Hector, but he wasn't cheering this time. Instead, he sat in silence with a look of sorrow and guilt. A minute later, Jamaal walked away, turned his back, and then lowered his head in shame.

"This Heretic here tried to attack some of our congregational staff members, and they had to defend themselves! It is claimed that he attempted to summon a demon, but failed because they are protected by the holy ghost!"

The audience began to boo Hector, who was feeling very dazed because of his head injury, and some of the blood loss. Shortly after, the sound of police sirens could be heard, and then the cops entered the church. Officer Lives walked to Abraham, and demanded an explanation

"This man attacked my staff! They defended themselves, and now I am teaching my church members a valuable lesson when it comes to dealing with demons like him," Abraham explained.

Officer Lives reflected on this for a moment. "Hmm, makes sense. Gotta protect yourselves. However, you should have called the cops after you restrained him. Your congregation just practiced vigilantism. I'll have to arrest you and him, then—"

Before Officer Lives could finish, Abraham wrote him a check for a thousand dollars, and handed it to him.

"Err, what I meant to say was that I'll have to arrest him for domestic disturbance."

The officers tied Hector down, and then carried him to their police car.

A few hours later, in jail, a police officer approached Hector's cell. He said,

"You are bailed out. You can go now."

This news confused Hector, and he tried to think of who had bailed him out. Once he is allowed outside of his cell, he walked to a room to meet the person who had helped him, but he'd never met the person before. The man shook Hector's hand.

"Hello, my name is Michael, and I attended that church ceremony just like you did."

Hector gave him a wary look. "Thank you, but why did you bail me out—you are one of them!"

"For one, they aren't true followers. It says in the Good Book to respect people's beliefs, even if they are different from yours. There are a lot of people who claim that they are evangelicals, but they don't follow what they preach. I don't consider these people followers, but hypocrites, who make us real followers look bad. Also, if I were to jump in right away, then I would have been eaten up by the crowd just like you, so I needed for things to die down."

Hector was still skeptical. "If you are so different, then why did you attend service?"

"Abraham is Jerome Incompetence's brother. I wanted to see if he is as messed up as Jerome, and apparently he is. I am running for mayor, and I am just looking for leverage to have on my opponents. Whether he knows it or not, I recorded these events on the phone. I showed them to the police, but it seems like Abraham bribed them against you."

Hector shook Michael's hand again. "Well, you got my support, and if you need me to speak up, I'm here."

The two parted ways.

The next day, Hector headed to his store to work a shift in a vain attempt to forget what had happened yesterday. He was shocked as he saw that there were cops parked in front of his store. He got out of his car, and approached one of them.

"Hey, what happened, officer? This is my store!"

The cop motioned for Hector to follow him, showing him the damage.

"Looks like a bunch of people vandalized your store last night."

Hector saw that the windows were broken, the door was broken, and there was graffiti all over the walls that said various things, like "heretic," "devil-worshipper," "demon-channeler," "witch," and "non-believer."

"These are the people of that church, officer!"

The officer sighed, and shook his head. "Nobody wants to speak up, man. I'm sorry, but we have no evidence of who did it so far."

Hector stood in front of the store with his head low. He looked up, and heard Marisol's laughter as she walked by.

———

Out in the streets, near a church, Cecil walked peacefully towards his destination.

Cecil, remembering the experience that he had had with the irate man, immediately held out his arms in front of him defensively as a group of shady-looking men approached him. They appeared to be gang members.

"I don't want any trouble! I'm just trying to walk to the junior football stadium!"

The men chuckled at Cecil. "Don't worry, bud. We aren't here to hurt you. We simply wanted to hand you this."

Cecil lowered his arms, opened his eyes, and observed what they'd presented to him. It was a pamphlet for Abraham's church. One of the other shady men said, "We are members of this church, sir, and would like for you to become a member as well. Please consider it, bud. Abraham is doing whatever he can to save as many souls as possible, and he is helping out the community."

Cecil took the pamphlet. and said thank you.

"No problem, sir. For your own sake, we hope that you attend service. We don't want to see your home destroyed and looted."

The other shady men chuckled. Cecil didn't know what to make of this, and decided that it was best not to think about his interaction with these church members since there were other matters that he must attend to.

An hour later, at the junior football stadium, Cecil was having a motivational speech with his football team. He stated, "All right, kids, remember what I taught you—good sportsmanship, fair play, and a positive attitude! This will conquer all. You all have been training for this for months, and now is the time to put what you have learned to the test!"

Cecil's junior football team cheered after his inspirational speech was over. The team and the coach waited patiently for the opposition. The crowds were already sitting in the bleachers, and they cheered for their children. Eventually, the opposing team, as well as the referee, entered the field. Cecil looked at the coach, and saw that he was a strongly built man who had a crewcut. The opposition approached them. One of the kids stuck his tongue out at Cecil's team. Cecil was about to tell his team not to be rude like them, but their coach, Mr. Tank, beat him to it.

"Cretins! I told you over and over again to be honorable during our games!"

Immediately, the opposition snapped to attention, and saluted. "YES, SIR! WE APOLOGIZE!!"

Mr. Tank turned to Cecil, and then extended his hand.

"Hello. My name is Metal Tank. Feel free to call me Metal or Mr. Tank, whichever you prefer, as long as it isn't an insult."

Cecil shook his hand. "Nice to meet you. I'm Cecil."

Mr. Tank saluted. "We wish you good luck in the game."

The game started. Cecil was very proud of his team as he saw that they were doing very well. The team was working well together, and were winning by a long shot. Mr. Tank would occasionally nod at him, and praise Cecil for a coaching job well done. So far the score was twenty-eight to zero. The opposing captain paused the game, and called his team for a meeting.

Cecil praised his team, and afterward he observed Mr. Tank, pondering what he was up to. There was no way in hell that his team was going to catch up, no matter what Mr. Tank did. After the meeting was over with, they resumed the game, and it was Cecil's team's run. Once the ball was hiked, the runner tried to run past their tacklers until he was met by one. Instead of tackling, the tackler clenched his fist and punched the runner as hard as he could in the face, instantly knocking him out. The punch was so hard, that the assaulter punched through the face guard of the helmet. Cecil was in complete shock over this. The audience, on the other hand, cheered happily. What also shocked him was the fact that this seemed all right with the referee, as he was nonchalant about it, calling a first down. Cecil, alarmed, blew his whistle, and went to talk to the referee.

"What the hell?! One of his teammates punched one of mine square in the face! That's illegal!"

Jerome, the referee, shook his head at Cecil. "It's clean. He took down the runner, and there was nothing wrong with it. This isn't tag football!"

A few minutes later, the runner attempted again, except this time, he was met with a tackle. Shortly after, he was tackled, and then he was picked up and choke-slammed to the ground. This type of game went on for a while. The opposing team caught up, and then they passed Cecil's team by six points.

A few minutes later, at the opposing team's side, Cecil argued with Mr. Tank.

"You said that you and your team play clean! There is nothing clean about punching my team, kicking them, and slamming them!"

Cecil just glared at Mr. Tank, who sighed at him.

"Looks like someone is a sore loser," he said. "I thought you had more class than this, since your team seems well behaved. Perhaps you should stop blaming your failure on illusory factors, and focus on the real reason why you are struggling—because your team isn't good enough. Now get out of my sight, sir, and please try to chill out. The crowd is happy, my team is happy, your team is happy, and the referee is happy, so you need to be happy with them."

Cecil left in anger, and he tried to call off the game, blowing his whistle. "No more! We are finished!"

The audience protested angrily. "This is the best game ever!"

"Let them play! Keep the game going!"

"Booooooooooooo! You suck!"

Jerome looked at Cecil, shrugged, and then continued with the game.

Half-time arrived, and Cecil gazed at his battered and bruised team. Half of them were crying, while the other half were just rubbing their wounds.

"Coach, we are doing what you taught us. Why are we losing?" asked one of the players.

"Because they are playing dirty. You all are good kids, and regardless of this outcome, you all are way better than they will ever be!"

"We need to do what they do!" said one of the other players. "We need to punch them back, pile drive them, and kick them! This is more than a game...THIS...IS...WAR!"

All of the kids cheered, and they agreed to this philosophy. Cecil was against this, and he blew his whistle. "No! You are better than that! You do not need to stoop down to their level in order to beat them!"

Some of the kids snorted in annoyance.

"How about this?" asked Cecil. "Even though the referee doesn't seem willing to call off the game, you all can leave right now. You have been through enough already, and I don't want to see anymore of you get hurt."

There was silence from all of them for a moment, until one of them spoke up.

"My dad will kill me if I back out." The rest nodded, agreeing that their parents had also put a lot of faith in them, and pressure.

Cecil calmed down, and he tried to remain optimistic. "On the bright side, it is their go. We are on the defensive, and they are on the offensive. Also, just let them win the game. If you see them with the ball, let them get the touch down. Do not try to tackle them or win the game. Simply stay out of their way as best as possible. Also, if you have the ball, then toss it to one of their players so they can get another touchdown. Do not put yourselves at risk. I know it sounds lame, but your well-beings are at stake here. Don't be heroes this time."

The team approved of this, and they had finally agreed on something.

The crowd cheered as the game resumed. Once the ball was hiked, rather than going for the ball, Cecil's team just allowed the opposition to get the touch down. He was relieved, because if they did this, then none of his team would have to go to the hospital. This caused the audience to boo, and call Cecil a loser. Jerome laughed at him, and Mr. Tank just looked at him, shaking his head. The opposing coach had another talk with his team and shortly after, they resumed the game again.

Cecil's runner was given the ball, but instead of going for the touchdown, he tossed it to the opposing team. Instead of the opposing team running the ball, the ball holder threw the ball as hard as he could into the face of the one who had given it to him. Then the whole team tackled all of the teammates, punching and kicking them repeatedly.

The audience cheered. "More! More! More! More!"

Cecil looked away. This was too much for him. After they were finished, they finally ran the ball, and made yet another touchdown. The battered team just lay on the ground, groaning in pain, and some of them got up to tend to their wounds. Jerome blew the whistle, and called the game off, giving the explanation that Mr. Tank's team was way ahead and it was impossible for Cecil to catch up. The opposing team cheered, and they rushed for the stragglers that recovered.

Eventually, they caught them, and started punching and stomping them. Cecil called an ambulance, and his team went away to the hospital. Some of his teammates glared at him, and they blamed him for all of this. He had always told them that if they played clean, and treated their opposition with respect, regardless of what happened, they would prevail. This plan however, had been derailed today.

Mr. Tank extended his hand to Cecil. "Even though we disagree with your coaching methods and how your team plays, it was a good game."

Cecil crossed his arms and looked away from Mr. Tank, not saying anything. Mr. Tank put out his hand again.

"You know why you lost, correct? For one, your team are a bunch of cowards. Second, your plays weren't as good as mine. Third, your team lacks discipline. And finally, your team didn't play clean. Your team played so dirty that it makes me want to throw up just thinking about it."

Cecil still didn't respond. Mr. Tank left with his team as they celebrated their victory. One of them gleefully tackled one of Cecil's players as he was being strapped to the hospital bed.

Jason walked down the street toward his college. Maybe if he was lucky, he would catch the lunch special at the pizzeria place. As he walked, he reflected on a report that he had been doing for his physical education class. Even though he was not an athlete by any means, what had been concerning him lately, was that many athletes had been using any means necessary to win games. They had been taking steroids, cheating, and engaging in many other types of foul play, and yet, many of them were getting away with it. Even though these were just games, bad sportsmanship could translate to bad sportsmanship in life.

Jason eventually arrived at the traffic light. He waited patiently for the light to turn green. After it turned green, he didn't cross right away, but looked back and forth to see if there were any oncoming cars. After realizing that there was nothing, he crossed calmly. On his left side, as he was halfway across the street, he heard a screeching sound, but was unable to move quickly enough, and the car ran him over. He bounced off of the hood of the car. Jason lay in the street, and the driver got out of the car. Jason's eyes were closed, and he could barely hear the voices of the ones who were present.

"Holy hell, what have I done?!"

"Yeah, look at that dent on your car!"

There was nothing but silence after that.

Jason quickly woke up from his nightmare. Malik was present, and looked at Jason.

"Hey, are you all right?"

He nodded at his best friend. "I'm fine, but it's that same nightmare again. It just won't go away."

His best friend attempted to comfort him. "Perhaps you need to atone for what happened."

Jason nodded, and sat back in his seat on the train that was heading back to Harshtown. The group of them had decided to return there for vacation, and had taken a break from robbing places all over the world. So far he felt like he wasn't missing much being away from this town. He had been doing nothing but watching the news, and what he had witnessed appalled him. There was a kid's football game in which one team was brutally beating up the other team. The news reporters were talking about how entertaining the game was, and showed some high-lights of the game. These highlights consisted of slow-motion replays of the kids getting punched in the face, and many other brutal acts. There were also cheesy sound affects added onto it for laughs. Fortunately for Jason, there had been a commercial break. An ad came on the television that caught his attention.

"Hello, everyone. My name is Jerome Incompetence, and I'm running for mayor. You're probably wondering why I should become mayor. For one, I am a renowned counselor. I have a lengthy history of helping out those who have personal problems. This isn't just help for the person, but for society in general. Second, I am now a school counselor, and I help out with the children a lot. One of my major goals is for all children to be properly educated. There will be additional funding for the Typical Nursing Home, and the streets will become much cleaner. We will have more cops like this guy, Officer Lives, patrolling the streets."

"How are you all doing? My name is Officer Fuxup Lives. Be good, or else I'll send your ass to prison. And by the way, don't drop the soap!"

Jerome has stated, "Next we have Mr. Tank here to assist with education!"

"Hello, my name is Metal Tank. Jerome is a very good school counselor, as well as a referee. He helps out a lot with the cretins in school."

"And finally, we have Marpha Geewiz, a patient that I assisted in the past!" said Jerome.

"Jerome helped me out so much! I had a coworker who said that I worried about everything, but Jerome's expertise as a counselor has really set things right!"

Jerome said, "Vote for me—for a much better future!"

The commercial ended with inspirational music. Jason's jaw completely dropped as the memories of Jerome resurfaced. *This town is filled with a bunch of fucking morons!*

After the group of criminals arrived at their destination, Jason decided to split up from them. He had grown up there, and needed some alone time. He took a walk around town, but to his dismay, not too much had changed except for the fact that there was a new restaurant, as well as a new church. Jason decided to visit the restaurant. He ordered some food a few minutes later. As he waited, he looked around at the others who were present. The restaurant itself wasn't very crowded, which was fine with him because he didn't like crowds. He glanced at two women who were gossiping with one another. After Jason looked away, he looked back at them immediately in shock. As he listened to one of their voices, he suddenly realized who one of them was. and he heard in his head, "Holy hell! What have I done?!" He realized it was the woman who had ran run him over.

After five minutes of reliving the nightmare, he got up to go to the bathroom. He went into a stall. He took out his gun, loaded it, and then put it back in his pocket. Jason walked to the table where the two women were. One of them looked up at him in disgust, and the other asked nervously, "Y-you need anything, sir?" Jason took a deep breath, and said a prayer. The other woman looked at Jason closely until it dawned on her.

"Hey! I know you! You are that man who vandalized my car five years ago!"

Jason swiftly took out his gun, shot at the roof, and then pointed at them.

"Don't fucking move!"

Everyone panicked, and ran out of the restaurant. Marisol, the woman who had run over Jason years ago, was terrified, but trying to keep a calm demeanor. Her friend Marpha was breathing heavily.

"Oh no! He's gonna kill us! He's psycho! Where did he come from?! Are you associated with the mafia?" she asked Marisol.

"I need to do background checks on my friends! What if my other friends are associated with the mafia? Then that means this could happen again! If I survive this, and it happens again, then—"

Before she could get another word out, Jason shot at the ground near her, and yelled, "Shut the fuck up!"

Marpha did as she was told, but was breathing heavily, terrified. Marisol spoke up, like she was being inconvenienced.

"You know how much counseling I needed in order to get over the trauma you caused me from vandalizing my car?! And now here you are causing some more terror in my life, regardless of the fact that I put a restraining order on you."

Jason shook his head, unable to believe what he was hearing.

"Shut the fuck up! You seriously have no idea what you did, huh?! Are you that much of a fucking moron?!"

Marisol thought about this for a moment, but was completely confused, as she had no idea what he was talking about.

"I was driving, then out of nowhere, you vandalized my car! Afterward some caring citizens came to my rescue, and sympathized with me! I called a police officer, and then the gentleman arrested you. I was traumatized from the experience, so I received counseling. I was thinking about suing you, but decided to let bygones be bygones and let it go, and here you are with a gun pointed at me and my friend! Just tell me what you want, and we can probably work this out."

Shortly after Marisol's speech, police sirens could be heard as they closed in on the restaurant. Jason did not care at all. What he cared about was setting things right.

"You ruined my life! Before this whole incident, I was a straight-A college student who was gonna become a doctor! I can't believe that you can't register it in your head that you ran me over with your car! I did not vandalize your car. I was simply crossing the street, minding my own business, the light turned green, and so I crossed. Afterward, you came out of nowhere, and you ran me the hell over! You only cared about your fucking car, and so did the witnesses! I was arrested for no reason, and sent to jail for five years! Then, that dumbass counselor Jerome put me in the insane asylum."

Marisol scratched her head in confusion like he was speaking another language. She tried in vain to compute what he had told to her, but was unable.

Marpha gasped as she looked at her friend. "Oh my God! You hurt this man, and ruined his life over a car dent?! You are such a bitch! Were you always such a bitch? Of course you were—I met you after this incident happened. What if the same thing happens to me? Would you care about me or one of your material possessions? Oh my God, what if my other friends are like this? Then this means that I really don't have friends. This would mean that I'm truly alone. Then who would have my back? What if—"

"SHUT....THE FUCK....UP!" Jason yelled again.

A familiar voice yelled on a microphone from outside.

"Jason, I know it's you. Perhaps we can talk out a deal. All I ask is that you don't have another psychological fit, and shoot those two women, since we all know that you are crazy, and aren't fit to be around the general public."

Jason easily recognized the voice as Jerome's.

"I'm coming in, Jason, and I will be alone to negotiate."

A few minutes later, Jason was face to face with Jerome. With his arms crossed, Jerome said,

"What do you want, Jason? Money? Dope? Crack?"

"How about my life back? Can you do that?!"

Jerome chuckled. "I'm no miracle worker, Jason. How about you put down the gun so we can work this out?"

The criminal shook his head at the counselor. "It's apparent that you aren't a miracle worker. You're a pathetic excuse for a counselor! You lost your wife and family, and your ego is heavily inflated. Your ego is so heavily inflated that it plays tricks on you, and makes you think that you are helping out the world, when in actuality, you are doing the opposite." Jason glanced at Marisol. "And apparently, this psychopath here is no different! You know? Every night I still have that same dream over and over again, and all I want is some type of atonement, but seeing you two here makes me feel that none of you are even worth the effort, so I will be leaving now."

The last bit caused the counselor to chuckle. "How? There are cops everywhere!"

Jason reached into his right pocket for a smokescreen ball. "Like this."

He threw it down like a ninja, and a smoke screen appeared. Everyone except for Jason covered their eyes, and he was able to escape. He easily exited, and made his way behind the restaurant. He ran through the alley and into the streets, but was met by a screech to his right side, and was run over. Jason bounced off of the hood of the car, and fell to the ground, unconscious.

It was one of the cop cars. The officer got out. "What the hell?!" He looked at the front of his car. "Look at this big-ass dent on my car!"

The officer called for backup, and once it arrived, the officers talked about the dent, ignoring Jason, who was unconscious on the ground.

The officers took the car to the shop, and a mechanic got rid of the dent. An hour later, Jason was still unconscious as the cops returned to the scene to arrest him and send him to jail. He was sent back to the Harshtown Correctional Asylum. Since his crimes after he had escaped from the asylum were so well done, he wasn't even convicted of them. Jason was sent back to the cell that he had escaped from. There was much higher security in his area to prevent another escape from happening again. Jerome's negotiation attempt with Jason had made everyone in the town strongly consider him as mayor, and pictures of him were on just about every building. Even children were wearing shirts that had his image on them.

———

A week later, in Michael's office, Jason ranted:

"I'm crazy, you know I'm crazy, the world knows I'm crazy, so just put me back in my cell so I can finish rotting and dying here!"

Michael crossed his arms, and gazed at Jason. "You're not crazy, Jason, so you can just cut the act now!" He shook his head at him. "The reason I called you in here is because I want to work things out with you. I do apologize for the past. I seriously thought that Jerome and the others were genuine, but I should have just thought for myself, rather than go with their opinions."

Jason chuckled sarcastically. "Oh, wow! Your apology just makes my life a whole lot better now."

"You know, I could easily just sign the papers and let you go since I am your counselor," Michael continued, "but because of what you did back there, I just can't do it."

Jason banged his hands on the desk, glaring at Michael. "Why the fuck not?! You know that I'm not crazy, and you know that I'm the victim in this situation!"

Michael leaned forward. "You took a gun and held a couple of people hostage! What you did is a criminal act! Are you a criminal now? For that matter, how did you and Malik escape?!

And what did you do this whole time?"

There was silence from Jason, as he looked away and crossed his arms.

"I'm not signing any papers until you at least talk," Michael said. "Now go back to your cell, and think about how you handled things! From this point on, I expect to see you here every day. I won't do any negotiations until you tell me the whole story. Keep in mind that I'm willing to work with you, so don't put up your guard with me."

Jason rolled his eyes, and stated, "Fine then." A minute later, Jason was escorted out of the office by a couple of security guards.

A couple of hours later, in the recreational area, Rachel said to herself:

"I'm at my job right now, just working another shift. I did not shoot Milena! It never happened, and everything is just going on as it was."

Rachel diligently organized a book shelf, and continued to say this over and over again. Jason sat on the right side of the book shelf thinking about what Michael had said. He would occasionally look at Rachel with an annoyed expression on his face.

"I'm at home now, straightening my room! Everything is normal! Everything is—"

"Shut the fuck up, and get back into the real world!" yelled Jason. "You shot Milena and fucked up! You are in an insane asylum, and you have been here for a couple months now."

Rachel looked at Jason, and then slowly shook her head no. Jason grabbed her shoulders and shook her.

"GET....WITH...THE...PROGRAM! Accept responsibility! You fucked up, now own up to it!" Jason slapped her in the face a few times, and said this over and over again.

He let go of Rachel. The whole room just observed the

situation in awe, and a few of the people applauded. The guards separated the two, and then sent them back to their cells, concluding Jason's day.

A day later, in Michael's office, Jason said,

"All right, I have been here for a little over a week, and I already want to get the hell out, so this is what happened. Me and Malik escaped. I can't explain how we did it or what happened after we escaped, but I haven't lived an honorable life according to society's standards."

Michael took out a pen, then jotted down what Jason had told him. "I see."

"After I got run over, my eyes were opened. Malik taught me that you need to take what you want in life, or else the world will continue to take from you. This all made sense, since nobody gave a shit about me while I was unconscious, and during the aftermath of the incident. There is a code of conduct that we live by in order to not be ruthless, since everyone else is. Sure, I held those two women hostage, but I didn't intend to kill them. All I wanted was atonement. After hearing her perspective, I learned that me holding onto this isn't worth it, and for the first time in years, I don't have that same dream anymore."

Michael reflected on all that he'd been told. He could easily tell that Jason was being genuine, and he wrote this down in his notes. After ten minutes, Michael had made a decision.

"I'll sign the papers so that you can be released from here. I have no idea what your plans are outside of this world, or what you have done, but if I ever see you here again, then don't expect me to bail you out a second time. You have been genuine with what you have said, but I don't like your pessimistic philosophy—regardless of legitimate reasons for believing in that. If there's a next time, you're on your own." Jason nodded at him in silence.

A week later, Jason was released from the asylum. As he walked out of the gates, he saw a familiar woman approach him. It was Rachel dressed in proper attire. She shook his hand with gratitude.

"Thank you, Jason. If it weren't for you, then I wouldn't have come to terms with things."

She gave him a hug. Jason returned the hug without saying a word. He had a lot on his mind as he reflected on the counseling session with Michael, as well as what he'd been doing with his life the day that he'd escaped with Malik. He arrived at an intersection traffic light that was red. He waited patiently for it to turn green as another guy stood next to him. The light turned green, but Jason's instincts told him to wait patiently because of what had happened years ago. The man next to him walked across, but to his left there was a screeching sound, and the man was suddenly run over by a car. He bounced off the hood, and then fell to the ground unconscious. Jason's eyes widened. *That could have been me again!* The driver of the car got out, and was clearly alarmed.

"Holy hell! What have I done?!"

Some witnesses arrived, and one of them spoke in the same alarmed tone as before.

"You ran over this poor guy!"

Another person piped up. "Yeah! We need to call 9-1-1 now, and get him some medical assistance!"

One of the witnesses took out their cell phone to call the police. Jason just observed the situation blankly. The driver paced back and forth, crying out, "This poor man! Why?! Why do I have to be such a terrible driver! He didn't do anything wrong to anyone!"

One of the witnesses tried to calm her down, and told her that everything would be taken care of. Shortly after the accident, sirens could be heard, and an ambulance arrived. The workers carefully picked up the man, and then placed him on a stretcher. The ambulance drove quickly to the hospital. Five minutes later, a police officer arrived to the scene. The driver explained the situation to him. After things were cleared up, the driver and the witnesses headed toward the hospital to check to see if the victim was all right. Jason just stood there, frozen, and thought, *Now why the hell couldn't that happen with me?!*

CHAPTER SIX

Mark hastily entered the fast food restaurant to work his shift. He was thirty minutes late because he'd had to help a poor guy who had been run over nearby. Fortunately for him, the other onlookers had been very caring, and were quick to help out. What bothered him a little about the situation was the one guy who had just observed with a blank stare on his face. Mark shook his head The guy had just stood there, watching everyone help the guy, without lifting a finger. How would the guy have felt if he had been the one run over? Mark put his thoughts aside, hastily clocked in, and entered the break room. Apparently he had made it just in time for the day's meeting. He slowly walked to an empty chair, and sat down. Mark listened intently to his store manager, Tim, who had previously been a manager of some crappy toy store.

"As you all know, our CEO Fatima is really expanding when it comes to the fast food chain. We are going to need a new supervisor for this store, and we only hire from within, so all of you will be evaluated, but one of you will be promoted to the supervisor position. What I am looking for is an individual who has the ability to lead as well as work very hard. Regardless of the outcome, you are all hard workers, and just keep doing what you're doing. If you don't get the position, then keep in mind that since we promote from within, there will be more opportunities in the future. All of you joined at the perfect time, so make us proud!"

This was very good news for Mark. Shortly after finding the Shelter for Eighteen-year-olds, he was able to get a job. Regardless of how hard things were, Mark was still determined to make his dreams come true. After the first month, he was able to find a place where he and a few others from the shelter could stay and rent out. Getting the supervisor position would help his business resume, and would help with tuition money for school next year. Mark felt certain that he would be able to get the job since he was the hardest worker, and already knew ahead of time that he was going to become the employee of the month. Getting people to follow him was also no problem.

An hour later, in Tim's office, Tim asked curiously, "Why are you here, Mark?"

Mark attempted to hide his confidence as he spoke. "I came here to get your input about the supervisor position, sir. I'm curious whether you think I'm a good fit."

Tim didn't need to think about it too much. "Things are looking good for you, Mark. For someone who has no prior job experience, you are extremely impressive and—"

Tim was interrupted suddenly as Andrew, the same guy who had stolen Cecil's vision, walked inside the room. He was just as lazy as he'd been when he'd worked with Cecil, and just about everyone knew this.

"Hey, boss. I came to talk to you about the supervisor position. I'm wondering if you think I'm up for it."

Mark sighed, looking at Andrew, and then shook his head. He found it ridiculous that this underachiever was actually considering this position.

Tim shrugged. "Well, I was about to talk to Mark about it, so you'll have to wait."

Andrew rushed to his manager's side. "Tim, you're an awesome store manager. Whenever I get a child, you will be their number one role model. Better yet, if it is a boy, I'll name him Tim."

Tim opened his mouth to reply, but Andrew walked behind him and began to give him a massage, offering increasingly flattering compliments.

Mark was in complete shock over this. "Boss, do you think I'll be a good fit?" Tim didn't pay attention, and was very relaxed as he listened to Andrew's compliments.

"Hey, Mark, why don't you do something useful, and get back to work, will you?" Mark, dismayed, was about to protest, but Tim repeated himself. "Did I speak Spanish? Get your ass back on the grill, and do something useful!"

Mark sighed, nodded, and then closed the door in frustration.

Mark was determined, and he continued to work extra hard, regardless of his poor treatment. He looked at Andrew who just purposefully took forever to work while having a smug look on his face. Mark shook his head at him, then continued with his work. He was approached by coworkers who constantly praised him, and said he would definitely become a supervisor—not to worry about Andrew, since he was a worthless tub of lard. Regardless of being told this, Mark was still very worried.

Two days later, in Tim's office, Mark said, "Hey, Tim, a couple of days ago I tried to ask you if I would be a good fit for the position."

Mark stopped suddenly in his tracks, seeing that Andrew was present in the office. Tim had his feet on the desk as Andrew cut his toenails.

"For your age, you are a very healthy man. I mean, look at these feet! You probably should consider taking Tae Chi Foo! These are the feet of an athlete. These are feet that should be feared."

The manager chuckled. "Hmm, I never considered taking martial arts, Andrew, but I'll definitely consider it."

After Andrew was finished, he stood up. "All right, sir, I'm going back to my hard work. Keep in mind what I said."

Tim nodded at him. "Will do."

Andrew closed the door behind him. Mark then repeated what he had said two days ago. Tim reflected on this deeply, which worried Mark. The last time he had asked the question, Tim hadn't had to think too much about the answer.

"I'm not sure. It's a very tough decision. Like I said, I'll think about it, and—" Andrew had quickly returned.

"Hey, Tim, I bought you this antique hat that I think you will like."

Mark sighed as he shook his head again. Tim took the hat without any hesitation.

"Awesome, Andrew! Thank you so much!" Andrew went back to giving complements to Tim. Eventually, Mark, the over-achiever, left in frustration.

One week later, in the break room, Tim announced, "All right, workers! I'm going on vacation! I expect you all to behave very well while I'm away! Keep in mind that your performance while I'm gone will be evaluated if you are interested in the supervisor position." Tim left the room, and the fast food restaurant.

Andrew muttered in contempt after his manager had left. "What a douche bag." Mark gave Andrew a surprised look as he tried to believe what he'd heard. He hoped that Andrew had been talking about someone else.

"Who are you talking about?"

Andrew snorted. "Who do you think?! Tim is a douche! Just look at him! He is a piece of shit. He can't manage for shit, he lives in a fucked up apartment, his children are a bunch of losers, his wife is a whore, his car reminds me of the huge shit I took this morning, and his hair cut is fucked up."

Andrew paused for a moment as he paced back and forth. "He dyes his hair to hide the fact that he has grey hairs. Tsk, tsk, tsk. Also, have you noticed how fucked up his teeth are? The man cheats on his whore of a wife. What a pathetic excuse for a human being. It's a pity that he is wasting the air that we breathe."

Mark gasped at him. "You give him a lot of compliments and buy him gifts! Hell, the other day you went to the football game with him since you two both like the Crazy Town Crazies."

Andrew cackled. "Everyone and their mommas know that the Crazy Town Crazies *suck* as a football team! The reason I'm doing all this shit is to get the promotion."

Mark got in Andrew's face, and glared at him. "You're no hard worker! My father always told me, before he placed a gun to my head, that if you work hard, then you will move up in this world! Before you worked here, you were homeless because you're a lazy, fat, tub of lard, and even here, now, you don't do anything."

Andrew chuckled, and his demeanor changed to one of arrogance. "I *am* a hard worker! I work hard at kissing Tim's ass so I can get the promotion. Stupid kid, that's how you move up in the world! Hard work can be good at times, but at the end of the day, if you aren't liked, your ass ain't going anywhere, no matter how much you contribute to the work force, and no matter how much time passes. You need to get with the program, kid! That's how the corporate world works."

Mark raised his fist in anger. "I'll beat you!" Andrew smirked at him. A few of the coworkers pulled them both back, as things began to heat up.

Mark and Andrew had started a rivalry from that day on. Mark tried his best to avoid his rival, but every time he saw that cocky smirk, he just wanted to punch the older man square in the face. Every time he walked past him, Andrew gave Mark that smirk. In order to take out his frustration, Mark worked much more effectively and efficiently. Mark worked three times better than he did before, and he was by far the best worker in the fast food restaurant. He heard a rumor that he was the best worker out of everyone in all of the stores. Mark received a lot of praise and rewards from the other supervisors. Andrew, however, started to call out of work three days in a row, and one of Mark's coworkers told him this.

Mark was nonchalant about it. "No biggie. He won't get the position, and we don't need him. We are much better off without him. I'll call Tim and tell him this just to sabotage Andrew even more. Maybe he will get fired, and thank God for that." He decided to call Tim, but was greeted by his manager's voice mail.

The next day, Tim returned from vacation, and walked through the door with Andrew. Mark narrowed his eyes at his rival, then looked at Tim.

"Hey, Tim. Andrew called out three days in a row, and his absences were unexcused."

Tim's demeanor was very calm. "Don't sweat it. Honestly, Andrew was with me those three days. He volunteered to be my man-servant." Andrew walks past Mark with a smirk on his face.

A day later, Tim had finally made his decision as to who would become the new supervisor. He decided that it was best to promote Andrew, much to everyone's dismay. Mark was so furious, because he had worked so hard for the position. His coworkers were also disappointed with the choice.

Andrew called a mandatory meeting for all of the workers the next day. Mark arrived with his arms crossed, looking away from the new supervisor. He could not bear the sight of Andrew after what had happened.

"All right everyone, the reason I called you here is to let you know that you all are very good workers. There is, however, a new position that is available. The pay is slightly more, and I have come up with a decision as to who's going to do it. The position is called A.S.C., and this position goes to Mark—if he accepts." Mark looked very confused, along with his coworkers, because everyone knew that Mark and Andrew didn't get along. "So, Mark, do you accept?"

Mark shrugged. "You were very vague about the position. What exactly would I do?"

"For one, you won't be working on the food anymore. You'd be doing custodial work. You have been laboring a hell of a lot on that grill, so you definitely deserve the break. You get paid two dollars more, but you have to work the shifts that I work."

Mark didn't see why not. The pay increase seemed nice, and he was very sick of making food. Ever since Tim had made his announcement, Mark had lost a hell of a lot of motivation, and it showed in his performance.

Mark signed up for the position without any hesitation. What he wasn't aware of was that A.S.C. stood for "Andrew's Shit Cleaner." Even though this implied that Mark would only clean Andrew's shit, he actually had to clean everyone else's as well. Before his next shift, Andrew made sure to eat a big meal so he could take a huge dump. Mark walked into the building begrudgingly for his shift. Technically, to him, this was a better job, considering he made more money, but it was a kick to his pride. The problem was that he needed this job since it was so hard to find one due to the economy. It was either this, or he could go back to the shelter. Shortly after Mark clocked in, he got his spray and gloves, and waited patiently outside of the bathroom.

Andrew opened the bathroom door, fanning the wind with his hand. "Man, I had ten chili dogs! Thank god my shit cleaner's here!" Andrew left in a fit of laughter. Mark was greeted by a horrible smell, which was accompanied by the sight of a toilet that was almost over filled with Andrew's shit.

Andrew shook the vice president's hand. "Hello, Jamaal! It is nice to meet you! Thank you for visiting Eat Healthy Fast Food."

Jamaal shook the supervisor's hand. "Nice to meet you, too, Andrew. You have provided nothing but good services, your store is clean, and the morale here is high. You all are doing a very good job of representing Happy Sunshine, Inc. If you will excuse me, I have to go to the bathroom."

Andrew nodded, and the vice president headed to the bathroom.

Ten minutes later, Jamaal approached Andrew. "Well, this is awkward."

"Is everything okay, sir?" asked Andrew.

"Well, the toilet seems to have malfunctioned, and I was not aware that it was like that before I went, so—"

Andrew held up his hand. "Do not worry, Vice President. We will take care of the situation. It is no problem at all."

"Mark! Get over here!" Andrew yelled.

A few seconds later, Mark arrived, wearing cleaning gear. He gave Andrew a dubious look.

"Mark, I need you to—ahem—do your job. The vice president had to use the bathroom, but you know how it goes with the toilets. Ever since I became supervisor, for some odd reason, they have been malfunctioning. So do the usual."

Mark rolled his eyes at Andrew, put on his gloves, opened the bathroom door, walked inside, and then slammed the door shut. The situation caused Jamaal to feel more awkward, which prompted a confused look at Andrew. This worker seemed to be the only one in low spirits out of all of them. It had been a week since Mark had become a shit cleaner, and he clearly hated his job.

"Don't mind him, Jamaal. He comes to work like this all the time. Every place has at least someone who hates their job, someone who's unappreciative of the benefits they receive."

"Huh? But that's not the problem. Does that kid have to clean my—"

Before Jamaal could finish, Andrew hastily began to escort Jamaal out. "Ah! Don't worry about that! Surely a vice president such as yourself has places to be, and things to do."

Jamaal, remembering his task, said, "Yes! I need to be somewhere. Thank you again, Andrew, and continue to hold down the fort here!"

Jamaal rushed out of the fast food restaurant, much to Andrew's relief.

Thirty minutes later, Jamaal arrived in the Underwater Basket Weaving Professional's Building.

Jamaal stood in front of the receptionist, ready to be disappointed again, until he heard something unexpected.

"You qualify for the job, sir."

Jamaal stood there, completely dumbfounded. He could not believe what he'd just heard, and he wondered if he'd gone insane.

"Pardon me, can you repeat what you just said?"

The receptionist nodded. "We reviewed your application, as well as your job experience. It appears that you are very well educated, and served in the military. In the past, we required for you to become a CEO of a corporation, but when you applied that day, it was April Fool's Day." The receptionist laughed hysterically. Jamaal narrowed his eyes.

"Don't play with my emotions like that! And for that matter, is this a joke?!"

The woman shook her head no. "You qualify, sir. Due to a high turnover rate, the fact that you served an extra year in the air force is something we'll overlook. You can start next week if you like. All you have to do is sign here."

Jamaal did so without any hesitation. After all this time, his dream was finally going to come true.

An hour later, at Happy Sunshine, Inc., in Jamaal's office, Fatima said to Jamaal, "I don't see why you are even still bothering with it in the first place. Ever since you turned eighteen, you worked so hard on becoming an underwater basket weaver. You spent so much money and time on it, and again and again, you kept on being turned down. Sometimes a person needs to learn to quit, and pursue something else. Hell, you are my vice president, for god's sake! How is this going to work out with your schedule?!" Fatima gave Jamaal a serious look as she spoke. To her, this was all ridiculous, and it would mean that she would have to find someone else to take his place.

Jamaal sighed. "You know that we aren't in the office twenty-four-seven. I could very easily fit this job into my schedule on my days off, and during mornings. I could do the vice president thing at nights. It won't be an issue at all, so don't worry. Go home with your husband, and chill out for the day. It's all good!"

"Okay, but you better not back out on me now after we've come so far."

Fatima left Jamaal's office, and then headed home. Jamaal sat back in his chair with a grin on his face. "At last! I can do my life's work!"

A week later, Jamaal walked into The Underwater Basket Weaving Professionals building, and approached the receptionist.

"All right, ma'am, I'm ready to do my job."

The receptionist yawned, bored. "Sir, your interview is tomorrow afternoon."

Jamaal slammed his hands on her desk. "What the fuck?! You said I could start in a week last week!"

The receptionist sighed, and then looked away. "Indeed, sir, but it is protocol that you get interviewed first. Everyone is aware that before they can start a job, they need to be interviewed. I scheduled you for one tomorrow afternoon. I tried to tell you this, sir, but you skipped out of the building while singing songs before I could, and your voice mailbox was full."

Jamaal got up, and then stormed out of the building.

The next day, in the Underwater Basket Weaving Professionals building, Jamaal said to the receptionist,

"All right, ma'am. I'm ready for my interview."

The receptionist nodded at him, and asked him to sit down with a bunch of other people who were waiting. He was curious as to whether these people were before him, because he clearly was told that his interview was at 1 p.m. It was 12:30 p.m. He waited patiently, but started to worry once it reached 12:55 p.m. Jamaal approached the receptionist, concerned.

"Hey, my interview is supposed to be at one o'clock, but I see that these people are going before me. How long is this gonna take?"

"There is only one person doing interviews, and she has her

hands full. It could be anywhere from now to midnight. We are open twenty-four hours."

Jamaal's eyes bulged. "What the heck?! It could take the whole day?!"

The receptionist nodded slowly. "I apologize, sir. It is protocol. If you wish to back out now, then the front door is right there." She pointed to the door. "Otherwise, you may wait with the others. They have worked hard on trying to make their dreams come true, and aren't willing to just let a long wait stop them after they've come so far. As I said, if you want to back out, then there is the door."

Jamaal clenched his fists at her, sucked it up, and then sat back down to wait as patiently as possible.

He wasn't sure how long he waited, because he fell asleep in his chair an hour after his talk with the boring receptionist. Jamaal was poked by another receptionist. This one was cheerful, unlike the previous one. He smacked his lips as he woke from his dream, and then looked at his watch. It was 7 p.m. Fortunately for him, this was his day off from his job as vice president, otherwise he would be sweating bullets, because his shifts there normally started at 5 p.m.

"Sir! It is now time for your interview!"

Jamaal stood up to head for the office.

Once, inside, he saw that the interviewer was a young woman. This baffled Jamaal, because she appeared like she could be eighteen or nineteen years old. *What the hell?! How did this kid get the job as an interviewer, and it took me this long just to be considered for the job as an underwater basket weaver?* He refused to let his thoughts botch up the interview, and maintained a calm demeanor. The interviewer extended her hand.

"Good evening. My name is Tiffany, and I will be doing your interview today."

Jamaal shook her hand. "Nice to meet you. My name is Jamaal."

Tiffany's cell phone rang. She asked for Jamaal to wait so she could answer. Jamaal crossed his arms as she talked casually on the phone with her friend.

After an hour, Tiffany hung up the phone.

"I apologize, sir. I had some professional work to take care of. I thank you for being patient while I took care of that." Tiffany took out a few papers. "All right, Jamaal. I looked through your files, and I see that you have a PhD and some military training. You also are the vice president of Happy Sunshine, Inc. My question for you is why you chose this job when you have so much going on?"

"It has always been my dream to become an underwater basket weaver," Jamaal hastily replied. "Even though I'm a vice president, that isn't my dream job. It just happened due to circumstances."

Tiffany nodded at him. Time passed until the interviewer finally came to a decision.

"Well, Jamaal, based on what you presented to me, I'm still not sure if you would be a good fit, but I'll go with my gut on this. I decided to hire you for the thirty-day probation period. When can you start?"

"Tomorrow is fine!"

The next morning Jamaal began his training period.

A day later, in the Underwater Basket Weaving Professionals building training room, Jamaal saw that he wasn't the only one who was being trained. What he saw shocked him. All the people he was training with were much younger than he was. In his mind, he knew damn well that these people couldn't have finished college, and yet here they were, working the same job that he was—the same job that he had worked so hard to get in the first place.

He curiously asked one of them, "Hey, how did you get this job?"

One of the young workers gave him a confused look. "Excuse me, sir?"

"How did you get this job? I had to get a PhD, and needed military training."

"Easy. My friend got me inside. I'm a high school dropout who sold crack on the streets before I got this job. I asked my friend to hook me up, and he did, so now I work here, dawg. It wasn't that difficult really. If you have friends on the inside, then anything is possible."

The young man went on, but Jamaal ignored him because he knew being pissed off during his training period would give a very bad first impression. One of the male trainers spoke up.

"All right, people! You have been chosen because we feel that you have what it takes to become an underwater basket weaver! Before you can start with the training class, you must complete the computerized tests."

The tests themselves didn't seem too terribly hard to Jamaal. The problem was that he needed to take ten of them, and each test took about thirty minutes to complete. After five hours, Jamaal finished.

"All right, sir. I'm done. Can I get started with the training?"

The training leader shook his head no at Jamaal. "Nope, you gotta wait until tomorrow."

Jamaal sighed, sucked it up, and went straight to his second job very early. Fatima could easily tell that her vice president was distraught, so she gave him his space. Later that night while doing paper work, Jamaal received a phone call.

He picked up his phone and was greeted by a young woman's voice.

"Hello? May I speak to Jamaal Johnson?"

"This is he."

"We looked through the results of your tests, and it turns out that you failed. You will have to re- take them. Otherwise we will have to let you go, sir."

"Are you sure that I failed? That test was easy!"

"Sorry, sir, but you failed. You were required to get an 80 percent on the test, and you got a 79.99 percent. You can re-take it tomorrow morning if you like."

Jamaal stormed out of his office after his call had finished, and then out of the building in frustration. Fatima decided to have a talk with him once he'd cooled down, because she was concerned.

The next day, at his new job, Jamaal turned in his retake of the test to the proctor. He then stated,

"All right, I'm done with the test, sir."

The trainer nodded, and began to grade the tests. Jamaal waited patiently and nervously until the trainer had finished.

The trainer took a deep breath. "You passed, sir, but you will have to wait two weeks until you start. You failed the test yesterday while the other workers passed, so you have to wait for the next training class."

Jamaal stood there for a moment, stupefied. The trainer looked at Jamaal.

"Did I stutter, sir? You will have to come back next week to start your training, so you can get the fuck out now."

Jamaal narrowed his eyes. "Excuse me?"

The trainer replied nonchalantly, "I said you are done now. You can leave, go home, retreat, get the fuck out, retire, rest for the day, whatever registers in your head—just get out of my face. Comprende?" The trainer was very casual about this, and continued to do his paper work. "Is there an issue with what I said, sir?"

Jamaal decided to just leave it be, because this was his dream job, after all. He left for his second job, his head low. Fatima tried to comfort him, but Jamaal asked her politely to give him some space.

———

Two weeks later, Jamaal was finally able to start his training. He was very disappointed that he had had to wait this long, but it was all worth it now. He, as well as a few others, waited patiently for their teacher. Many of his coworkers were between the ages of eighteen and twenty-two. Jamaal would have asked them how they got here, but as before, he didn't want to get pissed off, after all the hard work he'd done. Eventually, the trainer entered the classroom. Jamaal was relieved to see that at least this woman was about the same age as he was. He also noticed that everyone seemed to be divided. There were about thirty people in the training room, but the people all sat in cliques, like it was high school. The trainer spoke up.

"All right, everyone. I will be your trainer for this period. Even though you all have earned your PhD's, and did all that it took to be here, you will need to unlearn what you have learned in school."

This confused Jamaal. What was the point of all of that schooling in the first place if he was going to have to just unlearn it in the end? When it came to the lessons, the trainer herself seemed to know what she was talking about. He was easily able to follow the directions of the instructor. This was nothing to him.

Three hours later, the classroom instructor said, "All right, can someone show me a demonstration on everything I've taught you so far?"

One of the male employees raised his hand. The trainer called on him. The worker first put on his scuba gear, and then got the weaving equipment. He dove into the tank that was in the room as everyone observed. Immediately, the volunteer jumped out of the pool, shivering in fear. The trainer gave him a confused look.

"What happened? You were doing it right. Why did you stop?"

"I quit! Honestly, I'm afraid of water! The only reason why I got this job in the first place is because my uncle works here. I'm out!"

The young man left hastily in tears. Jamaal was shocked, but at the same time, he wasn't. It was apparent to him that none of these people actually qualified for the job, and they'd all gotten here by other means. Some of the other workers laughed about the guy who had just left, and bad-mouthed him.

The trainer sighed in disappointment. "All right, does anyone else want to give it a go?"

Jamaal raised his hand, and thought he would show them how a real pro did it. He was called on immediately. Jamaal gracefully put on the scuba gear, and then dove into the water with his weaving equipment. Instead of making one basket as instructed, he made ten of them in a minute, and for the hell of it, he wove a figurine that looked like a mini-roller coaster. Jamaal proudly got out of the tank. The trainer was shocked as she applauded for him.

"Well done!"

Jamaal heard some of the coworkers making negative comments under their breaths, but he ignored them.

"Fucking show off."

"Old-ass broken fool."

"Stupid-ass mofo."

Ten minutes later it was break time, so Jamaal headed for his locker to get his drink. He was approached by several guys from his training class.

Jamaal looked at them curiously. "Hello. Do you need help with anything?"

One of them sneered at him, and shoved him against his locker. Jamaal struggled to get out, but was held by two other guys. They all laughed at his futile attempts to break free.

The leader spoke up angrily. "You think you're cool, don't you?! Well, you're not! You are a piece-of-shit teacher's pet!"

Jamaal was dumbfounded as he stopped struggling. "What the fuck is this?! High school again?"

The leader kneed him as hard as he could in the stomach. "No! This is real life! Show off again and we'll beat the hell out of you, bitch!"

Jamaal was left alone at his locker, on the ground and holding his stomach in pain, curled up in a ball. Rather than going back to class, he felt like it was wise to talk to someone about what had just happened. That was extremely unprofessional, and it couldn't go unchecked.

In the manager's office, the manager stated, "Why aren't you in your training class? You are very aware that you are supposed to attend it one hundred percent of the time, or else you won't work in the water tanks, correct?"

Jamaal nodded. "I understand, ma'am, but the thing is, I was assaulted by a few young men when I was at my locker. I was asked by my trainer to demonstrate what she taught us, and I went overboard. These guys didn't like the fact that I showed off, so they attacked me."

The female manager reflected on this for a moment. "Do you remember their names?"

Jamaal shook his head no. "I can point them out to you, ma'am, and I'm sure that you have them on camera."

The manager stood up, a look of aggression on her face. "Show them to me!"

Jamaal wasted no time, and went back to the classroom. There was silence as they entered the room. He pointed them out. "Those are the ones who did it!"

The manager observed them with that same look of intensity for a moment, and then her face broke into a smile. "Andre, how are you doing, nephew?"

The leader, Andre, rushed to the boss. "Auntie Denise! How are you doing? Thanks so much for getting me this job."

The two hugged each other while Jamaal observed.

Denise spoke like a parent scolding a child. "Nephew! You know that it isn't right to beat up people you don't like!

Andre looked down with false guilt. "I'm sorry. I promise that I won't do it again."

He crossed his fingers behind him. Denise turned to Jamaal. "All right. I have taken care of it. He said that he won't do it again."

Jamaal was about to protest, but the manager left without another word. Jamaal was met with a paper ball thrown to his face as he turned around to sit back down.

An hour later, it was now testing time, and Jamaal blazed through the test with very little problems. Truthfully, even though he had had to relearn some things, it still wasn't that much more he'd had to learn in order to do the job. Once he was finished with the test, he turned it in. Shortly after, the woman next to him turned in her test, then more and more people finished. Jamaal snickered, seeing that Andre clearly didn't know what he was doing. He seemed to be picking answers at random. After thirty minutes, the trainer called Jamaal up for a private meeting.

Jamaal didn't understand if he'd done anything wrong or not.

Just outside of the classroom, the instructor said, "Jamaal, today you have showed me that you are very good at this, but something concerns me. I noticed that the answers to your test are exactly the same as the woman who was sitting next to you. You both even got the same two questions wrong out of fifty."

Jamaal was back in defensive mode. "Are you saying that I cheated?! Because I didn't cheat off of her test! If anything, she cheated off me."

"Whether that is true or not, this is a very serious matter. We don't condone cheating in our training classes, and if neither of you admits to cheating, then you both will be out of a job. There are still two more hours until the shift ends, so I'll give you both that much time."

Jamaal returned to his seat, glaring at the young woman who was seated next to his desk.

"You cheated off of me!"

She looked at him in disgust. "Wut are ya talkin' 'bout! I's smart! I's smart girl! Me know how ta tawk! Me is no cheatah. I know math. Five pwus five ecals one fity."

Jamaal scratched his head. "WHAT?! Can you speak coherently?!"

The woman gave him a confused look. "Uhhh, you use big words. Me no understand you."

Jamaal spoke slowly. "You. Cheated. Yes, cheated. Off. Me." Jamaal pointed to himself. "Me. Me." Jamaal grabbed a piece of paper, and pointed at it. "Test. Test."

The woman nodded at him quickly. "Me fogot how ta read. Me looked at youz paypa, den circled da dots ya circled."

Jamaal raised his hand to call the trainer. Jamaal quickly told her that the woman had confessed. It took nearly the remaining two hours just to get her to say what she'd said before, and then to translate it.

Finally, Jamaal's first day of training was over. He walked over to his car, and what he saw there shocked him. There was a lot of graffiti on his car, which said things like "snitch-ass bitch," "smart ass," "teacher's pet," "old-ass mofo," and "douche bag." He had had enough for the day.

He left to head to his first job. Fatima was in the parking lot preparing to leave for the day. She was about to ask him how his day had been at his new job, but she gasped when she saw his car.

"I'll call the cops!"

Jamaal replied with no emotion. "You do that."

———

"I didn't want to tell you this, but I have to, since you are my friend. You need to quit that job now! It is making you miserable, and it shows in your demeanor. You come to work either upset or depressed, and you have been very antisocial."

Fatima glared down at Jamaal, who was unresponsive, his head low.

"Did you hear me?!" she asked.

She lightly pushed his forehead back, but he lowered his head again.

"I hear you, and I appreciate your concern over me. You are a good friend. I was told by the trainer that the training is the worst part. Yesterday was my last day of training, and I have been training for a month now. Since it is finally over, we are actually going to be in the tanks, making our baskets. This is my dream job. I always wanted to do this ever since I was a kid. I'm as happy as I will ever be."

Fatima crossed her arms, and appeared unconvinced. "Fine, but keep in mind that I'm here if you need someone to talk to."

The next day, at the Underwater Basket Weaving Professionals building, Jamaal asked, "All right, I'm ready to get started. Where is my tank?"

The supervisor looked at Jamaal closely and curiously. "I remember you. You were the one who would have been in my training class if you hadn't failed. Well, technically, between you and me, you didn't fail."

Jamaal looked at him, confused. "What do you mean?"

"You passed, but one of the trainees requested for the proctor to fail you so that his friend could take your spot. The trainee is friends with the proctor, so it worked out—but you didn't hear it from me."

Jamaal simply shook his head at him. Nothing about this place surprised him anymore, and before he would have reacted angrily, but the training was finished. Now he could just work alone. The supervisor got back to the point.

"Back to what you just asked—our company was bought out by someone else. I forgot the name of the guy, so the plans have changed."

Jamaal's eyes widened. "How so? It says on the contract that after a month of training, we start making baskets."

"Well, you will be making baskets, but it won't be underwater anymore, and they won't be made by hand, but by machine."

"What the fuck?!"

"Yep, times change, my man. After I heard the news, I wanted to quit because I'd worked so hard to get here in the first place, but every corporation that specializes in this is doing the same. They hire some poor schmucks to just push a button, then the machines do the underwater basket weaving for them. I swear, people have it easy nowadays compared to how we had it when we were younger."

Jamaal went to his locker, feeling heartbroken. He sank to his knees, and covered his head with his arms. This had been his dream, and now because of technological advancements, his skills weren't needed anymore. These were the skills that he'd worked so hard to perfect.

A moment later, Andre and his gang approached Jamaal, laughing.

"What's up, bee-yotch? I'm talking to you, you old-ass broken motherfucker! Guess what? Your skills don't mean shit anymore! You learned all of that crap for nothing." He cupped his hands around his mouth, and shouted, "It was over nothing! All of that education was for nothing, bee-yotch!"

They all continue to laugh at Jamaal. Andre got down to Jamaal's level, and whispered, "I'm glad that you wasted all of that time. You are a piece-of-shit old man who doesn't deserve to live. You deserve to have your dreams crushed. How does it feel? I love your sorrow. Your sorrow invigorates me, and make me feel better. They sustain me. I hope your house burns down, and I hope you die of cancer. It feels so good beating the hell out of you every day. There's nothing you can do about it, since my aunt is the manager of this building. So, are you ready for your ass-whooping?"

To their surprise, just like that, Jamaal snapped. He didn't give a fuck anymore. He snatched at Andre's head, and started punching him in the face repeatedly. The other two guys who were with Andre tried to restrain Jamaal, but as soon as they grabbed him, Jamaal kicked them extremely hard into the lockers. Jamaal punched Andre furiously, as hard as he could, and then kneed him in the stomach repeatedly.

Thirty minutes later, Officer Fuxup Lives handcuffed Jamaal, and walked him to the police car. He threw Jamaal in the back of the car, and then drove straight to jail. The officer decided to have a little pep talk with Jamaal on the way there.

"You feel like a real hotshot, don't you? Picking on some guy who has to be about twenty years younger than you? What type of man are you, doing shit like that? Hmmm?" He waited for a response from Jamaal. "Just what I thought—you're no man. You are a piece of shit, you—"

"Shut the fuck up, BITCH!"

The officer gasped, and brought his car to a screeching halt. He turned to Jamaal.

"What the fuck did you say to me, boy?"

At this point, Jamaal didn't care about anything anymore.

"I said...Shut. The. Fuck. Up. BITCH! You think just because you're a cop, you can treat anyone any way you want? Well, I got news for you, you picked the wrong motherfucker to fuck with, pal. I worked so hard to become an underwater basket weaver. At first, I didn't qualify for the job after I'd gotten my PhD and I'd gone through military training—which took years! Then, I make it to the job only to find out that a bunch of underachieving young fucks got in effortlessly. Now I come to work to find out that the skills I've been working toward aren't needed anymore because of technological advancements. I have nothing to lose, and if you want to take me out of the car and throw down, then I'll throw down! You better not take these cuffs off me, because if you do, and I get a hold of you, then you will be breathing your last breath, motherfucker!"

Ten seconds later, Officer Fuxup Lives turned away from Jamaal, started the car up, and then drove to the police station without saying another word.

Twelve hours later, Jamaal was out of jail. He hadn't had to stay for very long because Fatima had bailed him out, and then had driven him home. They didn't exchange words, because she'd heard about what had happened. She completely understood why he'd placed so much value on becoming an underwater basket weaver.

The next day, to Fatima's surprise, Jamaal came to work with a completely different demeanor. He didn't seem upset or angry, but was surprisingly peaceful, smiling and helping out his coworkers. Even at the meeting, there was an unusual calmness about him. Later on that day, Fatima approached her vice president.

"Jamaal,.is everything all right?"

"Everything is perfectly fine, Fatima."

"Are you sure? Considering what happened yesterday?"

"Yes, I did a lot of thinking yesterday. Sure, being an underwater basket weaver was my dream job, and sure, I went through a lot of hell to try to get it to work out, but everything happens for a reason. I have no regrets over what happened. The reason things weren't working out for me is because I wasn't able to appreciate what I have, and I couldn't see what's in front of me. My name is Jamaal Johnson. I have a couple of wonderful children, my best friend is the CEO of the corporation that I work for, and I am her vice president. I make good money, my counselor is a wonderful person, and I'm living pretty well. I don't have to work at a corporation to do what I love doing. I could just start my own business if I like. Everything is fine, Fatima—my best friend."

Jamaal hugged her. Fatima was in complete shock, but at the same time, she was very happy for him.

"I thought Hector was your best friend."

Jamaal looked down, feeling guilty at the reminder of what had happened in the church. He pictured his former best friend hung up on the cross.

"Hector..."

An hour later, Jamaal was doing some paperwork in his office, when he was interrupted by someone knocking on his door. He opened the door to see a cop, a lawyer, and Andre. He narrowed his eyes, observing them.

"Can I help you?"

Andre pointed at Jamaal.

"I'm suing you! You attacked me in the locker room for no reason!"

Jamaal was alarmed, but he immediately calmed down.

"All right, can you all take a seat?"

He went to get chairs for everyone, and they all sat down. Jamaal sat down at his desk.

"What's the issue?"

"You know damn well what the issue is, bitch! You beat me up in the locker room!"

Jamaal reflected on this. "I see."

"Don't play dumb with me! You know damn well what happened. That's why you went to jail. You're lucky your ass is rich, otherwise you wouldn't have survived in there."

Jamaal chuckled at Andre, who he thought was a complete moron. "Are you aware that I am a veteran, Andre? I served in the military for five years, and during that time I was on the front lines, in close combat, so I can survive anywhere! As for beating you up, yes, I admit this. I did beat you up, and—might I add—quite badly. Caught you completely off guard, then let you have it. It was bound to happen sooner or later."

The lawyer wrote all this down. The officer was intrigued.

"See!" he said. "I told you! He admits it!"

Jamaal held up his hand. "Wait a second. Let me finish. I did it out of self-defense. You remember when I had my head down low? Well, I was using the audio recording device on my phone."

Jamaal took out his phone, and pressed a button. It played everything Andre had said that day, including the things that he'd whispered to Jamaal. Jamaal turned up the volume as loud as he could so everyone could hear it.

"I'm glad that you wasted all of that time," the recording played. "You are a piece-of-shit old man who doesn't deserve to live. You deserve to have your dreams crushed. How does it feel? I love your sorrow. Your sorrows invigorate me, and make me feel better. They sustain me. I hope your house burns down, and I hope you die of cancer. It feels so good beating the hell out of you every day. There's nothing you can do about it, since my aunt is the manager of this store. So, are you ready for your ass-whooping?"

Andre was about to respond, but Jamaal cut him off.

"Since your shitty aunt wouldn't do anything about the situation, I placed hidden cameras near my locker area, and I recorded the times when you beat me up."

Jamaal pressed another button on the phone, and a screen was lowered that began to show videos of Andre and his gang beating up Jamaal.

"You probably wondered how I could use cameras if you couldn't see them, but check this out."

Jamaal took out an object that was so small it could have been the same size as one of the little buttons. "Believe it or not, this is a camera, and I stuck them on the lockers. I decided to use the video as leverage just in case I needed it, and apparently now I do."

Andre was silent.

"Do you wish to continue this, gentlemen?" asked Jamaal. The rest of them looked around, confused. "If anything, you, your aunt, and the town should be paying *me*. You're lucky that I don't want to rob the taxpayers, *and* your broke ass. The officer on duty didn't care to listen to my side of the story, and the whole thing was completely one-sided. I had no say in any of this. Now get the fuck out of my office, and stay the fuck out of my life."

Everyone left awkwardly. Jamaal sighed, and shook his head.

"Children these days. I *could* sue the Underwater Basket Weaving Professionals for this." Jamaal reflected on everything, and his final thought was: *Owned.*

—————

John, the jolly, newly hired custodian, was working another shift. He whistled cheerfully as he mopped the floor. He suddenly stopped in his tracks when he saw an irate young man with his lawyer.

"That is some bullshit!" yelled the young man. "He attacked me in the locker room!"

The lawyer sighed. "Andre, he has recordings of you and your friends assaulting him on a daily basis. He has irrefutable proof that you are the one who instigated the situation. You are lucky that he isn't pressing any charges against you, despite what happened."

The two continued to bicker on and on until they eventually left the building. John wondered what that had been about. He continued working.

Not only did John enjoy his job, but he had also proposed to his fiancé Jane recently, and she was happy to marry him—so nothing could bring him down. John and Jane were a young couple who had been together for four years, ever since they'd both been violently kicked out of their parents' homes at the age of eighteen. At first they were together primarily for survival purposes, but they eventually started to fall for each other.

Even though their living standards could have been better, they weren't doing too badly for themselves. John was currently a custodian at Happy Sunshine, Inc., and Jane was a receptionist at C.J. Pickles. The two had decided to get married, and were currently working toward finding the perfect place to have their ceremony.

Later on, in their apartment, John asked, "How about here, love? We can have the wedding here in PC Town. I hear that it's peaceful, the area is clean, there are a lot of attractions, and it's overall a fun place to stay."

John looked at his fiancé, waiting for her opinion. She thought about it for a moment as she paced back and forth.

"Sure, I don't see why not. Let's get it set up there right now. I'll call the perfect place for us to stay."

Jane picked up the phone to take care of the wedding preparations. John was filled with complete joy over the fact that they were going to get married soon. Unfortunately they would have to wait just a little bit longer before they could say their vows, but that was fine with them. They decided that it was best to have a private wedding rather than invite their families. Both families disapproved of their marriage in the first place, and the couple didn't want anyone to object before they could say their vows.

A couple of months later the couple arrived near a hotel in PC Town. Jane was already inside the hotel while John was outside transporting the suitcases to the building. So far John had gotten very good first impressions of the town. The air was clean, the streets appeared safe, and the citizens seemed to get along with one another. What John found unsettling about these things, however, was that the town itself appeared flawless, and he was the type of person who believed that that was too good to be true. As he walked toward the hotel's front door with two suitcases in two, John was approached by an older couple who appeared to be in their 60s.

The man, presumably the woman's husband, stated warmly, "Hello there, stranger! I can tell that you aren't from around here. What's the special occasion? A vacation?"

"Nah, I'm actually here to get married to my fiancé," said John.

"A wedding?! Congratulations, young man!" said the woman. The wife looked around curiously to make sure that nobody else was listening. She then whispered, "We honestly are outsiders, too. We moved here from Unknown Town. Even though it seems like you're going to be here briefly, you may want to be careful, sir. This town ain't as nice as it appears to be—especially to outsiders."

"What do you mean?" asked John.

"For one," said the man, "you may want to change that shirt. It may offend someone. Second, I understand that you are trying to be cool and all with that tattoo, but you should probably figure out a way to conceal it as soon as possible. You're lucky we're the first people to meet you; otherwise you would have been reported to the authorities."

The wife simply nodded in agreement.

Confused, John looked down at his shirt, and had no idea how it would offend people. It was a holidays-themed shirt that said "Have a Merry Christmas and a Wonderful New Year." He then looked down at his henna tattoo, and back up at the couple in disbelief.

"You're kidding me, right?" John said. "I understand this shirt is out of season, but it's one of my favorite shirts, and me and my fiancé received this tattoo at a cultural festival. How is that offensive?"

The husband stated, "You got it all wrong, bud! We agree

with you completely. We're just trying to look out for you."

"But if you don't believe us," the woman added, "then that's on you. For your sake and for your fiancé's, please take our advice and be careful."

The couple then left for their destination. John was in complete disbelief over what he had just heard. It all sounded completely asinine to him. He began to head toward the front door of the hotel, but then, intuitively, he stopped in his tracks. He muttered to himself, "Goddammit!"

He opened one of the suitcases. John removed an all-black, long-sleeved shirt, and put it on. He then headed inside the hotel carrying the luggage. He was greeted by the sound of classical music that he soon realized was playing on a loop. He knew the song.

Curiously, John asked the receptionist, "Excuse me, sir, but why do you have this song playing on a loop like this?"

The receptionist immediately narrowed his eyes, and said, "Excuse me?" His voice sounded somewhat feminine.

John stated, "Sir, I was curious as to why this song is being played on a loop."

The music immediately stopped. There was a brief silence as the receptionist glared at John. Even more unsettling about the situation was that the receptionist wasn't the only person who was glaring at him, but everyone else in the area was as well. Men, women, children, and even the pets were glaring at John. One of the dogs snarled at him while all of the fish in the nearby tank swam as close to John as possible, staring at him, motionless. This further confused John, because he'd done what the couple had told him to do—change his shirt and hide his tattoos.

The receptionist then stated, "Did you just address me as 'sir' when I would clearly prefer to be addressed with female pronouns? And what's the problem with how the music is playing?"

"What?" asked John.

One of the children who stood near John suddenly pointed at him, and said, "Hey, Mom! Dad! Those white shoes he's wearing offend me! I thought that society wasn't about color or race anymore? Yet he's choosing to be intolerant, and offensive to others by wearing those."

This caused the crowd to gasp, and they slowly began to inch toward John, who was beginning to feel very nervous about all of this. Apparently, the couple from earlier hadn't been kidding, but they had failed to warn him about his shoes.

"Woah! Calm down!" said John. "I think you people are being overly sensitive here."

"'You people'?! What do you mean by 'you people'?!" shouted a woman in the crowd. "You need to stop getting angry, asshole! Lower the tone of your voice. Now! You're upsetting my daughter."

"What?! I'm just confused," said John. "I was referring to the people in this town when I said 'you people'—nothing more, nothing less. Sheesh! Is that really that difficult to understand?"

John's pleas didn't seem to appease the crowd, and more of them slowly shambled toward him. As they got closer, they began to claw at John, like deranged animals. Their eyes bulged, and they began to foam at the mouth as he saw their veins and muscles tense. They growled and hissed at him.

"Hey!" a man near the entrance suddenly shouted, which broke the tension. "What's the problem here?!"

John hastily looked over at him, and saw that the man was a police officer.

"Officer, you have to help me!" yelled John. "These people are going to attack me over nothing! All I did was ask this receptionist why the music was playing on a loop, and then he—err, *she*—got mad at me! You see, I'm from out of town. All I want to do is get married here. Please give me a free pass this time! I wasn't trying to offend anyone."

The officer simply nodded. "Sounds reasonable," He then looked around at the hostile crowd, and shouted, "Hey! Leave the out-of-towner alone! Break it up! Let's go!"

The crowd did as they were told, and began to back away from John. Oddly, the music started to play again on the same loop as before. Rather than questioning things further, John left it alone, and assumed the reason for it was because the full song was offensive to someone.

Ten minutes later, John had made it to his room. He wanted to explain to Jane what he'd just gone through. Even though they had planned their wedding out several months in advance, John now wanted to postpone it and hold the wedding somewhere else. He placed the suitcases on the floor, plopped down on the bed, and then turned on the television. Jane wasn't in the hotel room, but John assumed she'd probably gone out for a smoke.

He thought to himself, *I seriously hope that the act of smoking isn't offensive to anyone.*

John soon realized the television displayed every channel's programming in the same combination of sepia tones—nothing but a beige-colored screen each time—like watching black-and-white television in the 1950s. John thought to himself, *I guess programs in color are also considered too offensive...but what if someone gets offended by the color brown?*

Right at that moment, the news reporter on the TV said, "And in today's news, we've decided that in order to be more sensitive to others, we are going to air programs without any video feed at all. Since we are a progressive town that preaches acceptance and tolerance, this change will be in response to those people who are color blind. The changes will go into effect immediately."

The picture was suddenly gone, but the audio could still be heard. John simply turned off the television in disbelief, and muttered to himself, "Wow. Just...wow."

Ten minutes later, John began to feel concerned about Jane. She hadn't returned yet, which made him start to wonder. He really didn't want to return to the lobby, but he had no choice. Jane might need his help. John got up off of the bed, and exited the hotel room. He began to look around for Jane, but did not see her anywhere. He approached the receptionist, and said, "Excuse me, ma'am, but—"

"Did you just call me by a feminine pronoun?!" The receptionist's eyes narrowed as she said in a deep voice, "I clearly want to be referred to with male pronouns."

John held his hands in front of him. "Whoa, whoa, whoa! I'm sorry! I..."

The receptionist chuckled. "Just messin' with you, dude! That was my transgender twin brother—err, sister—you were speaking with earlier. Between you and me, people are too sensitive here."

John calmed down. "Phew! You got me good, man! And yeah—tell me about it. Did you see what I went through earlier?"

"Yeah, I was the one who called the police officer over."

"Thanks, man. There's no telling what they would have done to me if you hadn't intervened. Also, have you seen a young woman around here? She checked into the hotel earlier."

John began to describe Jane's appearance to the receptionist, but the receptionist shook his head.

"Sorry, dude. I haven't seen anyone like that at all today, but then again I only started my shift shortly after that mob antagonized you."

"What?! Are you kidding me?" asked John.

The receptionist nodded, and said, "You should probably check around town. She may not be that far."

John thanked him, and he decided to take the receptionist's advice and leave the hotel.

Three hours later, John returned to the hotel, having had no luck with finding Jane. He felt extremely concerned, to the point that he went to the police to have them issue a missing person's report. The police could not find her anywhere. They questioned whether she was even still in town. John had returned to the hotel because it looked like a thunderstorm was brewing, and he needed to clear his head.

He'd also been attacked by another crowd of people who'd been after him because of his nearly bald head. They told him that his balding hair was offensive to monks, and the crowd had forced him to wear a hat that had the words "intolerant asshole" on it.

"Hey, sir!" the receptionist called to John.

John stopped, giving the receptionist a depressed look, and his expression said it all. As John approached, the receptionist looked back and forth to make sure that nobody was listening.

"Sir," he said to John. "It's very possible that the SJWs kidnapped your fiancé." Suddenly, right after the receptionist finished his statement, a lightning bolt struck near the building, and the lights inside of the lobby dimmed briefly.

John's eyes widened. "What?! SJWs? What does that even mean?!"

"Social Justice Warriors. They don't mess around, man. They're the main reason this town is the way it is now."

Another lightning bolt struck nearby. As a result, all of the lights in the lobby turned off except for the lamp on the receptionist's desk. John gulped nervously as he continued to listen to the story.

"We went from being a town where everyone was very tolerant to a town where people are really bigoted and intolerant—and operate under the guise of being progressive and culturally sensitive. When it comes down to it, we're pretty much no different than any extremist group that practices intolerance, like the KKK or the Nazis."

There was a brief awkward silence from the two as John reflected on what was just told to him. He then chuckled timidly and said, "You're messing with me man."

The receptionist shook his head, "No joke. Hell, when it comes down to it, we don't even believe in freedom of speech anymore, and we resort to bullying. Even though we say that we believe in this country's values, we really don't."

The receptionist opened the desk drawer, took out a picture, and handed it to John. John looked down at the object and saw a professionally dressed elderly man. As John gazed down at it, the receptionist said, "That picture is the picture of the douche-bag conservative guy who ran for mayor years ago who talked about building a wall to prevent immigration. His catch phrase was, 'I'm going to make PC Town great again.' None of us thought that he would win, but *boy* were we proven wrong. He ended up winning the election, and then half the townspeople rioted. The crazy thing is that one of the main reasons he won is that half of the population didn't even vote. Yet many of them got all up in arms, protesting about an election they didn't even take part in. Talk about hypocrisy," he finished.

The receptionist shook his head. "Personally, I was on the fence. I didn't want the guy to win, but the general population pretty much stated that they would go against the principles of this town and country by rioting and destroying small businesses—unless their appointed person won. Doesn't sound like a democracy to me; more like a dictatorship. The malcontent even paid a shit-ton of money to get a re-count of the votes—money that could have been used to fix the streets, solve the homeless problem, feed the children, or stop the crime back then. All that re-count did was waste money, and prove that the guy won fair and square. I was fine with at least giving the douche bag a chance, but he conveniently died of a heart attack before his term started."

John shrugged. "Okay, what you said pretty much aligns with my first impressions of the town here, but that doesn't matter too much. I *really* need to find my fiancé! The politics of this town don't really matter to me. Honestly, ever since you explained all of this, my opinion of this town couldn't possibly get any worse. I really should have held the wedding somewhere else, maybe in Rainbow Town. And just when I thought that Harshtown had problems..."

The receptionist whispered ominously, "Shhhhhh! Not so loud, man! They have surveillance all around. They know when you are sleeping, and they know when you're awake. They know when you're bad or good, so be good, for goodness sake! All I'm trying to say is that you better watch out, you better not cry, you better not pout. I'm tellin' you why! The SJWs have taken over this town."

"Okay, I understand, but how do I get her back? Where do I find them? This is the love of my life here. I'm not going to just sit around and do nothing."

"You don't find them...they find you. Sir, this is going to be hard for me to say, but it may be too late for your fiancé. When it comes to that douche bag who ran for mayor, many of us believed that the SJWs kidnapped and murdered him, and then covered it up. You may be best off leaving her behind. I under-stand that you are determined, but, believe me, the SJWs are nothing to mess with. Grab your suitcases, take them to your car, and leave town while you can."

"What?! I'm not going to just abandon my future wife, and head back to Harshtown alone!"

The receptionist sighed. "Well, that's all that I'm willing to share. I wish you the best, man. Stay safe."

John thanked the receptionist for his advice, and then head-ed back to his hotel room, mentally exhausted and now more stressed out than ever. He laid down on the bed in the dark, sighing. The lights were still off. He felt a lot of anxiety over Jane. He could not stop thinking about her and worrying about her well-being. He began to sob, thinking of the good times they'd had together. Now it seemed there was a chance she'd been caught by the SJWs—or worse, if such a thing was possi-ble. Perhaps she'd simply gone home after she figured out about the problems in this town. If that were the case, then he didn't understand why she hadn't called him.

After an hour of wallowing, John stood up, and then exited the hotel room. He really needed to find a better way to clear his head. Perhaps finding a bar to hang out at would help calm his nerves, and help him think clearly. As John walked through the empty hallway with his cellphone in hand as his light source, he wasn't aware of the prowler lurking nearby until it was too late. From behind, John was swiftly grappled, and held in a sleeper hold. John struggled to break free, but the prowler's hold was too strong, and John began to lose his sight. Right before he lost consciousness, he heard the prowler, a man, say, "You…are on the naughty list."

John gradually awakened. As his vision returned, the last thing he remembered was being attacked in the hotel by a male Social Justice Warrior. The receptionist from earlier hadn't been joking. *The SJWs find you; you do not find them.* However, he hadn't expected for the situation to be this extreme. He now found himself somewhere very dark, unable to move his arms or legs. As his vision continued to return, he eventually saw that he was tied to a chair—and that he wasn't alone.

John heard the sounds of groans all around him. There were at least two men who were tied near him. John immediately recognized the two men; one was the friendly receptionist from earlier, and the other was the police officer who had saved him. His main concern right now, though, was still Jane. He wondered if Jane was even in the same room. The thought of her receiving the same treatment as he was pained his heart. He began to yell, "Hey! Is anyone here?! Please, let me go! I have a fiancé, and we're supposed to get married a couple days from now! Please let me go!"

The receptionist was to John's left. He said, "It's no use. They aren't going to let us go like that. The SJWs are very vindictive, and we will be lucky to get out of here unscathed—if at all. I suspected that something like this was going to happen. I shouldn't have warned you about them. Otherwise, I wouldn't be in this mess in the first place. I should have just kept to myself."

John's eyes widened. "What?! Why are they doing this to us?!"

"I don't know," said the receptionist. "It could be for many reasons. Maybe we did or said something to offend them or someone else. What PC Town and the SJWs don't understand is that anyone can be offended by anything. It's all perspective, and what may offend someone may not offend another. Their goal is to convert the world to think like them. Just check out politics and the media! They have been on the move for quite some time now."

As the receptionist spoke, John attempted to break out of his binds, but the rope was tied too tight. A minute later, the police officer awakened. He looked around, confused, and then said, "Hey! What's going on?! Where am I?!"

Once the police officer realized who had captured him, he began to weep. "Oh, no, no, no, no! Not the SJWs! Why me?! Was it because of that striped sweater I wore a few days ago? I'm sorry about that! I'll be more culturally sensitive!"

A female voice that came from a loudspeaker said, "The fact that you have no idea why you were taken away offends me, and makes my blood boil. It infuriates me so much that I want to come down there, rip out your tongue, and then shove it down your throat. Fortunately, I have people who are more than willing to do that for me."

Suddenly the lights turned on in the room, which initially blinded the three men. Once they'd regained their sight, they saw that they were sitting at desks inside of a classroom. They weren't the only ones present. There were men and women tied in their seats and sitting in front of desks. Half of them were asleep while the other half slowly began to awaken. John spotted a familiar woman in the far right corner.

"Jane! Is that you?!" yelled John. "Honey! Wake up! Please!"

John received no response from her, because she was still unconscious. He felt relieved to at least see her, but now he had to figure out a way to escape. Just then John was approached by a strong-looking, well-built man. The man glared down at him. While John was focused on Jane, a group of people he assumed were SJWs entered the room. They wore white shirts that had "SJW" written in what appeared to be blood. Many of them were armed with guns, and they were pointing them at everyone.

John's heart was beating fast; he'd never had a gun pointed at him before. The people wielding guns appeared emotionless, and ready to pull the trigger if needed—just as they'd done many times. They were like hardened soldiers or mercenaries who had experienced the harshest conditions. John looked up at the intimidating man in front of him, tried to rid himself of his fear, and yelled, "You bastard! Let me and my fiancé go!"

The man crossed his arms, and glared down at John. One of the gun wielders then said,

"'Bastard'? D-d-did you just say...'bastard'?" The man began to weep. "My dad disowned me when I was a kid," he said, and wept some more.

John thought to himself, *Are you serious?!* The distraught man knelt down, covered his face, and began to cry again. Some of the other gun wielders sat down their weapons to console the crying man. Some of them even cried with him.

"There, there," said one of the women in a soothing voice. "It's going to be okay. Here is your pacifier."

She reached into a nearby pink bag, and removed a pacifier. She handed it to the crying man. The crying man threw it on the ground, and stated with a pout on his face, "No, it's not okay! I used to get picked on a lot as a kid because I didn't have a dad. The kids were like, 'Hey, what are you going to get your father for Father's Day? Oh yeah, that's right! You don't have a dad!" He began to cry some more. "I-I-I-I'm so glad that we got rid of Father's Day. It always reminded me that I never h-h-had a dad, and it always o-o-offended me!"

He continued to sob. The woman knelt down, picked up the pacifier, and handed it back to the crying man. This time, the man took the pacifier and placed it in his mouth. The woman hugged him, and patted him on the back.

"There, there. Everything is going to be okay," she said, soothing him.

As the group consoled the man, they continued to glare daggers at John. One of the other women of the group said, "You're gonna pay for being a big, meanie pants to him!"

The man in front of John nodded, and stated coldly, "Indeed he will." He swiftly grabbed John by the head, then slammed it on the desk, causing John to yelp in pain. The aggressor shook his head, and stated, "Cis-gendered, able-bodied, male, privileged, young, middle-class assholes like you piss me the hell off. You privileged fucks have no place in our society."

He lifted John's head back up, and then slammed it back on the desk even harder. This caused the onlookers to wince, feeling John's pain. He continued to bang John's head on the desk.

John yelled, "Go to hell, you bastards! You all can suck my nuts!"

This caused the crying man to gasp, and begin to cry even more, breathing heavily. The man in front of John said coldly, "That's enough, you insensitive prick."

He banged John's head one final time on the table as hard as he could. Afterward, he motioned for one of the female members to approach them. She did as instructed. John noticed she was carrying a hammer and a nail. The man in front of him opened John's mouth with one hand, slammed John's chin against the desk, and used the other hand to grab John's tongue. He then he pulled the tongue out. The woman then placed the nail against John's tongue, and held the hammer above it, ready to nail his tongue to the wooden desk. The man, no emotion in his voice, said, "Now apologize to my comrade, unless you want your tongue nailed to the desk."

Beads of sweat poured down John's forehead. He knew that

the safest thing to do was to apologize, but he was too stricken with fear to focus.

"I'll give you ten seconds." The man began to count down.

John attempted to apologize, but his words were incoherent.

"What's that? I can't hear you," said the man. "Five...four... three..."

Jane must have woken up at some point during all of the confusion. John heard her yell, "John! Just do it, and get it over with!"

After he'd calmed down enough, John said—at the last second—"I-I'm sorry...for...calling you a bastard."

"What was that?" asked the man.

"I'm sorry...for c-calling you...a...bastard."

"Good job. What was your name? John, was it? Good job, John! But you're only halfway there. He has to forgive you next." He then turned to the sobbing man. "Do you forgive John? He said he was sorry, and he said it in a non-offensive way."

The sobbing man stopped crying, and then he looked over at John. He removed his pacifier, and said, "D-does he mean it?"

John swiftly nodded as best as he could despite the fact that his banged-up head was being held down.

The sobbing man then said, "Okay, I'll forgive you this time."

Immediately, John was released. Even though he'd been released, his nerves simply wouldn't calm down. The other captors sighed in relief.

Hours passed after John and the others were kidnapped. Shortly after the incident, the perpetrators introduced themselves as PC Town's SJWs. John had been kidnapped because of the incident that had happened in the hotel earlier. The police officer had been taken away because he'd told the crowd to leave. The receptionist from earlier had been kidnapped because he'd used the word 'dude'—which was a problem because there were at least eight genders who resided within the hotel. Jane's situation was different. She had been taken away because she'd presented a picture of herself wearing a braided hairstyle on a social media site. This was considered to be too culturally insensitive.

Ever since the incident, the group had been undergoing video lessons on the topic of sensitivity. None of the captors spoke a word. John assumed that it was because they did not want to get harmed with the threat of possibly offending someone. As John observed the others, he suddenly did not feel right about the situation. Not only were they quiet, but their eyes were glazed over as they watched the television, completely absorbed in the lesson. Some of the captors even had their mouths open, and were drooling.

He thought to himself, *Are they being brainwashed?* John looked at Jane, and she had the same look as the rest of them.

"Jane! Snap out of it!" yelled John. "They're brainwashing you!" He looked around at the rest of them. "Hey! Close your eyes, people! They're trying to brainwash you!"

The receptionist said, in a daze, "Brainwash? That's a politically incorrect term! We are being properly educated."

The cop then said, "Yes, properly educated."

One of the SJWs then approached John. He pointed his gun at John's head, then said, "It seems like you aren't paying attention to the lectures. Here is a question for you: There are five apples in a basket. If a kid takes away two of them, then how many apples are left?"

John looked at him in confusion. "What?"

"There are five apples in a basket. If a kid takes away two of them, then how many apples are left?" The SJW cocked back the trigger.

John said nervously, "T-t-the answer is three apples."

Jane then stated out of the blue, "That is totally wrong, love! The answer is cultural tolerance, no body shaming, acceptance of one's sexual orientation, and compassion!"

The SJW said, "That is correct, ma'am."

The rest in the classroom, including the captors, agreed with the answer as they nodded in approval.

John gasped. "What?! That was a fucking math question! That answer doesn't make any sense!"

The SJW laughed. "No?! It makes complete sense!"

"You're insane!" yelled John.

"I don't know why the lessons aren't getting through to you. My guess is because you are a Conservative or a Republican or something."

"Or maybe it's because I have common fucking sense!"

The SJW chuckled. "No matter. If you can't think like us, then this world does not need intolerant people like you. Out of compassion, democracy, freedom of speech, and freedom of expression, I shall shoot you dead for not thinking like us."

The captors in the room chanted, "Kill the deviant! Kill the deviant! Kill the deviant! Kill the deviant!"

John simply observed them all in disbelief and confusion. This could not be happening. He had come to this town because he'd heard that it was a good place to visit. He and Jane were supposed to marry one another here. He looked over at Jane, and saw that she was chanting along with the rest of the crowd to kill him. It seemed like the brainwashing had taken root. The woman he loved no longer existed anymore. All that was left was a shell of the woman—if there was even that. John shed a tear, and then he closed his eyes, ready to meet his maker. "Do it," he said. "I have nothing to lose anymore."

The male SJW said, "Very well. I'll make this quick."

Right before the SJW could pull the trigger, a group of police officers hastily broke down the door. They pointed their guns at the SJWs, and they heavily outnumbered them. One of them yelled, "Freeze! Put your weapons down, or else we will open fire!"

The SJWs did as told without any resistance. Over time, all of the captors were released from their binds. John explained to the cops about the brainwashing lessons. Instead of allowing the captors to return home, they were sent to the hospital.

A couple hours later, in the police station, John spoke to a detective about the situation.

Ironically, the detective himself was originally from Harshtown. He told John that he had been working hard on taking down the SJWs for years now, ever since the last mayoral election. He also explained that not all SJWs took things to the extreme like this group did. Even though they had taken down one of the SJW's bases, there were still many more of them all around.

John talked about what he had gone through, along with how he and Jane were supposed to have gotten married in a couple days. Although the detective easily understood, he told John that there was no telling how long it would take for the others to recover from the brainwashing. In the hospitals were the best doctors, psychiatrists, and counselors. Despite all of this, John decided to wait, no matter how long it took. Every day he waited at Jane's bedside. Most of the time she was asleep due to the medication, but he refused to abandon her. He loved her unconditionally, and nothing was going to change that. Even if she became an SJW, he decided that he was still going to love her no matter what. Time continued to pass, and John's determination to see this through remained strong.

Four weeks later, Jane had finally recovered from her brainwashing:

From what John could tell, she became her usual optimistic self that she'd been prior to the brainwashing. The couple had received protection by the police ever since the incident with the SJWs. Currently, the two walked side by side, ready to say their vows of marriage. It had been a long journey, but they had finally made it. They stood in front of the judge, ready to move onto the next chapter of their lives. The judge looked down at them, and then silently motioned John over. John nodded, and did as instructed.

"I congratulate you on your marriage, John. After reviewing your wedding application, we noticed that there is one critical piece of information that is incomplete. It is something that is very minor, but is a necessary policy of PC Town. You must choose between either of these two preferences," said the judge.

The judge presented him with the marriage application. The question read: "Are you a Democrat or a Republican?"

John chuckled to himself as he thought about the stupidity of the question, and how dumb it was for it to be their policy for a marriage. He decided to answer the question anyway, since it wasn't serious. He circled "Democrat." Jane, however, had been looking over at his choice curiously.

"Umm, why are you circling that option?" she asked.

John looked over at her. "Because I'm a Democrat."

"Huh? Why?! How could you believe in the same things as the Democrats?! They are ruining this country! Look at the Unaffordable Healthcare Act."

"Umm, Jane? It isn't that serious, honey."

"Not serious?! We are talking about the country here, and everyone's rights! You know what? Maybe this marriage was a bad idea."

John thought to himself, *Is she being serious right now? This has to be a joke! There is just no other way around it.*

John then chuckled, and said jokingly, "If it bothers you that much, then maybe you should leave then."

Jane said, "Fine! I will!"

She immediately turned around, and began to storm out of the chapel.

"Jane! Wait! I'm joking! Come back here! Jane! Jane!" John yelled. He rushed after her.

A month later, back in Harshtown, John sat at the bar with his childhood friend:

He was single again since Jane had been serious about leaving him over a political party. He bitterly explained to his friend everything that happened in PC Town.

"It just didn't work out, man," John explained. "I loved her unconditionally, too. It didn't matter to me what political party she was a part of—or hell, if she was still a brainwashed SJW. I loved her, man!"

John's friend, Horus, said, "Not to be that guy, but you kinda fucked up. You should have taken her seriously. Otherwise this wouldn't have happened. Women can be sensitive at times. Perhaps the SJWs were right about you to some extent. You probably should be more sensitive to other's emotions."

"Hell no! The problem is that people are becoming *way* too sensitive! People in general need to chill the fuck out, because life does not have to be that serious. All I tried to do was apologize to her, and she kept avoiding me. She then left town without me, and once she got home, she packed up her things and left before I arrived home. I tried calling her, but I think she blocked my phone number."

Horus said, "Give it some time, man. She needs to calm down." He looked at his watch. "Well, time to go. I hope things work out for you, man."

Horus waved goodbye to John, and then exited the bar. John sighed in disbelief, and then banged his head on the bar in frustration.

CHAPTER SEVEN

AT THE PARK IN HARSHTOWN, a young man grumbled:

"She...won't talk to me! I tried to explain the situation to her, but she completely shut me out. I think...it may really be over."

Marpha comforted him. "I am sorry to hear about your relationship problems, and I truly do hope that things work out for you in the future."

Marpha looked at her clock, and saw that it was time to go. Every now and then she would take a walk in the park, and that day she'd encountered a troubled young man that she never met before. Prior to their talk, she noticed that he was sitting alone in the park with his head low, and then he simply opened up to her despite being strangers. Marpha exchanged hugs with the distraught one, and left to head to her destination, the hospital. Abraham was supposed to give a wonderful sermon there to provide moral support to the patients.

Marpha had been heavily involved with the church ever since it had been built. She had volunteered a lot for the establishment, and had provided a lot of support for her saint, Abraham.

Thirty minutes later, at the hospital, Marpha observed her

priest, Abraham, preach the will of the Lord.

"It doesn't matter if you are terminally ill! It doesn't matter that you may die in the next hour! If you give me all of your money right now, then your soul will be saved! Even if you were to use the money to pay for the operation, then your soul will be cast away into the Lake of Fire, and your pain will be one hundred times what it is now!"

One of the terminally ill hospital patients stood up, wrote a check for Abraham, handed it to him, and then shook his hand in admiration.

"Logically, this doesn't make sense. I may die next week, and this was the money for the operation, but I really believe in your words, Abraham. It matters not, for even if I did live and die of old age, then my soul wouldn't be saved!"

Abraham took the check without any hesitation. More and more patients stood up to give the priest money and checks. Marpha just stood there, smiling in admiration. In her eyes, he was helping out so many people. She imagined his life was filled with happiness because he could look at himself in the mirror every day and feel proud of the service he was doing for humanity. Marpha felt that the volunteer work she had been doing for Abraham, and the church, were both great justices to society. The priest bowed to the crowd.

"I thank you all for your commitment to the Lord." Abraham handed the basket of money and checks to Marpha, and then they both left the hospital.

A day later, in the breakroom of C.J. Pickles, Marpha argued with Rachel.

"Abraham is such a great man. He saved so many souls in the hospital that day," said Marpha.

Rachel glared at her. "You mean 'killed'? Yeah, I saw on the news. Thirty people died in the hospital later that night."

Marpha glared back, and then slowly walked closer to Rachel. "Regardless of the fact that they died, they are experiencing eternal life right now! That is eternal bliss, and it is all thanks to Abraham. How can you question him so much? You are such a terrible person."

"Listen to yourself! The only person that this man cares about is himself. What happened last night proves that he is willing to do anything to get what he wants, which makes him a very dangerous man! He is doing a disservice to humanity, and to our religion! Don't feel self-confident just because you are taking pills to control your What-if Syndrome! It doesn't mean you are sane now."

Marpha chuckled at Rachel, pointing at her. "You have the nerve to question my sanity?! You tried to kill Milena! If anyone is doing a disservice to humanity, then it's you. How the hell did you get the idea that Milena was going to hurt you? Who put that in your head anyway?"

Immediately, Rachel pounced on Marpha, and began to strangle her while banging her head on the ground. Even though Rachel ended up losing her job that day, to her it had been worth it. She couldn't stand Marpha.

The next day, Marpha entered Hector's Store.

Marpha had been spreading the word about Abraham and his wonderful teachings. Even though she and Hector had been on bad terms, it did not stop her from trying to reach him.

"Excuse my French, Marpha, but fuck that church. They beat me up, and then hung me up on the cross because I have different beliefs than they do. On a side note, I don't hold a grudge against you for firing me, and I'm glad that you fixed your What-if Syndrome."

Marpha glared at Hector, who was cleaning up his store. She didn't care at all about the polite comment directed toward her, rather what he'd said about the church—the church was more important than her dignity and self-respect.

"Abraham's teachings are the only true teachings in the world! The reason that happened to you in the first place is because you're a heretic! You follow false teachings, and you will pay for it once you're dead, because all of your choices are going to be weighed against each other. Because you chose to go against the one true teachings, you are going to hell!"

Hector stopped cleaning for a moment, turned to Marpha, the fanatic, and wondered if this was the same person he'd worked with in the past.

"What happened to you? You were annoying as hell back then, but sometimes we had good conversations. Now you are very closed-minded and intolerant. There is more than one path to enlightenment. There isn't one path!"

Marpha held the Bible up in his face. "Not according to the Good Book! I'll do anything for my religion! I am the Lord's disciple, and since I think you are a good person, I want to save you."

Marpha then corrected herself. "No—you WILL be saved!"

Hector sighed, and then went back to work. "You know what? Stop taking those pills. You were much more tolerable when you were worrisome. The only thing that is going to be saved, is my sanity. Now get out of my store before I throw you into the dumpster."

Thirty minutes later, in a park, Marpha observed her surroundings.

Marpha walked around town preaching the will of God all day. After her talk with Hector, she decided to visit the park. She spotted a little girl who was nearby playing by herself.

"Hey, child. I see that you are alone here in the park. I have something important to tell you."

The young girl, who happened to be Carmen, looked up at Marpha warily. "My mother always told me not to talk to strangers."

Marpha approached her, reached into a bag, and then pulled out a child's edition of the Good Book. "But I'm not a stranger. I'm a disciple of the Lord."

Carmen rolled her eyes, knowing damn well where this was going. "Here we go," she said.

Marpha handed the book to Carmen. "Have you ever heard of the Good Book? It is the one true book in the world. It is the only book that you will ever need to read, because—"

Carmen suddenly threw the book in the sandbox, and then went back to playing alone. Marpha narrowed her eyes at the young girl, then immediately snatched her up, dragged her to a bench, pulled out a belt, and then threw her over her lap. Carmen began to scream in terror.

"She's crazy! Let me go! Let me go! Someone help me! Anyone! She's not my mother!"

Marpha raised the belt, and then whooped the young girl's behind.

"I smite the sin out of you! In the name of the Lord! Darkness! Leave this little girl!" She beat Carmen over and over again. "Demons! You will not claim this girl, for her soul will be saved!" Carmen cried as she was beaten. It was apparent that nobody was going to come to her rescue.

"In the name of the Lord! Leave this little girl, demon! For you have no hold on her! For she is a child of God!"

Marpha did not get in trouble for her actions. Even though this was the case, she'd still gotten many strange looks by many of the townspeople. As a result, she decided that she had done enough for the Lord, and for Abraham, so she devoted the rest of her day to reading the Bible at home.

A day later, at church, Marpha spoke to Abraham:

"Abraham, even though I have been doing a lot of work for God, and am trying to get people saved, I realize that I'm not saved myself, so I would like to be saved. My life has been nothing but chaos, and there are so many issues with the world. Ever since I started going to the church, you opened my eyes and showed me the only way to live life. Life is something that will end eventually, one way or another. The main goal is to work your way to heaven. Nothing else matters." Marpha shook his hand in admiration. "Thank you for opening my eyes."

Abraham smiled at her, and placed his hand on her shoulder. "Marpha, you have been a huge help to the church, and it is much appreciated. However, there is a trial that you must undergo in order to be saved. It isn't for everyone. Actually, there are hardly any people in the world who can be saved, but I have faith in you—even though the Lord thought you were a nobody, a worrisome piece of garbage who probably shouldn't have been born in the first place. He has faith that you will prove him wrong this time." A tear of joy rolled down Marpha's eye as she listened to him. "Are you ready to go on your journey to be saved?"

She nodded.

The priest smiled as he walks away. He returned with a bag and a basket.

"All right, for your first trial, there are people in the convenience store who need to hear my teachings. What I want you to do is go there, preach for them to stop drinking alcohol, smoking, and gambling, and then—" He whispered in her ear. Marpha gasped, giving him an alarmed look. Abraham reassured her. "As I stated before, the journey to being saved is a difficult one. If you wish to back out, then it is understood. It's only an eternity of fire and brimstone...that's all. So feel free to back out. No big deal, right?"

Marpha shook her head no, took the belongings, and did as instructed. "This is the one true way. I haven't been more sure of anything else in my life."

Fifteen minutes later, Marpha walked into the convenience store. She looked around, and spotted a couple of people—the clerk and a customer. She cleared her throat to get everyone's attention, and began to preach the word of the Lord without anyone's consent. The customer rolled his eyes as he checked out the beer section. The clerk, however, just gave her an amused look. Rather than kick her out of the store, he was rather entertained, since he hardly got to be there at the store.

Marpha approached the clerk. "Since my lesson has been given, if you want to be saved, you must donate to the church, for it is the will of the Lord!"

The worker laughed at her. "Get out of my store, ma'am. You are embarrassing yourself."

Marpha reached into her bag, pulled out a gun, and held it to the clerk's head.

"This is the only way for me to be saved! This is the only way that you can be saved! If you don't donate money to me right now, then your life I shall take, because it is the will of the Lord!"

The customer tried to run away, but Marpha turned to him, and shot him in the leg without feeling any remorse. The customer instantly fell to the ground, screaming in pain, and holding his leg. She had great aim due to having taken shooting lessons after she'd become worried that a group of straight-A high school students were going to mug her. The clerk opened his register, gave Marpha all of his money, as well as all the scratch tickets. Marpha put them all in the bag, and then left the store hastily to head back to the church.

Ten minutes later, Marpha returned to church, and spoke to Abraham.

"Abraham, I did as you asked. I preached the good word, then gave the clerk a choice of either being saved by donating, or by me delivering divine retribution. He chose to donate." Marpha placed the bag on the ground.

Abraham approached her, and opened the bag with a smile. "You did the Lord a great service, Marpha."

"Am...Am I saved?"

Abraham shook his head no, and placed his hand on her shoulder. "There is just one simple thing for you to do. All you have to do is wait here, inside this room, and say a few prayers. You must not stop until I say you can."

Marpha nodded.

She knelt down and began to pray. The priest left her alone in the room. Thirty minutes later, a few policemen, and Abraham, entered the room. Abraham pointed at Marpha, who looked at him, confused.

"She is the one who robbed the convenience store," he said.

"What?!" Marpha yelled.

The cops restrained Marpha, and then put her in handcuffs. Marpha was still looking at Abraham, very confused. It hadn't yet registered that she was being betrayed.

"Am I saved?" she asked.

Abraham glared at her. "I got a message from God ten minutes ago. He says that you aren't saved, you are an abomination, and he wishes that he had never created you. He also said that you are better off in jail, and hopes you rot and die, and then burn in hell for all eternity! You aren't welcome at this church anymore, so get out and stay out!"

Marpha was completely speechless as the police took her to their police car.

———

In the break room at Happy Sunshine, Inc., a few workers gossiped about a recent event that had stirred up a little bit of attention on the news.

"Hey, did you hear?! There was some crazy woman who robbed the 96-69 last night! One of my friends got shot there!"

"Yeah! I heard that it was some Muslim. Preaching about their god, and doing it in his name."

"Sounds like a bunch of terrorism bullshit."

"You got it wrong, and I find that very offensive! It wasn't a Muslim, and not all Muslims are terrorists. Some of the nicest people that I have ever met are Muslims, and they generally are very peaceful people! Don't do the bigoted thing by lumping them all in one category just because they have a few bad apples."

John listened to his coworkers for a little while, until his break time was over. He walked over to the clock-in kiosk, punched in, and spotted another custodian. It was Marisol, and he saw that she was wearing a popular brand of shoes.

"Hey, Marisol. I like your new shoes."

Marisol looked down at her shoes curiously. They were new work shoes, but she didn't really care about the nice compliment, because she was having another bad day. Rather than respond to John right away, she walked away from him, pretending that she hadn't heard him.

"Hey, Marisol, I'm not sure if you heard me or not, but I said that your shoes look nice," he said again.

Marisol rolled her eyes. "Whatever."

"What's wrong? Having a bad day?"

Marisol, annoyed, turned to him, clearly frustrated. "Leave me alone. Give me my space!"

John sighed, dismayed. "All right, but if you need a fellow coworker to talk to, then—"

"I said, leave me alone!" Marisol yelled angrily.

She quickly left to continue working. Three hours later, John approached her again.

"Hey, Marisol, are you still feeling upset?"

Marisol was silent, and simply glared at him.

John decided to just leave. "All right, I'll continue to give you your space, but keep in mind that if you need someone to talk to, then I'm here."

Thirty minutes later in Fatima's office, Marisol stood in front of her—Fatima, the person Marisol most despised, second only to Jason, the car-vandalizing psychopath.

"Wow, Marisol. What a surprise. I thought you said that you hated me, and never wanted to talk to me again."

"Yes, I did say that, but this is something serious. Even though we had our falling out, because we're both women, we need to stick together."

Fatima raised an eyebrow. "What's the problem?"

"It's about John. I didn't say this before, because I tried to be nice, but he has been coming onto me, and it has been lowering my work performance."

Fatima crossed her arms, and gave Marisol a serious look. "What happened exactly?"

Marisol looked away. "Earlier today, he said that I looked sexy in my shoes. He constantly keeps looking at me, and blowing kisses in my direction. I tried telling him to stop, but he kept on coming onto me, saying that everything would be all right, calling me baby, and that if I needed someone to ease my stress, then I should come to his place for the night—or every night." Marisol began to weep. "He's creeping me out, Fatima! All I want to do is my work! I have no choice but to charge him for sexual harassment!"

Marisol hugged Fatima as tightly as possible as she continued to weep. Fatima tried to comfort her, hugging her former rival back, regardless of the fact she felt very awkward about it.

"I'll look into this immediately. I apologize that you have had to go through this. Nobody should have to endure that. Action will be taken now!"

The next day, John was still giving Marisol her space. Marisol looked at him as he walked past her, and was completely filled with disappointment. *He still works here?* she thought. *Gotta work harder to get him out. He's an annoying little prick.*

Marisol approached her victim.

"Hey, John. How are you doing today? Sorry about yesterday. I wasn't feeling very happy, but I'm feeling better."

John looked at her, and nodded. He continued to walk away.

Marisol walked over to him, and made him stop in his tracks. "Hey, John. I would like to have my talk now about why I had such a bad day. Would you like to meet up during lunch, or some time after work?"

John looked at her, and sighed. "I appreciate your concern, but just like how you needed your space yesterday, I need mine."

He continued on his way.

In the break room, John sat by himself in complete silence, reflecting on the whole situation. Coworkers constantly looked at him like he was crazy, because rumors had spread fast in the workplace. Just about everyone was completely aware that he had been charged with sexual harassment, which had created a very hostile environment for him. Just about all of the women, except for Marisol, steered clear of John, while the men just glared at him with contempt. Most were convinced that he was guilty, regardless of the fact that he was very pro-woman, and tended to be very reserved in the workplace.

Meanwhile, in the breakroom, Marisol wiped away a fake tear from her eye. "So are you girls in? He has been doing this to me for months now, and the company still allows him to work here! Even after his charge, he still comes onto me!"

The female coworkers all came to an agreement to help Marisol, and they all went to Fatima to accuse John of sexual harassment. Because of this, he was placed on suspension without pay until further investigation was made. Marisol was relieved, but it still wasn't enough, because John hadn't been fired yet. She needed to work harder on this. She wondered why she hadn't thought of this idea sooner since she knew society was quick to crush males who had been charged with sexual harassment. After she had tried to get people on her side for a week, she was called into Fatima's office.

Marisol gave Fatima a concerned look, as Fatima glared at her.

"Is there anything wrong, ma'am?" Marisol asked.

Fatima's voice was filled with anger, but she was trying to conceal it. "John has been receiving counseling, and we performed another background check on him. We also contacted his previous employers. It turns out that, for the most part, he kept to himself, aside from caring about whenever his coworkers were feeling down."

Marisol scratched her head, confused. "What are you trying to say?"

Fatima leaned forward on her desk. "I talked to all of his coworkers and supervisors only to find out that he is the least likely person to be convicted of his current accusations. Hell, when I talked to him in person, he didn't give me a pervert vibe at all."

Marisol shrugged, and tried to do the math in her head. "And?"

Fatima banged her fists on the desk. "You better stop with the false charges! Now! You are doing the exact same thing that you did with me to him! You see someone who you don't like or understand, so you try to force them out, and it is going to backfire on you hard, again! Stop this now, and I'll forget that this ever happened."

Marisol began to cry, and covered her face. "We are supposed to stick together! We're both women! You know how men can be, and we gotta watch out for each other! I cannot believe that you are even considering that I might be lying about something as serious as this." Marisol, sobbing, got down on her knees.

"Get the fuck out of my office! NOW!"

Fatima pointed at the door. Just like that, Marisol stopped sobbing, shrugged, and then left the office. Honestly, Marisol didn't see what the big deal was. All she was doing was trying to get rid of someone she didn't like, and it certainly wasn't the first time that she had done something like this.

A couple days later, John sat down at the bar with Horus,

"They suspended me for these charges, man. The thing is, I have a hell of a lot of respect for women. What have I done wrong? On the other hand, maybe I deserve these charges."

Horus grabbed his shoulders, and shook him. "Don't say that, man! I know that you wouldn't do that, and you sure as hell know that you wouldn't! These are false charges, and you need to do something about it! The only thing is, with this situation, it's your word against theirs."

John looked away from him. "I still miss Jane. I always had problems with women before these charges. I try to be respectful to them, but they always screw me over in some way. It has always been like this, one way or another, ever since I hit puberty. Jane was the only woman I really liked, but it turned out that she was a lot less tolerant than I expected, or perhaps you were right about me. Perhaps I need to be more sensitive and just apologize to her."

Horus tried to comfort him. "Do what you feel is right, man. Also, keep in mind that not all women are like that, and there are just as many guys who are just as bad. I hate to make things worse, but rumor has it that it was Marisol who started it."

John froze for a moment as he thought of Marisol, the woman he had tried to comfort.

"What the hell?! I have always been nice to her! Why the hell would she do this to me?! This is what I'm talking about! I try to be nice to women, and they treat me like shit. Yet if some guy is rude or mean to them, then it's all good."

His friend sighed. "Dude, keep in mind what I said. Just because you have had a bunch of bad experiences, that doesn't mean that all of them are that way. Yes, this society can be fucked up at times, but please don't fall into the category of people who lump groups of people together."

An hour later, disregarding the fact he was on suspension, John stormed into Fatima's office. She was taken by surprise as he glared at her.

"Fatima! These sexual harassment charges are false! I may not have the proof in order to debunk this, but I'm not going to just sit by, idle, and let this build up even more."

Fatima smiled at him. "It's about time you fought back. You are late, though, because the whole issue has already been investigated. You will be returning back to work soon, and Marisol has been demoted to the position of Shit Cleaner in one of my fast food stores—so you won't have to worry about seeing her again."

John smiled, and cheered. "Have a good day, ma'am—and thank you!"

He closed the door, and then took out his cell phone to call Jane. However, he wasn't able to get in touch with her as usual.

———

Marisol begrudgingly opened the door to the fast food store to begin her shift. She clocked in, got her gloves and mask, and then walked to the bathroom. She spotted Mark in front of the bathroom door, who simply waved at her.

"You're a shit cleaner, too? It's good to know that I finally have help for a change."

Shortly after Mark greeted her, Andrew opened the door, fanning the air.

"Phew! Those chocolate sundaes and that extra-large pizza really hit the spot! Thank god my shit cleaner's here!" He paused for a moment, looked at Marisol, and then at Mark. "Who the fuck is this?"

"She's our new shit cleaner. Looks like I have help for a change."

"Good. Teach her the ropes of cleaning my shit. She should be able to master it today, since she has a huge load to clean up."

Mark turned to his trainee. "All right, you heard him. You are doing all of the work while I monitor your progress. Let's get started."

Marisol glared at him, and then peered through the door to the sight of a toilet overflowing with Andrew's shit, which caused her to throw up.

"Hey! Look at the mess you made!" Andrew yelled at her. "You gotta clean up that shit, too!"

———

Tony walked past a disgruntled-looking janitor. From the look of it, the janitor had just come from the restroom. He grumbled about having to clean other people's crap. Tony's focus shifted as Lee hastily rushed toward him.

"Hey! Tony! I got something very serious to tell you!"

Tony looked at Lee skeptically, and crossed his arms. "What is it this time? You gave five kids swirlies?"

"No, you dumbass! This is even more important than that." Lee looked to his left and to the right to make sure nobody was watching or listening, and then whispered, "But we need to lower our voices."

Tony could care less whether anyone heard him or not. He just wanted to get this over with so he could go straight to class.

"Just spill it out already!"

"Tony, I'm scared! Have you ever heard of the Illuminati?"

"Nope, don't know. Don't really care too much."

"They own the whole world! They own this school, they own our homes, they control our education, and they hold people back from succeeding in life by using black magic. We gotta look out for one another, man. At first, I cared the most about owning this joint, but ever since I heard about the Illuminati, my eyes have been opened."

Tony thought there was no way in hell that this could be real. "Are you talking about a TV show?"

Lee shook his head, and grabbed his friend's shoulders. "This is reality, man. Just check out the internet! They may have the masses fooled, but they certainly don't have me tricked."

The bell rang, signaling it was time for them to go to class.

Ten minutes later, in class, Mr. Tank said, "All right, cretins, are you ready to learn about physics?"

Everyone replied together except for Lee, "May we have permission to speak, Master?"

"Yes you may, cretins."

"We are ready to learn about physics, sir. We are finished, our superior elder."

Lee's lack of a response instantly caught Mr. Tank's attention, and he walked over to Lee's desk, glowering down at him. "And what's your problem?" he asked Lee.

Lee crossed his arms, looked away from Mr. Tank. He was no longer concerned about rules or consequences.

"Why the hell are we learning about physics when we need to learn about more important things—like the Illuminati?" Mr. Tank narrowed his eyes at his student, but Lee couldn't care less. "The Illuminati is the biggest threat in the world! They are a bunch of shape-shifting reptilians that are holding back humanity with their black magic. This whole system is controlled by them. You are controlled by them! They are our world leaders!"

The class listened in awe, as Tony just shook his head at Lee.

"We need to unite, and take them down and reclaim this world from these reptiles," Lee continued. "I won't see humanity fall!"

Suddenly, rather than discipline Lee, Mr. Tank left the classroom without a word.

Tony decided to debunk Lee's theories, so the class could just go on with learning physics.

"You are speaking a bunch of nonsense!" said Tony. "Anyone with common sense can easily tell that what you're saying is a bunch of lies! There is no such thing as the Illuminati!"

Lee quickly turned to Tony. "Mr. Tank is fully aware of them. The reason he left is because he knows about this secret, and his eyes are now opened to the truth of the world."

"That's not why he left! He left because he was simply amazed at how much of a fucking retard you are, and he needed a breath of fresh air—especially because that was probably the first time that he's ever laughed." Tony pointed at the door. "Look at him right now!"

The whole class observed Mr. Tank through the window. His face was red from laughing so much and so hard. Lee stood up on his desk, not caring about what Tony had said.

"Classmates! We need to unite and take back our planet!"

Mr. Tank entered the classroom ten minutes later.

"Class, out of all the years that I have lived, this has to be the second time that I have ever laughed. I was disappointed over the fact that only two of you are above the line of retardation, but after this moment, it was worth teaching you all. Stay retarded."

30 minutes later, in the counselor's office, Jerome said curiously, "So you are saying that there is a secret organization filled with reptile-like beings that perform black magic, and are taking over the world? And the only way that we can counter this is by uniting?"

Jerome shook his head in confusion as he tried to understand where Lee was coming from.

"It gets worse!" said Lee. "The government is also working with the aliens. There are different factions of them. There are the greys, and of course I told you about the reptilians! The greys and reptilians hate us. Many of these aliens walk among us right now, because they can shape-shift. It's mind-blowing, man! Your friends could be aliens without you even knowing it."

Jerome wrote in his notebook as Lee continued to speak.

"Even though these reptilians and greys are against us, there are good aliens that are on our side. They are called the Nordics. As a matter of fact, this race is actually a race of humans who have been evolving much longer than we have. It isn't enough support, though."

Jerome discarded his notebook, and reflected on what Lee

had told him. "Well, Lee, I apologize for sending you to the insane asylum a little while ago. Based on what you have told me, I can see that you are a guy who thinks outside the box." Jerome extended his hand to Lee, and then shook Lee's hand. "Keep doing what you're doing. You are onto something, kid! You have a very bright future ahead of you!"

The next day, right before class started, Tony was baffled as he walked down the hallway. He saw a bunch of people talking to one another about the Illuminati, and to top it off, Lee was giving people a bunch of articles about the secret organization. Eventually, Kenny approached Tony.

"Hey, dude, at first I thought you were right about what you said, but then I went on the internet to check out what Lee was talking about, and now I'm scared! I have never been this scared in my entire life, dude!"

"Are you serious?" Tony asked him.

"Yeah, dude! The point of our existence is to sustain the reptilians! We are cattle to them!"

"All it takes is common sense to know that this is false. If there is a race of reptiles that lived on this earth way before we were created, then why is it that we are the dominant species? For that matter, why is it that we haven't seen one yet?"

"It's because our earth is hollow, and they live underground, dude!"

Tony sighed, and shook his head at his best friend. "I'm finished. Now you are just being even more retarded than Lee." Tony began to walk away, but Kenny handed him an article.

"Read this! This will open your eyes!"

Kenny walked away contentedly to his locker, like the article had completely made his point.

Ten minutes later, in class, Mr. Tank said, "All right, cretins. Rather than go through our normal class routine, today we will dedicate this day to talking about what has been popular topic, and that is the"—Mr. Tank made air quotes—"the Illuminati." Mr. Tank approached Tony. "Since you are the most skeptical guy, and the unofficial third person in the class who is above the line of retardation, you will debate against Lee and whoever else agrees with Lee. Now you have my permission to speak any way you choose until I say so. This is very rare, and the only time that I'll give you this privilege." Mr. Tank took out a bowl of popcorn, and then sat down at his desk. "Now discuss."

Without wasting any time, Kenny quickly spoke directly to Tony. "Hey, Tony! Did you read the article that I gave you?"

"Yes, I read some of it. It documented the story of a woman who interviewed a reptilian in person. I didn't need to go into too much further detail."

"Why is that? Because it opened your eyes?"

"Nah, it's because the person who wrote it is a science-fiction author. She wrote about how she interviewed a reptilian, and you expect me to believe that crap? She specializes in making up shit like that!"

Kenny shrugged, and looked around for support from his peers. "Well...."

Kenny went silent. Tony sat there, twiddling his thumbs, waiting for the next person to argue with him.

Lee yelled, "You have always been such a dumbass, Tony! The proof is everywhere! Turn on the television, and you will see a bunch of Illuminati logos!"

Tony wasn't stressed out at all. He was just surprised that nobody else seemed to agree with him, apart from Mr. Tank. "Or," he said, "they're just logos for whatever it is they are advertising."

"The media constantly hides stuff," said Lee. "And the purpose of school is to keep us dumbed down! They don't want critical thinkers, because then that would cause the enemy to have problems with taking over the world."

"What enemy?" asked Tony.

"I already told you over and over again yesterday."

"All you told me were a bunch of fabrications you conjured up from the Internet. For that matter, how credible is the Internet? Do you all simply just believe everything you read and hear?"

"This is information from experts, and people who have seen this in person! Hell, there is a guy whose fingers were blasted off by a Grey! I saw the video of his fingers after it happened!"

"So if a person says they are an expert, and have interacted with the Illuminati, then that means it's real? Well, if that's the case, then I am the President of the Unites States, Inc., because I said I am! Also, there are a hell of a lot of ways for a guy to lose fingers."

Tony stood up, and began to count the ways. "They can be chopped off, they can be blown off, they could decay and rot off...."

The debate went on and on for a while. There was a power outage in the school that caused all of the lights and power to turn off, but this didn't slow down the debate's progress. In the end they agreed to disagree.

The next day Kenny invited Tony to go to the park. Fortunately, Tony's mother was generous enough to allow him outside despite the Milena Alert. It felt very odd to him, considering that usually Kenny and Tony planned their time spent together in advance, but it didn't play out this way. This time Kenny had called and told Tony that it was an emergency.

Tony arrived at the park, and looked around curiously. Strangely, there was no one there.

Tony yelled, "Kenny! Are you there?! Is everything all right?!"

Out of nowhere, Tony was tackled by a group of kids who yelled, "Illuminatis!" Tony tried to break free, but was unable to as they restrained him, knocked him out unconscious, and threw him into a sack.

———

Tony found himself at an unknown location during an unknown time. He couldn't remember anything. He was tied to a chair in some type of warehouse, he was alone. The last thing that he could remember was going to the park, and before that, he could remember his classmates being a bunch of fucking morons. He tried in vain to break through the ropes, but this was to no avail. He began to yell for help, but there was nothing but silence, until five minutes later, a crowd emerged from the darkness.

Tony saw that Kenny was among them. "Kenny?! What in the world, dude?!" The memories of the conversation he'd had with his friend resurfaced, and he remembered how he'd gotten there all of a sudden.

"You set me up!" Kenny shook his head at Tony, as Tony pointed angrily at him.

The crowd split as Lee, their leader, emerged. "Shut up, dumbass!"

Tony focused on Lee, and narrowed his eyes. "And you are supposed to be my friend, too! What is this all about?!"

Lee walked over to Tony, his prisoner, and began circling him. "I knew that there was something off about you. It wasn't the fact that you were a lame kid, and it wasn't the fact that you got your ass handed to you by Kenny, here."

"Then what is it?! Is it because I don't believe in the Illuminati?!"

Kenny yelled furiously, "You are one of them! I saw it!" The crowd was in an uproar now.

Tony tried to make sense of this. "How so?"

"Your eyes! They changed in class yesterday around the time when the lights went out, and then they changed again when the lights turned back on!"

Tony shook his head at Kenny, who had betrayed him. "You're a dumbass, Kenny! That's what's supposed to happen with your eyes! Haven't you paid attention to Mr. Tank when he taught us science?"

Lee glared at him. "No, we haven't, but we have paid attention to the fact that you are a shape-shifting reptilian! Tell me, what are your plans for world domination?"

Tony went blank as he was interrogated. It like time slowed down as he observed his classmates. They all had looks of hatred and anger on their faces. He had never experienced something like this before, as they continued to yell. He couldn't understand them, because they were speaking in slow motion. Without a single doubt, Tony was convinced that this was over nothing. He wondered how many times something like this had happened throughout history. Kenny appeared to be just another face in the crowd. Tony couldn't even call him his best friend anymore. It was just Tony versus them.

Time seemed to revert back to normal. "All right, Lee. I'll talk. You finally stumbled upon my secret."

Lee turned around, told everyone to shut the fuck up, and then turned toward Tony. "Speak up then, or else we'll kill your reptilian ass."

"Thank you for showing me mercy. The truth is, I am an agent sent by the Illuminati. The reason my eyes changed is because my shape-shifting abilities have weakened ever since you caught onto me. My job is to play the role of the skeptic in order to throw people off." This caused a few in the crowd to gasp. "They didn't tell me anything more about my role just in case something like this happened. However, if you let me go, then I can go back to my home underground to gather more information. I really don't like what they are trying to do to you humans, but they told me that they would kill my family if I didn't comply."

There was nothing but silence in the crowd. Lee motioned for someone to hand him something. Someone handed him a switchblade knife, and Tony's eyes widened a little. Lee held the knife in his hand, and glared down at Tony as he held it against his throat.

"How do we know that you are telling the truth?"

Tony tried to hold his bladder as he replied nervously. "Y-you don't, but you can take the top button on my shirt as proof of my word. It may appear to be a regular button, but it actually can summon my spaceship."

Lee cut off the button, observed it, and then looked at Tony. "Amazing." Lee cut off Tony's ropes. "Go back to your underground home, then get information. If you don't, and if you don't get more proof about what you say, then you're dead when you come back to school Monday."

Tony nodded at Lee, and got up. He left immediately, and as soon as he was away from his location, the abandoned warehouse, he ran home, screaming in terror.

After Tony arrived home, he screamed,

"Mom! The kids at school are gonna kill me!"

Tony's mother looked at her son curiously. "Are you being bullied again? Or"—she crossed her arms—"did you start trouble this time?"

"No, this is much more serious than school politics! They are literally going to kill me! They knocked me out, put me in a warehouse, and held a knife to my throat!"

Tony began to explain the situation to his mother. She listened intently.

"All right, son. Come with me!"

The two decided to visit the school. There were hardly any faculty there since it was Saturday.

In the principal's office, Tony said,

"And that's what happened, sir. I lied to my classmates so they would let me go! The reason I lied is because, regardless of what I said, they are going to believe what they want to believe, and I didn't want to get stabbed over some made-up garbage. It happened enough during the Holy Crusades—or so Mr. Tank says."

The principle reflected on this. "I see, but the thing is, how do we know that you are telling me the truth? Your story sounds just as ridiculous as the Illuminati stories that are on the Internet. It's hard for me to believe that any of my students are capable of murder—even Lee!"

Tony's mother protested. "My son wouldn't lie about something like this! Sure, he has had his share of trouble-making, but making up a fib like this is way out of his league! It is now, and it was back then."

"Even if this is the truth, I can't do anything about it, because all you are doing is making accusations without having anything to back them up. If you can prove to me what you say, then action will be taken."

Later on, in the police station, Tony explained, "That's what happened, officer. My classmates will kill me if I don't come up with something."

Office Lives reflected on this. "I see."

Tony continued to protest. "I don't believe in the Illuminati. I questioned everyone, so they knocked me out and tied me to a chair."

The officer took a deep breath, looked at Tony, and then at Tony's mother. "What I can do is visit their parents, explain the whole thing, and talk them out of it. If they keep harassing you, then action can be taken."

Tony's mother smiled. "Thank you so much, officer."

The officer smiled at her. "No problem, ma'am. I'll work on it right away."

Officer Lives stood up, shook their hands, and then left.

A day later, Tony woke up before his mother had, and he heard the phone ring downstairs. He quickly picked it up.

"Hello?"

He was greeted by Officer Lives's voice. "Is this Tony?"

"Yes, this is."

"Tony, I talked to the parents of those children, and learned a lot more than I expected. I went to the first house, and a child explained to me about to Illuminati. It blew my mind away, because I didn't know that the world was like this! Afterward, I went to the next house to learn more, and the child gave me an article about a woman who had interviewed a reptilian. I thanked the child, then shook his parents' hands. I went from house to house learning things that I never would have learned in school. I didn't know that this was the reality of the world. It certainly does explain a lot. Well, your situation is taken care of, and it won't be a problem again. Take care."

Officer Lives hung up on Tony, who sat there with his mouth wide open, shocked.

Monday approached, signifying that it was now time for Tony to go back to class, much to his dismay. Earlier, his mother had attempted to convince him that the children were merely bluffing, but Tony was skeptical of that, too. He arrived at school, and walked down the hallway nervously as everyone glared at him and called him reptilian spawn. Rather than going to his classroom right away, he waited in the hallway, terrified as his classmates waited for him and continued to glare.

Lee patted his pocket, and smirked. Tony could tell that Lee had his pocket knife in there. Mr. Tank was about to enter the classroom, until he saw Tony standing in front of the doorway. He sighed, and then looked down at Tony. Before Mr. Tank could speak, Tony nervously said first, "M-may I have permission to speak, sir?"

Mr. Tank nodded at him. "Yes you may, cretin."

"You may be by far the worst person to ask for advice, but I'm desperate right now. My classmates want to kill me because they think I'm a reptilian. What am I supposed to do? I am finished, my superior elder."

"That's simple. All you have to do is make up something else that is just as ridiculous as the idea of the Illuminati."

"And what could possibly be as ridiculous?"

"That's easy—religion."

"Religion?"

"That's right." He motioned for Tony to wait as he gave someone a call on his cell phone. "Wait out here."

Mr. Tank walked into the classroom while Tony waited patiently and nervously, hoping some random person didn't shank him in the hallway. He sat against the wall waiting defensively. Thirty minutes later, a tall man wearing a robe approached Tony, and motioned for him to go inside the classroom. Tony did so without a word.

In the classroom, Mr. Tank has stated: "All right, cretins. You will be presented with an exorcism."

Everyone in the class looked confused, including Tony.

The man in the robe, Abraham, said, "All right, kids! What I'm going to do is perform an exorcism on this poor boy, here! He may appear to be a normal boy, but he isn't—and yet he is! He isn't a reptilian either, but rather he is possessed by one! All I ask of you is to give me your lunch money in order to do humanity this justice! This isn't just for your sakes, but it also is the will of the Lord!"

Kenny reached into his pocket, and then took out five dollars, his lunch money. The rest of the class followed suit, and they all passed their money to the front row. Abraham took the money, put it in his wallet, and then ordered for Tony to lay down on the table in front of the classroom. Abraham waved his hands above Tony.

"Reptilian! Let go of your hold on this young boy! Leave him be, for he is a child of the Lord! And out...YOU GO!"

Abraham removed his hands as he looked down at Tony. Tony looked around, confused. He had no idea what was going on. Mr. Tank walked over to him, and whispered in his ear, "They are morons. Play along."

Tony coughed. "What happened?!" He looked around. "Wow! He did it! He actually did it! I'm not possessed anymore!"

The class began to clap cheerfully. Abraham bowed, then left the classroom.

Mr. Tank said in relief, "All right, cretins, back to your lesson. No more of this Illuminati garbage."

Lee crossed his arms, because he knew that even though Tony wasn't a reptilian anymore, the Illuminati threat was still at large.

Two hours later, Lee stood in the hallway during lunch, handing people pamphlets about the Illuminati. He had given all of his lunch money to Abraham, so it wasn't like he could eat if he wanted to anyway. He was called into the principal's office, which confused the boy, because he hadn't done anything wrong this time. Lee sat down in the chair, looking up at the principal.

The older man said, "It has come to my attention that you still are going on and on about the Illuminati. Most people have moved on."

"Of course! They are the biggest threat to the world!"

The principal sighed, and stood up. "I didn't want it to come down to this."

Five seconds later, the principal's eyes turned into those of a reptile, and his skin turned into green scales. He spoke with a hiss, "You know too much, kid!"

Lee's eyes bulged, and his mouth dropped. He turned around, and rushed out the door. Ten seconds later, the principal laughed, and was joined by Mr. Tank, who had a camcorder in his hand, and was laughing for the third time in his life. The principal instantly appeared human again.

"Man! That was an awesome idea, Metal! You could pull all kinds of crazy pranks with multimedia technology nowadays! I always wanted to scare the hell out of that annoying little shit."

Hector sat down at a restaurant during lunch time. He was with his former friend, Jamaal, who constantly pleaded for Hector's forgiveness. Similarly to the time that Hector had attended church, he zoned out. Hector really didn't want to put up with Jamaal's bullshit. Hector had been hung up on the cross that day, and Jamaal hadn't done a goddamn thing about it. Instead, he'd just chosen to blend in with the crowd.

Hector listened to some teenagers nearby. They briefly discussed what seemed to be the popular topic of the moment, The

Illuminati. Hector shook his head, and decided that it was best to just listen to Jamaal. He would lose a lot fewer brain cells compared to listening to the Illuminati garbage. Deep down inside, Hector believed that there was some truth to conspiracy theories, but some of them were ridiculous. He decided to focus his full attention on Jamaal so he could get this over with. Jamaal continued to ramble.

"Hector! I'm sorry! I went through a lot of internal conflict that day. My religion states that our way is the right way, and the crowd intimidated me a lot."

Hector shook his head at his former best friend. "Doesn't matter to me. I could have been killed that day. There is no telling what that mob would have done to me if the cops hadn't shown up."

Jamaal pleaded with his former best friend. "Is there anything that I can do to make this up? I heard that your store was vandalized. Do you need any cash? Any help at all?"

"No! I don't want your help! I don't care if I'm going through problems right now! I want you out of my life. Hell, asking for your help would be the last thing I would do. Doesn't even matter to me if my life is at stake, or if I'm terminally ill. Get the hell out of my life!"

"If this is how you feel, then I will comply. From this point on we don't have to have anything to do with each other, regardless of what you say." Jamaal stood up, and then left the restaurant.

Hector muttered, "Good riddance." He then stood up to head to his store. In thirty minutes he had to conduct an interview.

Later, at Hector's retail store, in the manager's office, Hector eyed his interviewee up and down, thinking he got a pleasant vibe from him. He seemed like a very well-educated man who was reliable, and very-well spoken.

The interviewee spoke up articulately. "Sir, I earned straight A's in school, and was a very good team player in my previous job. Hobby-wise, I like to write, go hiking, and practice playing on the piano."

"How is your availability? Will working this job interfere with your other job in any way? Because all I need is a night-shift worker."

"It won't interfere, sir. I will always be punctual and reliable."

Hector nodded at him, and then shook his interviewee's hand. "Excellent, then you are hired. I depend on you to close the store, and give good customer service. It shouldn't be a problem with your history and background. I have faith in you, man."

Hector's new hire, Andre, smiled at Hector. "Will do, sir."

A few days later, Hector went to work after doing his usual routine of exercising and eating something healthy. He worked his normal morning shift. Everything went well, until he began to feel sick to his stomach. He ran to the bathroom to throw up, and then felt a little bit better an hour later. As he continued to work diligently, out of the blue, he collapsed on the ground. Nobody was in the store except for Hector.

Thirty minutes later, Andre walked in for his first shift. He headed toward the clock-in kiosk, and then stopped dead in his tracks at the terrible sight in front of him. He saw Hector, lying down face first, in a pool of his own vomit. He was motionless, and Andre thought he could possibly be dead. Andre looked around him to see if anyone else was in the store.

"Boss?"

He continued to look around. Once he was sure that nobody else was in the store, Andre took out his cell phone to call his friends. His behavior and words completely changed compared to when Hector had interviewed him.

"Yo, homies! Get yo' asses here! My boss is knocked the fucked out! Get over here now, dawgs!"

Once his friends arrived, they all began to steal from the store while Hector was out cold. None of them even cared about Hector's well-being. They only cared about how many things they could get before Hector woke up—if he ever did. Hector began to stir, and Andre's friends ran out of the store. Andre pretended to tend to his manager, and began speaking like he had during the interview.

"Boss! Are you all right, sir? I was about to call the cops and an ambulance, but you woke up just before I had a chance to."

Hector got up slowly. He shook his head, feeling somewhat dizzy. "What? The cops?"

Andre nodded at him. "Some delinquents robbed the store when you were down. I was about to run to the back to call the police, but as soon as the thieves saw me, they left the store, sir."

Hector walked to the door. "Don't sweat it, man. Just work your shift."

A couple hours later, in the hospital, at the receptionist's desk, Hector pleaded, "I'm sick, lady. I think I need to see a doctor, fast."

The receptionist looked Hector up and down. "All right, here is the form that you need to fill out in order to see one."

Hector did as instructed, and then waited patiently with the other people who were waiting to be served. This sickness had caught him completely off guard. The only other time that he had gotten sick was when he worked with Marpha, but that had been a while ago, and it wasn't as bad as this. He had been eating healthy, exercising, and monitoring his activity every day, and everything seemed perfectly fine. The other people who were waiting looked like they needed help much more than he did, however. There was one man with a knife in his arm. There was a boy who had one of his eyes hanging outside of its socket. The boy held the dangling eye in his hand. There was a passed out woman who was carrying her left leg in her arms. Hector tilted his head, confused, and thought to himself, *These people need assistance now!*

Hector approached the receptionist again. "Hey, lady, these people need assistance fast!"

"We all need assistance in this world, sir. They will have to wait until someone is available to help them. Currently, many of our doctors are on their hour-long break, while others are doing more important things—like watching the baseball game."

"Just look at them! They seriously need help now!" Hector got in her face. "How the hell can you look at them and tell me they don't need help?!"

The receptionist simply sighed. "Once it is their scheduled turn, and once the doctors feel like doing their jobs, they'll be called back. Until then, they have to wait—crippled limbs or not."

Hector sat back down, and turned to the ones who were in horrible shape. "You all need to do something about this!"

They all groaned in pain, and it was apparent to him that they were in no physical condition to have much of a say.

Thirty minutes later, the receptionist said,

"Hector, the doctor is ready to see you."

He looked at the three injured people, trying to register why it was his turn before they had been called back. "They can take my turn."

The receptionist shook her head no. "Sorry, sir. It doesn't work that way, and they will have to wait longer for service since our emergency doctors are still on their breaks. If you wish, you could reschedule your appointment."

"If I do that, then will these people be serviced sooner?"

She shook her head no again. Hector sighed, and decided to just take his turn. As he walked to his room, he noticed that the people who were being helped were people who didn't really need it. He spotted a woman who had slipped and fallen on her back, but Hector thought that wasn't a problem worth seeing the doctor over. He then turned to his left to see a boy who seemed to have a common cold.

In a nursing room, the nurse said, "All right, sir, this is the room. I need you to change into these clothes." She presented Hector with a patient's uniform. "I'll return once you've finished changing, I'll perform some tests, and then the doctor will be with you." The nurse left the room to give her patient some privacy.

A minute later, Hector did as instructed. He felt extremely weak.

The nurse returned to the room to do some tests. After she was finished, the doctor entered the room.

She looked at Hector curiously. "Sir, what type of problems have you been experiencing?"

"I collapsed in my store, ma'am. I don't know what happened. I always eat healthy and exercise. I got sick once, but it wasn't like this before."

The woman reflected on this. "How have you been feeling?"

"Weak, ma'am. I can't lift things anymore because they're too heavy, and I have been feeling very sleepy."

"All right, Mr. Sanchez, we will need to perform some tests to see what is going on. Fortunately, your insurance covers these tests."

Hector nodded his approval. "Do it."

The doctor performed some tests on Hector, which took an hour.

Later that day, in the Doctor's office, Hector asked curiously, "All right, ma'am. What do I have?"

"We need to wait a couple hours until the results are in, sir. We will give you a call once they are obtained."

Hector nodded, and then left the hospital. On his way out, he saw those three people were still waiting for service, and it had been over an hour. He left feeling like there was nothing he could do about it.

Three hours later after he'd gotten home, Hector awoke to the sound of his phone ringing. He picked up the phone and was greeted by the same doctor.

"Is this Mr. Sanchez?"

"Yes, this is he."

"Mr. Sanchez, the results of the tests have come in." There was an uneasy and awkward silence as Hector waited for her to give him the verdict. He waited patiently, however, the doctor remained silent for nearly a whole minute.

"Well?! Is it bad?" Hector asked somewhat impatiently.

"I'm sorry to inform you, sir, but you have Hyper Cancer."

Hector's mouth dropped. "What?! How? I have been a very healthy man!"

"Sometimes you may appear normal, but once it is fully developed, that's when you can tell you have it."

"Well, when can I have the operation? And is there a cure?"

"Unfortunately, your insurance doesn't cover this. The estimated cost for the operation is five hundred thousand dollars."

"And there is no cure?!"

"Well, it depends. How much is your life worth to you, sir?"

"What the hell type of question is that?"

"There is no cure, sir. I cannot tell you anymore than what I've already told you. You will need to come to the office if you want to talk about this further."

Without no hesitation, Hector hung up the phone, and then headed back to the hospital.

In the doctor's office, Hector asked the doctor nervously, "When I asked you if there was a cure, was it really true that there isn't one?"

"Well, it really depends how much your life is worth to you—or perhaps you know a wealthy friend."

Hector thought about Jamaal, as well as the argument that he had had with him earlier. Jamaal was the only friend of Hector's who could pay it off. He thought about the last few things he had said to his friend who had betrayed him. *No! I don't want your help! I don't care if I'm going through problems right now! I want you out of my life! Hell, asking for your help would be the last thing I do. Doesn't even matter to me if my life is at stake, or if I'm terminally ill. Get the hell out of my life!* The doctor interrupted his thoughts.

"There is a place where you can go in order to obtain an unofficial cure. It really is a cure, but it's been kept secret from the general public in order to profit off of them—this is what we do in the medical field, profit from the suffering of others."

"Why are you telling me this?"

"Truthfully, I put in my two-week's notice a week ago, and don't enjoy working here, so I don't really care anymore." She said with a small hint of sorrow, "I hate to tell you this, but people who are diagnosed with having Hyper Cancer usually die in two years without treatment. Since you are so late in the stages, you only have a week."

Hector's eyes widened The doctor gave him a piece of paper with an address.

"If you go to this place, then you may be able to get the cure. I wish you the best, sir. Also, not to put any pressure on you, but I'm giving you this." The doctor immediately put a watch on

Hector. The watch itself says the following: "Countdown until your death." Underneath the words were numbers that were constantly counting down.

A day later, Hector entered the building of the address that was given to him. He was amazed at the number of people there. He talked to a few of them, and saw that all of the people had Hyper Cancer just like he did, and also didn't have the means to pay for the operation. The place itself appeared to be a huge auditorium, there were seats everywhere. Hector took a seat, and tried to wait as patiently as possible.

Eventually, a man with a cowboy hat walked to the podium. He held a microphone, and began to speak like a salesman.

"Ladies and gentlemen, welcome to the auction for the Hyper Cancer cure! Now the cure is hidden in a stash somewhere out in the world, so if any of you try to shoot me or any of my workers to try and steal it, then you will be *out of luck*. But I suppose in a few weeks, you will already *be* out of luck! Now let's get started with the auction of the century!"

A few people cheered, but for the most part, everyone was taking this as seriously as Hector was. Shortly after, the bidding started. Hector is baffled, because he hadn't expected an auction. No matter, he knew he must use all of his money. The bidding had started at five dollars, and had steadily increased from there.

An hour later, the auctioneer said, "Do I have anyone for twenty thousand? Anyone? Going once? Going twice?"

Hector yelled, "Thirty thousand!" This caused the last bidder to grumble in dismay, and then storm out of the building.

"Anyone for forty thousand? Going once?"

A sophisticated man spoke up. "I'll go for fifty thousand, sir."

The auctioneer did the countdown again, so Hector decided to go all the way. "Ninety thousand!" he shouted.

He was relieved he'd gotten lucky with a lot of scratch tickets lately, and also for the fact that he had saved a hell of a lot just in case something like this happened. The auctioneer began his countdown.

The sophisticated man considered the amount for a moment. "One hundred thousand dollars!"

Hector was completely shattered after hearing the man. The auctioneer began another countdown, but nobody could beat the man's offer.

"Sold! Cure for Hyper Cancer for one hundred thousand dollars!"

Most of the people had already left before they'd even reached twenty thousand dollars. The remaining ones were wealthy-looking people who Hector even wondered had the sickness. The wealthy man observed everyone cheerfully right before he gave his speech.

"Thank you all for believing in me! Don't worry. I won't add this rare cure to my collection of important things that I don't need—like the hidden single solution to solve the world's problems. Instead, I'm going to do the humanitarian thing, and auction the damn thing off online for three hundred thousand dollars! That is two hundred thousand less than the cost for the operation."

The wealthy audience cheered him.

———

The next morning after the auction, Hector desperately spoke to the doctor on the phone.

"Are you sure that I have Hyper Cancer, because I feel great!"

"Yes, sir. We are certain. We looked through the results ten times. Hyper Cancer is very complex. Even after you faint the first time, you will feel great shortly afterward. Once your time is up, you will definitely be able to tell that you're sick. After the countdown, your head will explode. Until then, you will feel physically fine."

Hector's mouth dropped as the doctor continued with the gruesome details. "Yeah, according to our computers and the doomsday watch that I gave you, you still have five days, six hours, thirteen minutes, and twenty-two seconds until your head goes boom. Is there anything else that I can help you with, sir?"

"And there is no type of payment arrangement that we can work out? Or any other way we can do this? I have been a good citizen. Why can't we work something out?"

"Sorry, sir. We need the money if you want the operation to happen. One recommendation I have is that you create a will if you don't have one. You should also prepare your own funeral if you like. Another thing—try not to be around people right before you run out of time. After your head explodes, it will leave a big mess, and will annoy a lot of people. Having brain goo on your freshly pressed business attire is very annoying."

Hector immediately hung up the phone on the insensitive and lackadaisical doctor.

Thirty minutes later, in some type of alternative healing store called "The Mystic Shop", Hector pleaded, "So that's the situation! I have a very deadly disease, and will die five-and-a-half days from now. Is there anything you can do to help me? I was hoping that maybe I had looked into the wrong type of cure, and that you could help me. Can you cast some type of spell on me? Give me some type of potion? Give me a psychic reading? Anything!"

The clerk looked Hector up and down. "Hector, you are generating a lot of negative energy right now. What I ask of you is to center yourself, and calm down. We can do a deep-breathing exercise together if you want. This is all happening for a reason, so try to be optimistic and focus on the positive aspects of your situation."

"What positive aspects?! My head is going to explode in five-and-a-half days, and nobody is willing to help me because it isn't their problem! Can you help me or not?!"

The clerk nodded at him, and closed her eyes. She took a deep breath, and then opened them a minute later. "Wait...and relax. Let the witching hour come upon you, but welcome it just like you welcome anything else. I apologize that I can't help you anymore, but this is all that I can say."

The woman turned around to look behind the counter. "I do have some herbs that relieve stress and—"

Hector had already slammed the door behind him on his way out.

At night, on some abandoned highway, Hector drove recklessly.

He didn't care about the fact that he was speeding. He didn't care much about anything anymore, since his life was at stake, He drove to the man's address who had won the auction. In his glove compartment, Hector had a gun, but hopefully he wouldn't have to use it—so long as the buyer was cooperative. Once he arrived at the mansion, he snuck into the back, then climbed through a window to enter a kitchen. It was night time, and it seemed like everyone was asleep. The lights were off, and there weren't any sounds. Hector snuck into the mansion with his gun clenched in his hand, looking for the buyer.

A minute later, Hector was stopped by a voice. "Stop right there!"

Hector turned around slowly to see a man holding a gun at him. To his dismay, it wasn't the guy that bought the cure, rather, someone else.

"Put down that gun, or else I'll shoot you!" yelled the man.

Hector put the gun down, and raised his hands. The man motioned for him to kick the gun to the side.

"Now tell me...what are you doing here?" whispered the man.

"I came here to get the cure for Hyper Cancer. I only have five days now."

The man chuckled. "Good plan, but you failed. You thought you were the only one going for the cure, but it's mine! This is the only way that I can get it. I will live—"

Before the man could finish, he was shot in the chest, and he collapsed on the ground.

Hector quickly ducked as a woman yelled at him, "The cure is mine!"

She began to shoot at Hector, who ran to hide behind a couch as bullets flew over his head.

Another person yelled, "No! It's mine! My head isn't going to blow up!"

The whole mansion turned into a big gunfight. Hector counted five people in the mansion. More and more entered through the windows while people were shot in the crossfire. Hector stayed where he was, too terrified to think logically as he tried to regain his composure. Escaping this place was his top priority. Eventually, the shots were interrupted by a loudspeaker since the man who had bought the cure finally made an appearance on the scene. As he talked, the sound of his voice caused everyone to stop doing what they were doing.

"Hello there, ladies and gentlemen! I hate to burst your bubbles, but the cure isn't here, because surprisingly, I had someone buy it! The only reason I bought it in the first place is because I'm a homicidal maniac, and the only way that I can get away with murder is through having the excuse of self-defense! So since you all are on my property, shooting up the place, I can kill you all for fun!"

As soon as the announcement was finished, everyone resumed shooting. Hector, having regained his composure, ran and ducked for cover as he tried to leave the mansion. The cure's buyer arrived to the scene at the top of the stairs. He gazed down at the desperate people gleefully, took out his rocket launcher, and yelled, "It's time to get my fix for murder! Say hello to my little friend!"

He shot a rocket toward a group of people, blasting them away from each other as he cackled. Hector barely made it to the window, climbed outside, rushed to his car, and drove away as fast as he could. In the background he could hear explosions, gunfire, and insane laughter.

As soon as he arrived home, Hector hastily turned on the computer to research who had bought the cure. His mouth dropped open when he saw that it was Jamaal Johnson who had bought it. Hector knew that Happy Sunshine, Inc. was closed right now, so he decided it was best to go there first thing in the morning. Just like the previous nights, Hector wasn't able to fall asleep. His anxiety was completely taking him over. Every ten minutes he would look at the countdown watch on his left arm, and then sigh in dismay.

The next morning, at Happy Sunshine, Inc., Hector asked, "Can I speak to Jamaal Johnson?"

The receptionist, Rachel, gave him a curious look. She was fortunate enough to have found a job shortly after she had gotten fired from her last one after fighting with Marpha.

"Do you have an appointment, sir?"

Hector shook his head no. "This is an emergency, ma'am. I do know him. He and I used to be friends. All I ask is that you get someone to tell him that Hector Sanchez wants to speak with him. Please don't give me any problems, ma'am! This is really important!"

The receptionist nodded at him, and without another word, picked up the phone in order to get the vice president downstairs. Hector thanked the woman as he tried to wait patiently for his former friend. He paced back and forth over and over again, until fifteen minutes later, Jamaal walked up to him. Hector grabbed Jamaal's shoulders, and shook him.

"Jamaal! You gotta help me!"

Jamaal gave him a skeptical look, recalling the last conversation they'd had.

"I have Hyper Cancer, and you are the only person who has the cure! I only have four days left until I die."

"You told me that you didn't want to have anything to do with me. You also said that if you were terminally ill, that you wouldn't accept my help—even if you needed it. And I complied."

"I need it, man! And I forgive you for what happened in the church! Just give me the cure, so I can live!"

Jamaal pondered this for a moment. "Oh, I get it. This is a test. You are testing to see if I can honor my word."

Hector shook his head. "This isn't a test! Give me the fucking cure! Now! Why the hell did you buy it anyway? You don't need it!"

Jamaal calmly said, "Right now, even if I could give it to you, I can't. That cure is being used to make copies in order to make this world a better place, since the medical industry just allows people to die without a care in the world. I decided to take matters into my own hands. It's going to be four days before I can help you. The cure itself isn't even in the country right now. If you aren't alive by then, then I apologize." Jamaal looked down in pity. "Even if it were here, I can't give you this cure as is, because it will save thousands of lives."

Hector pushed Jamaal in anger. Rachel observed the hostility between them. She quickly called for security. Hector reached into his pocket to pull out his gun.

"You're not telling the truth! I have nothing to lose! Give me the cure, or else I'll shoot you dead!"

Jamaal calmly raised his hands. Rachel had a shocked look on her face as she continued to observe the situation. Immediately, out of nowhere, a few guards restrained Hector, and removed his gun from his hands. Jamaal looked down at his former best friend with pity.

"I'm sorry, Hector."

An hour later, Hector was in jail, pacing back and forth, looking at his countdown watch. That evening, during recreation time, he watched a commercial on television. He observed a young man walking across the street, when, thirty seconds later, out of the blue, the young man's head exploded. At the bottom of the screen, there was a caption that said, "Hyper Cancer...the only disease that catches people completely off guard."

This caused the inmates to applaud and chuckle. Hector, however, went back to his cell, and sank to his knees after seeing a preview of his near future.

Three days passed, and they were by far the hardest three days that he had ever experienced. Hector woke up early on his last day to the sound of a guard banging on the bars of his cell.

"Hey, fuck face! You got a visitor."

Hector nodded, and got up to follow the guard. He was taken to a room, but to his surprise, Jamaal was there.

"Hector, I decided to drop the charges, because I felt that if I were in the same situation, I probably would do the exact same thing." Hector was about to reply, but Jamaal told him to wait.

"Our first copy for Hyper Cancer has been created! We need to hurry. Now! We may be able to make it if we take our jet!"

Hector didn't need to be told twice, and the two immediately left.

Later on, in a jet, Hector yelled, "Come on! Thirty minutes left! Can't you guys make this go any faster?!"

The slightly annoyed pilot turned to Hector. "I'm going as fast as I can, sir!"

Jamaal patted his friend on the back. "We will do it. You will live. Just have faith."

Twenty-eight minutes later, Hector stood up and began pacing back and forth in the jet, observing his watch as time kept constantly going down.

"Shit! I'm going to die, Jamaal! Two minutes left!"

This caused some of the passengers to give Hector his space, because they were expecting his head to explode. They didn't want to get brain goo on their freshly pressed suits. Hector looked away from his watch as the countdown reached the final seconds. He held his head and closed his eyes, but once the watch beeped, nothing happened. He heard his phone ring. He was shocked. He was still alive. A moment later, he answered the phone.

"Hello?"

Hector recognized the voice of the caller as the doctor.

"Hey, Hector, it's me, Dr. Lackadaisical. I apologize to you deeply."

"For?"

"We messed up when we said that you have Hyper Cancer. It turns out that the reason you fainted was because of food poisoning. You're perfectly healthy. As a matter of fact, you are the most healthy person that I've ever seen."

Hector was completely awestruck, but then he was filled

with anger. "Don't do that ever again! Do you have any idea how scared I was, and what I have been through because of your mess up?!"

"We apologize, sir, but we confused you for Hector Sonchez. He is the one who has Hyper Cancer."

"Don't sweat it. I'm alive and grateful." Hector hung up the phone.

Jamaal looked at him curiously. "What happened?"

"Guess what?! I don't have Hyper Cancer! It turns out that they mixed me up with a 'Hector Sonchez.' He has Hyper Cancer!"

Jamaal's eyes bulged as he turned his attention to the pilot who seemed just as surprised as Jamaal.

"Did you say 'Hector Sonchez'?" asked Jamaal.

Hector nodded at him "Yes."

"Oh, shit!" yelled the pilot. "I'm Hector Sonchez!" Just like that, out of the blue, the pilot's head exploded. Shortly after the explosion, the jet began to spiral downwards, and then crashed into the ocean. Fortunately for everyone on the plane, nobody was seriously hurt—except for Mr. Sonchez. However, now the survivors were stranded in the ocean.

CHAPTER EIGHT

IN AN ELECTRONICS STORE, one of the televisions was broadcasting the following:

> "And in tonight's news, a jet has mysteriously crashed into the ocean. There was an evacuation squad that was deployed to the site. Unfortunately, there have been reports of one casualty, the pilot. A few of the passengers were terrified and traumatized. Many stated that the most horrible thing about the experience was the fact that their freshly pressed business suits were covered in brain goo. Once the survivors were evacuated, they were taken to receive counseling and therapy."

Laura briefly looked up at the television, listening to the news reporter explain the gruesome details of Mr. Sonchez's death. She shrugged, and approached the customer service desk. Fortunately for her there wasn't a line. She and the staff members were the only ones present. She cleared her throat, and spoke to the gentleman behind the desk.

"Excuse me, sir. I want to return this. I have the receipt right here, and here is the phone."

Laura placed the device on the counter, as well as the box that had contained it. The worker looked at the receipt and the phone.

"Was there anything wrong with this, ma'am?"

"Yes, I thought the phone would work underwater, as advertised on the television. As a hobby, I like to do underwater basket weaving, so after I got out of the tank, the device stopped working."

The worker leaned forward on the counter, and glanced down at the phone. "Well, it only works in shallow water, ma'am."

"I understand that now, but the commercial showed a man perform some deep-sea diving with the phone in his hand. That is false advertising, sir. Please don't give me a hard time. I want my money back. I was here thirty minutes ago. You were the guy who completed my transaction. The receipt even has your name on it."

"It states in very, very small font that this device works only in shallow water, ma'am, but since you have the receipt, there shouldn't be any problems."

The worker tried to process the return, but was experiencing technical difficulties.

"Hmm, this is odd. I'm having some problems. I'll call my supervisor."

Laura nodded at him, and waited patiently. The supervisor approached the cash register as he tried to figure out what was going on.

"Oh, I see what happened. This phone isn't under warranty, and you used the phone, so I cannot process this as a return, ma'am."

Laura gasped. "What?! I only used it once, and it wasn't that long ago! I was lead to believe that I could do my underwater basket weaving just fine!"

The supervisor shook his head no. "I apologize, ma'am, but there isn't anything that I can do. However, if you want to talk to the store manager, then he will be here tomorrow afternoon. He should be able to handle things."

Laura left, feeling disgruntled.

The next morning, at the electronics store, Laura and Milena both entered the store. Milena was very pissed off over the fact that these people were giving them such a hard time over this. All of the customers who were in the store hastily rush outed, terrified, as soon as her presence became known. Some of them knocked down a bunch of goods on the floor as they left. Hardly anyone recognized Laura since she wasn't homeless anymore, in normal clothing, had a new haircut, and was clean. Milena stood in front of the counter glaring at the clerk, her hands on the counter.

The clerk shivered in fear, and sweat ran down his forehead. "M-Milena?! Oh no! Must stay calm...must stay calm...."

"Why the hell can we not return this phone?! We only had it for one day, and it already broke. We were under the impression that it works underwater since that is what the commercial advertised!"

Immediately, the clerk rushed to the back to get his store manager. The manager approached the two.

He whispered to his employee, "I thought the <u>Milena Alert</u> said that the streets were clear of hostile wildlife."

"It did," whispered the clerk. "However, this wild animal has developed some new patterns. We probably should report this change in behavior to the Animal Behavior Station. They need to update their documents on the Milena subspecies."

The manager then focused on Milena, and said as calmly as possible, "I was told about this issue from one of the supervisors.

I apologize to inform you, but there is nothing that we can do about this. The phone isn't under warranty, and our return policy on electronics is that you can only return them if you have the receipt, and the item must not have been opened or used."

Laura turned to Milena. "We probably should just let it be. The phone didn't cost that much, so it isn't that big of a loss."

Milena sneered at her. "No! This isn't right! We are going to get our money back one way or another!"

The clerk spoke nervously to the manager. "She's going to kill us, just like how she tried to kill that defenseless girl for no reason years ago. We need to refund this somehow—ASAP, sir."

Milena barely heard what he'd said as she focused her attention on the clerk, glaring at him.

"What the hell did you just say?!"

The clerk went silent. The manager reassured her. "That type of violence isn't a good way to solve problems, ma'am. Please don't pull out a gun on us. We can work this out somehow."

Milena looked at him, baffled. "I didn't say anything about pulling out a gun. All I'm doing is trying to get my refund!"

As Milena talked, the manager whispered to his coworker. "Call the cops. She's a psycho."

Immediately, he rushed to the back. The two women, with confused stares, watched him go, and then went back to focusing on the manager.

"Here is a phone number if you want to talk to the district manager, ma'am."

The clerk returned quickly.

Laura poked Milena. "I seriously think we should just leave. I have a very terrible feeling about this. I'm scared, and don't know why."

"Shut up! We are getting our money back, and I refuse to

take no for an answer!"

Laura went silent as she looked hopelessly at her friend.

"Well, it's pretty obvious who wears the pants in that relationship," whispered the clerk.

"What the hell did you just say?!" Milena yelled.

The two workers raised their hands in alarm. The manager responded like he was speaking to a dog.

"Nothing, ma'am. Stay cool. Stay cool. Good....good girl. I'll give you a biscuit."

Milena narrowed her eyes at them. "Our relationship isn't like that! We are just friends! We aren't lesbians!"

Laura turned to Milena with a sad look on her face. "You're not a lesbian? But you took me off the streets, helped me out, and said that you love me...you don't love me?"

Milena was completely shocked. "Uh, I took you off the streets in order to help you out. I consider you a good friend. The reason I said I love you was because you told me you loved me—even though that weirded me out hearing that from you."

Laura began to cry, burrowing her head in her arms. "I thought you loved me, too! Now I feel heartbroken!"

Milena shook her head, annoyed. "Go home, Laura! We will talk about this later. Now isn't the time!"

Laura ran out of the store, crying. The clerk whispered to the manager, "Told you, man."

Milena argued some more, but it went nowhere.

Ten minutes later, sirens could be heard as Officer Lives pulled up. He entered the store slowly.

"All right, now what is the problem here? Oh shit! Milena!" He took out his gun, pointing it at her.

Milena raised her hands, protesting, "All I'm trying to do is get my money back for the phone I bought yesterday!"

"Put down your weapons! Now!"

"I don't have any goddamn weapons!" she yelled.

The officer took out his walkie-talkie. "Hey, this is Officer Fuxup Lives. I'm gonna need some backup! Now! And send the snipers and helicopters. This is a hell of a doozy! Bring the crosses, the holy water, the silver bullets, the garlic, and plenty of mirrors!"

Milena just stood there with her arms in the air, and a very annoyed look on her face. *What the fuck?! I'm not a vampire! Why the fuck do I even bother with all of that volunteer work if I'm going to be treated like this every day?* she thought.

Five minutes later, there were a bunch of cops parked outside of the store, a dozen helicopters in the sky, a bunch of snipers on the rooftop, one tank parked nearby, and a bunch of news reporters. Laura was watching the whole thing at home on the television as she wiped away tears from her eyes. She was heartbroken that Milena had turned out to be straight, and wasn't in love with her.

Officer Lives just glared at Milena, holding his gun. "Just tell me what you want, and maybe we will be able to work this out."

"All I want to do is get my money back for this phone that I'm trying to returning."

Officer Lives thought about it for a moment until he came up with an appropriate answer.

"It's okay, Milena! You don't have to resort to this! You feel guilty for your attempted murder, and you want to be able to look at yourself in the mirror again. Well, committing a store shooting isn't going to help, so chill out!"

Milena started laughing at him. She wasn't even upset anymore. She just found the whole situation hilarious now. Officer Lives spoke on his walkie-talkie again.

"She is going crazy with laughter! We need a negotiator!

Get that counselor here—the one running for mayor!"

Ten minutes later, the counselor walked into the store. Milena immediately recognized him, and she gave him a look of surprise.

"Michael?!"

Michael nodded at her, turned to Officer Lives, and told him to calm down. He turned back to Milena.

"Milena, tell me...what's going on?"

"All I want to do is return my phone! All of these people are making crazy assumptions that I want to hurt them because of what happened years ago. I didn't even do anything to provoke them."

Milena motioned to the counter. "My phone is right there. My roommate thought that she could go deep in the water with it, but it broke. We bought it yesterday."

Michael nodded, and walked over to her. He picked up the phone to look at it. "Hmm, this is the phone from that commercial. That is false advertising if it broke as soon as you went deep underwater."

Milena sighed in relief. "Thank you! Someone understands what's going on!"

Michael turned to the manager. "By law, you need to refund this woman her money."

The manager chuckled. "It does say on the commercial that it works underwater, but only in shallow water. This is clearly stated in very, very small font."

Michael shook his head at him. "Even if it says that, nobody can read something that small, and that is a very dirty business practice that won't be tolerated after I become mayor of this town. How much did the phone cost?"

"Sixty-three dollars, sir."

Michael opened his wallet, and simply handed Milena the

money. She wouldn't accept it.

"No! This isn't right! The reason I'm here is more than just the money! It isn't right what they do!"

Michael nodded in agreement. "I know, Milena, I know. That's why I'm running for mayor. Sometimes you win some, and sometimes you lose some, but you can still continue the good fight. If you continue protesting as is, you may be sent to jail—or worse." Michael glanced at officer Fuxup Lives, who clenched his gun, and appeared ready to shoot at any second.

"Fine!"

Michael left the store, and explained the whole situation to everyone. The cops all left. Milena stormed out, pissed off that this was a political loss.

An hour later, at the mansion, Milena opened the door to see Laura in the kitchen, and it reminded her that she needed to talk to her friend to sort out the confusion. She approached Laura.

"Hey, Laura. We need to have a talk."

Laura turned to her, and she had two glasses of wine in her hands. "Hey, Milena. Yeah, I think we need to. Want a glass?"

Milena nodded at her. "Sure as hell need one. My day has been stressful."

Milena took the glass. The two went to sit down on the couch to speak.

"I'm sorry, Milena. I thought that since you took me in, and since everyone in this world hates me, then maybe you..." She began to cry.

Milena hugged her, still feeling uncertain as to whether Laura wanted a friend or a lover. She did not want to give her friend the wrong idea. "I'm sorry. It caught me off guard."

Milena began to feel dizzy, and she rubbed her head. That's strange," she said.

Laura looked at her curiously. "What's the matter? Feeling under the weather? I drugged your wine, and you will be unconscious for a while. You're going to learn to love me, whether you like it or not!"

Laura immediately stood up, went to the kitchen, and grabbed the butcher knife. She had a psychotic look on her face. Milena tried her best to escape, but everything appeared hazy. Laura returned, and then kicked the dazed woman as hard as she could in the chest. Milena collapsed on the ground in front of Laura, who clenched a knife in her hand. She looked at Milena intensely, and breathed heavily.

———

An hour later, in the attic, Laura ranted, "I tried so hard to be a reasonable person!"

Laura slapped Milena in the face as hard as she could. She had tied Milena up.

"I couldn't give the homeless man money, because I needed some financial support myself!"

She slapped Milena again. "I tried explaining this over and over again, but people didn't seem to care—even after I gave the guy money!"

Laura punched Milena in the stomach, and began to cry. "Everyone hates me. People always bullied me around, called me bad names, and put me in dumpsters for their amusement! I was nothing but trash to them."

Milena listened silently, in physical pain. She was trying to figure out ways to escape in her head as she observed her surroundings and tried to break through the ropes.

"I finally find who I thought was the love of my life, but it turns out that she mislead me this whole time!" yelled Laura.

"I apologize for misleading you, Laura. I thought that, based on my actions, I came off as wanting to just be friends."

Laura paced back and forth, shaking her head at Milena. "It doesn't matter at this point."

Milena was fortunate enough to loosen the knots. She could break out right now if she wanted, but her timing needed to be perfect. Laura clenched the butcher knife with both hands, and raised it above her head. She had a sadistic look on her face.

"Does this bring back memories? You did the same thing to Rachel at school years ago, correct?" Laura shook her head. "Then again, I guess it doesn't matter at this point."

She went in for the final blow, but Milena broke free from her binds, and caught the knife with both hands. She then used all the strength she had to stand up. Laura tried desperately to stab her in the head. Once Milena was up, she kneed Laura in the stomach, and punched Laura, who staggered back. Milena took this opportunity to rush out of the attic, down the stairs, and into the kitchen to reach the phone.

She frantically dialed 911. Once someone had answered, Milena whispered, "Officer, you gotta help me! My friend is trying to kill me right now! She went crazy!"

"And what is your address?"

Milena told the operator her address.

"That's the same address as Milena Purser! We are sending help ASAP!"

Milena dropped the phone to the sound of Laura coming from around the corner.

"Come out, come out, wherever you are!"

Laura came into view, and she had a gun at her side, in addition to the knife. She shot at Milena.

Milena barely dodged the bullet as she tried to escape the kitchen.

The two played cat-and-mouse for a while. Nothing could be heard but gunshots, screaming from Milena, and psychotic laughter from Laura. Eventually, the cops surrounded the mansion. Milena staggered out of the front door, and stumbled to the ground. She was all bruised up.

Unfortunately, as soon as the cops saw Milena, they hastily drove off, scrambling away in terror, and leaving her without any help. Laura caught up to Milena, who was completely exhausted and broken down. Everything seemed hopeless as she looked at Laura. Milena had tears coming down her face she was trying to hold back. She was backed into a corner, and she had never been in a situation like this.

Laura glared down at her as she pointed the gun at her. She pulled the trigger a couple times, but there were no more bullets, much to her dismay.

"That's all right. I still have the butcher knife."

Laura dropped the empty gun, and then raised the butcher knife.

"Stop it, Laura! Don't do this!" Milena protested.

Laura sneered at her. "No compromises!"

Laura raised the knife above her head. Milena closed her eyes in terror. Thirty seconds passed before she became confused. She opened her eyes a few seconds later to find out that she was still alive. Laura simply stood there, holding the knife to her side.

"I just came up with something. If someone doesn't love a person, then they shouldn't retaliate like this. It's impossible for someone to force someone else to love them. I apologize, Milena. How about this, let's start over like none of this happened. Do you forgive me?"

Laura dropped the knife as her demeanor changed back to normal. She gave Milena an innocent smile. "Well, it's Friday.

What do you want to do? Watch a movie? Go to a bar?"

Milena was speechless in disbelief as Laura helped her up.

"I want to just show you what I saw on the news," said Laura. "It's just mind-blowing."

"That's okay, Laura. I think I'll just...go for a walk right now."

An hour later, in Michael's apartment, Milena pleaded, "Michael, you gotta help me! I tried calling the cops, but they all scrambled away as soon as they saw me!"

Michael tried to comfort his former patient. "Is Laura still in your mansion right now?"

Milena nodded at him. "Her behavior just completely changed. She always seemed perfectly normal, so this caught me completely off guard. She needs to be committed to the asylum! I have a fucking crazy woman in my house, and I don't know what to do."

"This is why it isn't always a good idea to pick up random stray people. Your situation is complex, Milena, because of your reputation. The best course of action that I can think of is for me to go to your mansion and talk to her myself."

The counselor opened his closet, pulled out a gun, and put it in his pocket. "Just in case I need to use it in self-defense."

The two of them headed back to the mansion. After they had arrived thirty minutes later, Milena walked around nervously.

"Laura? Are you there?" There was nothing but silence.

Michael gazed around. "Perhaps she left."

Milena shook her head. "Something doesn't seem right."

The two patrolled the whole mansion, but Laura was nowhere to be found. They sit down calmly on the couch after their search.

"I don't get it. Normally she doesn't go out at this time," said Milena.

"Well, you can always spend the night at my home if you like."

Suddenly, a gunshot could be heard, and Michael was shot in the head. He slowly sunk down in his seat as death engulfed him. The one person who could fix the town was dead. Milena gasped as she saw Michael die before her eyes. It had happened so fast. She turned to see Laura glaring at her.

"I went to the store to buy some ammunition. Good timing on my part, I guess. I see that it didn't take you long to find a boyfriend! Didn't think it was possible for you to find anyone, since you're the psycho bitch who tried to kill a girl who was cooler than you are! It's too soon for you to be with someone. I'm still emotionally devastated."

Milena held up her hands, alarmed. "Laura! It wasn't like that!"

Laura shook her head. "Isn't like that?! You were on the couch with some guy who I never met! You were clearly cheating on me!"

Milena tried to protest once more, but Laura wouldn't listen. "Time to die," she said.

"Laura! Nooooo!"

Laura shot Milena in the head.

Immediately after the gunshot, Milena somehow woke up in her bed alarmed and confused and sweating. From what she could tell, she was in her mansion, but everything seemed fine. *Did Laura shoot me with some type of sedative or something? Or was it maybe all a dream?! What the fuck?! Please be a dream!* she thought. Milena looked at the time and date, and saw that it was the day Laura had bought the phone.

Milena grabbed her gun, and then headed downstairs to where Laura was, but she saw that Laura was simply watching television, and laughing.

After hearing footsteps, Laura turned around to see Milena, her eyes wide. "Milena?! What are you doing with that gun? Do we have an intruder here?!"

Milena, confused, said, "I...I thought I heard a burglar." She put the gun down, and looked at Laura.

"Did we ever go to the store to return that phone?"

Laura shook her head no. "Uh, no? Because it works perfectly fine, just as advertised." She picked up the phone off the table, and showed it to Milena.

"Hey, Laura, are you a lesbian?"

Laura looked at her confused, "No...I'm not. I'm honestly not sure why you would think that. Did I come across that way?"

Milena sighed in relief. "No, I had a crazy dream. That's all. You remember that time you said that you love me? That's why I was curious."

"I meant sisterly love...not romantic love. Sorry for misleading you."

Milena felt great now. The whole situation turned out to be a bad dream. This meant that Michael was still alive. It disturbed her tremendously because it had felt so real, this lasted for two days. This experience was something that she would never forget. What the two were not aware of was the figure who was observing them from outside of the mansion from an opened window. It was a middle-aged woman wearing a lab coat.

She had a smile on her face as she said to herself, "Or so you think it was just a dream. It turned out that the experiment did work after all. This young girl was probably traumatized from this experience, and will probably suffer some side effects that may negatively affect her cognitive abilities—but sometimes sacrifices need to be made in the name of science, and who really cares about Milena anyway? Everything is working out."

She slowly walked away from the mansion carrying a needle

and a bottle that contained some type of drug.

———

Officer Fuxup Lives patrolled the streets in his car. He'd decided to be mindful of the fact that Milena had been showing up in odd places at odd times. Even though she was still considered a dangerous villain, the officer admired her attempts at redemption. He simply wanted to meet the woman so he could shake her hand and tell her that she was a good citizen. The officer slowed down his car to come to a stop. He rolled down his window. He saw what appeared to be a drug dealer arguing with a woman. The officer recognized the drug dealer as the young man named Andre. Curiously, he opened his car door, closed it behind him, and approached the two.

The woman hastily beckoned the officer over as she yelled, "This man ripped me off, officer!"

Officer Fuxup Lives observed in deep contemplation. "How so?"

The woman yelled angrily, "He said that this crack is supposed to keep me extra high, but it is just like any other crack that I've smoked!"

The officer crossed his arms, and looked at Andre skeptically. "You offered her crack that is supposed to keep her extra high, and it doesn't do the job?"

The dealer shrugged. "Yo, you need to try it out yourself, dawg! This is the only time that I got a complaint from someone."

Andre handed the officer the bag of crack, who gazed down at the bag, and then looked up at Andre. Andre seemed calm about the whole situation. The woman on the other hand was still very irate.

"Don't mind if I do, but if this crack doesn't work as advertised, then you will have to refund this wonderful woman here her money, or else I will send you to jail for false advertisement."

Andre handed Officer Lives a pipe. He delicately put the crack inside while Andre took out his lighter. Officer Fuxup Lives began to smoke it. From time to time, he licked his lips like he was testing a dish, and then took another puff. Five minutes later, Office Lives handed it back to the dealer.

"Hmm, she's right. This crack isn't doing anything for me, sir."

Andre's mouth dropped open. "Dawg! That is my best shit yet!"

The woman smirked. "Give me back my money! Now!"

Andre grumbled, reached into his pocket, and handed the woman her money.

"Thank you for being cooperative," said Officer Lives.

He began walking to his car, but paused after he opened the door. "It's obvious that you didn't test out your product before you marketed it," he said to Andre. "A word of advice: actually smoke the crack before you sell it. On a positive note, a lot of people mess up like this, so overall, you are a good citizen. Just be more careful."

Andre nodded at him, thinking about this lesson. "Will do, dawg."

Officer Lives got into his car feeling very content that another problem had been solved.

An hour later, in the streets, a woman yelled, "Oh no! My purse! Someone help me!"

Officer Lives stopped his car and got out.

The woman screamed, "Help me! Someone! Anyone! That man stole my purse!"

Officer Lives hastily rushed toward the thief who was

heading his direction. The thief turned around, then back tracked. He ran past the woman he'd robbed. The officer immediately tackled the woman in distress.

"Gotcha!" he said to the woman.

The woman was completely dumb stricken as she fell on the ground. Officer Lives handcuffed her. "You are under arrest for causing a domestic disturbance!"

"What the hell?! How did I cause a disturbance? That man is getting away! He stole my purse!"

"Your screaming at this time of night woke up a bunch of people! You're going to jail so this doesn't happen again."

The woman looked in the direction of where the man had run. "You can still catch him!" she said. "He's getting away!"

Officer Lives immediately got up and resumed chasing the man. "Stop where you are, thief!"

Eventually he caught up to the criminal, then tackled him, and put him in handcuffs.

"Two crimes in one area...I need to patrol here more often."

He took the man to where the handcuffed woman was, who was furious.

"All right, you two. You both need to go to jail." He looks at the woman. "You, for domestic disturbance." He then turned to the man, "And you, for theft."

"He stole from *me*, and I have to go to jail because of it?! What the hell type of officer are you?!"

Officer Lives pointed at himself proudly. "My name is Officer Fuxup Lives, and I clean the streets of scum like you."

The thief pondered whether he could get away with his crime. It was apparent to him that this officer didn't know what he was doing, and perhaps there was a way to get out of this mess.

"Officer, I can explain. Do you see that ugly-ass mole on her face?"

Officer Lives looked at her face and easily spotted the mole. He wondered why he hadn't noticed it sooner. "Yes, I see it. Hideous."

"Well, the reason I took the purse from her is because I'm trying to protect it from that ugly mug. Such a delicate purse shouldn't be in the hands of someone as ugly as she is."

Officer Lives reflects on this, and decided he understood where the thief is coming from.

The woman glared at the criminal. "Fuck you!"

After coming up with a decision, Officer Lives took out his key, uncuffed the thief, and then handed the thief the purse. "You make a very good point. What you did is very heroic when you put it that way. You may be off, sir, and I apologize for causing you any inconvenience."

The thief bowed, and ran off with his stolen purse.

"All right, criminal! Off to jail you go!" said Officer Lives.

After taking the woman to jail, he continued to patrol the streets until his break.

Two hours later, Officer Lives sat in a restaurant. He drank his coffee, and thought about all the problems that had happened in the neighborhood so far. Usually the nights were quiet, but Harsh Town had become more and more dangerous lately. A few minutes later, a group of hooded, shady men entered the building.

They pulled out guns on everyone, while their leader yelled, "This is a robbery! Put your fucking hands in the air!"

Officer Lives turned to the commotion to see the robbers. They aimed their guns at the workers, who were all alarmed, holding their hands in the air.

"If any of you move, then we will shoot!"

Some of the customers looked at Officer Lives, trying to see if he would do something about the situation. Officer Lives just sat drinking his coffee nonchalantly. One of the robbers noticed him.

"Oh shit! A Cop!"

"Don't worry about me, gentlemen. I'm on my hour break, and I'm off the clock. I'm not being paid for this, so carry on with your business—as long as you don't steal anything from me. Everyone else is fair game."

The robbers looked at each other, confused, then did as they were told. After they'd gotten what they wanted, the robbers left.

Officer Lives nonchalantly finished off his food while everyone else glared at him. This did not stop him from enjoying his food or having a carefree attitude. Once he was finished, he paid the server without even bothering to offer a tip. He left the restaurant to resume patrolling the area.

He suddenly received a distressing phone call. Officer lives listened to the individual calling him on his cell phone. He found it odd that a civilian would contact him on his cell phone.

"Officer, you need to come here, quick. These people are being treated very poorly."

"Is this an emergency?"

"No, sir, but this is something that needs to be addressed ASAP. The reason I called you is because I hear that you are an excellent officer, and only you can help me with this."

"No need to say anymore. I'm on my way."

Fifteen minutes later, Officer Lives arrived at the Typical Nursing Home. He walked past people who were being abused left and right. He didn't have a care in the world until he spotted a situation with a caretaker and one of the elders.

"I said, go!" yelled one of the caretakers. He punched an old man in the face twice, and then said, "Eat. Your."—he finished off with a hard kick, knocking the man down—"MEDICINE!"

The officer observed the situation, appalled, and quickly got into the hack's face. "What the hell is going on here?!"

"This old fuck won't eat his medicine!"

Carl, the old man who was being brutally abused, was on the ground, unconscious and bruised. Officer Lives knelt down to the elder, and then glared at the hack. "Your methods are horrible!"

The caretaker gasped. "What?!"

Officer Lives nodded and turned to him. "You shouldn't punch a guy like that over and over again."

Carl got up slowly while Officer Lives continued.

"Your methods disgust me. I would have expected better from a nursing home!"

The hack was speechless as the officer ranted at him.

"The only thing that I have seen is poor and inefficient treatment."

Carl was relieved at finally getting help from the outside world—and from a police officer, to boot. "Yeah! They treat us like this every day! You tell 'em. officer!"

Officer Lives turned to Carl. "This is how it's done." He kneed the old man in the stomach as hard as he could. "Eat!" He kneed him again three more times. "Your! Fucking! MEDICINE!"

Carl fell down face first, unconscious again. This time he wasn't going to get up anytime soon. The hack's eyes widened when he saw this. He began taking notes of what he'd just witnessed.

"Thank you, sir. I will remember this."

Two minutes later, Officer Lives went to the room of the person who had called him. He wondered what could possibly be wrong at the Typical Nursing Home. There was a man in the room who appeared to be in his mid-thirties.

"Were you the one who called me?"

The man nodded as Officer Lives got a closer look. "Wait a minute! I know you! You're that guy running for mayor! Michael!"

"That's right. Care to take a seat, officer?"

Michael pulled out a chair from the side of the wall, and set it in the middle of the room. Officer Lives took a seat excitedly. He was meeting a famous person in town.

Michael said coldly, "This is the perfect place for this discussion, since there is nothing but injustice that takes place in this building. It relates to what we have to talk about."

Officer Lives shrugged. "Injustice? This nursing home is being operated very well. There is no injustice going on at all."

Several minutes later, several people walked into the room. Officer Lives observed them, and then it dawned on him that these people were people that he'd arrested or dealt with, including the woman he had just arrested tonight. Jason, Cecil, Fatima, Hector, Jamaal, Mark, and Tony, who was with his mother, eyed the officer like hawks, ready to snatch away their prey.

One minute later, Michael glanced at Jamaal, and then at Hector. "I'm surprised to see you two here, considering the accident with the jet."

"Well, we didn't land too far off land. Some of us were able to swim our way to safety, while others were evacuated. Unfortunately, we lost our pilot. We give our condolences to the family of Hector Sonchez," Jamaal replied.

Officer Lives looked back and forth, confused and anxious.

"What the hell is going on here?! If there isn't an emergency, then I need to get back to my nightly patrol. Is someone in danger right now?"

Michael turned to him, "No, not physically. However, the only person that is in danger, is you. What I have here is a group of people you've wronged in the past."

The officer chuckled for a moment. "I see. You all are bitter that I had to serve justice on you, and now you want revenge on the one who held the hammer."

Tony screamed, "I could have died that day! You were supposed to stop my classmates from killing me, but you sided with them!" His mother tried to calm him down.

Jason glared at the officer. "You didn't even bother to question Marisol after she ran me over. You just took her word for it, arrested me, and ruined my life!"

Cecil piped up, "I supposed it is your hobby to fuck up lives."

The rest of them nodded in agreement. Officer Lives was baffled by this as he attempted to figure out how he had wronged these people.

"It has always been my dream to be a police officer." Officer Lives had almost forgotten the fact that his son was there, and he slowly turned to him. "And what the hell are you doing here? My own son is going against me?! What for? I raised you, took care of you, bought you clothes. I even wished you the best after you left when you turned eighteen. And yet you do this to me— my own flesh and blood!"

Mark had a nervous look on his face as he listened to his father. He had never stood up to him before, and he was afraid. Officer Lives smirked at him.

"You're a pathetic excuse for a son. Look at you. You are eighteen years old, and you're already homeless. I guess all of those good grades were because you cheated, and after you made it to the real world, your true potential was shown." Mark looked down, as his father continued. "I hear that you are a shit cleaner for a living. My own son...reduced to a shit cleaner. Well, at least I'll know who to call after I take a huge dump. Maybe I should have kept you in the house for that sole purpose."

Fatima looked at Mark. "You are a shit cleaner?"

Mark shook his head at her, and looked down. "Some guy named Andrew kissed the manager's ass, so he got promoted over me. I'm the best worker in the store. Andrew made me his shit cleaner as a result."

Fatima looked at him, appalled. "Well, since I'm the CEO, you won't have to do that for long. We will talk about this some more later."

Officer Lives decided to continue to belittle his son. "I curse the day that you were born. If I knew you would be a fucking disappointment right now, I wouldn't have talked your mother out of going against the pregnancy." Mark covered his face as he tried to hide his tears. "Yep, I'm the reason why you are even alive, because she didn't want your ass. You were an acciden—better yet, you were a mistake."

Michael looked at the officer disgustedly. "That's enough!"

"What's the matter? This isn't working out how you expected?"

"On the contrary, it is. I have your actions recorded from tonight, including what you did here to Carl."

A few seconds later, the man who had robbed the woman opened the door and entered, waving at everyone. The woman who had been robbed walked alongside him nonchalantly, like they were buddies.

Officer Lives's eyes bulged. "Now what the hell is going on here?"

"He and this woman over here are siblings that are actors."

Michael motioned to the woman who was robbed. "We have that recorded. Also, Jamaal here has proof of your poor judgment. You arrested him purely based on accusations. He did what he had to do out of self-defense." Michael motioned to Hector. "I was at the church when Hector was put on the cross. I recorded the incident, including when you just ignored it because you were bribed. You're losing your job."

"What?! You're bull-shitting me!"

"No bull shit." He looked over to Cecil and Fatima. "You remember these two? You gave them the 'Jason' treatment, and Fatima here is the CEO of Happy Sunshine, Inc., the largest non-profit agency in the world. Do you not recognize her? You arrested her on the claims that she caused a domestic disturbance, but all she was doing was exercising her will to free speech by vouching for poor Cecil here—who is the biggest victim out of that situation. I hate to put it this way—but you're fucked."

Officer Lives went into panic mode, looking back and forth at all of the people in the room. "You can't do this! I always wanted to be a cop! It is my dream job!"

Jamaal chuckled at the moron. "I would have shown more sympathy if it weren't for the fact that you use that badge so crudely. I have had my share of dreams being shattered, but I've always cared for people."

The officer quickly took out his gun, which caused alarm from everyone. "You aren't going to show them shit! You show them this stuff, and I'll shoot you all dead right now!"

Tony began to cry. Officer Lives pointed the gun at his mother. "Shut that kid up! Now!"

She tried to calm him down. Michael raised his hands, but remained calm. "I would put down that gun if I were you."

Officer Lives pointed it at Michael, and then chuckled

insanely. "And why is that?"

Immediately, the door burst open as the police shot Officer Lives's gun out of his hand. He was soon restrained, then handcuffed. Michael looked down at him with contempt.

"All of your horrific deeds have been shown to the police department. You are a criminal now."

A day later, in the holding visitation room, a robed man asked:

"What happened, Lives? You were doing such a great job, and then it all crumbled away. I thought you had it all under control."

"I don't know. I just don't understand. I always strove to do the right thing, and yet I got shat on like this. Life can be so confusing at times."

"Don't worry. This is just a temporary thing. We still need your support, and people in this town love you, so you have their support. You won't lose your job. Also, this current situation is not helping out the election in our favor."

"And how am I going to get out?"

Abraham, gave him a somewhat sinister look. "Easy." The priest began to whisper his plan.

A day later, Officer Lives got off the prison bus, and was greeted by prison scenery. He hadn't said a word ever since he'd gotten there. All this time, he had always defended the law against criminals, and now he was one because he'd been set up by a bunch of criminal citizens. Lives walked toward the entrance, but then out of nowhere he heard a thud to his left, and a police car ran him over. He bounced off of the hood of the car, and landed on the ground, unconscious. The driver got out of the car, clearly alarmed.

"Oh, damn! Look at what this inmate did to my car!"

Immediately, the cops all rushed to the injured Fuxup Lives, and began to beat him with their clubs. Afterward, the car was sent to a mechanic to make sure there were no serious damages done to it. Officer Lives was sent to solitary for vandalism.

A day later, in the prison cafeteria, Officer Lives looked down at his food in disgust. There was no way that this was meant for a human. He fiddled with it. One of the guards glared at him, and approached.

"You got a problem, bud?" asked the guard.

"This food is terrible. I can't eat this. There are maggots inside."

"Eat your damn food."

Lives looked at it again. "I'd rather not."

The guard got in his face. "Eat your damn food....NOW!!"

Lives cringed as he took a spoonful of the food. He then took a sip, and immediately after threw up.

The cop grabbed Lives, and then punched him in the face repeatedly, as he said, "Eat your damn food!" The guard kneed him as hard as he could in the stomach. Lives collapsed, coughing.

The guard placed the plate in front of Lives, and then forced his face in it. The other inmates just cackled at the situation.

A day later, in the prison recreation center, an irate man asked furiously, "What the fuck is your problem?"

Lives gave the young man a confused look. "All I'm trying to do is go back to my cell. What the hell is your problem, kid?! I apologized to you for bumping into you accidentally."

"My problem is you! Look at you, trying to be all apologetic and shit! What's the matter?! Are you too good to fight me?"

"Look! I don't want any trouble! All I'm trying to do is go back to my cell!"

A crowd of inmates were attracted, and began to cheer the irate inmate on. "Go on! Beat the shit out of him!"

"Shank his ass!"

"You gonna just let him apologize like that?!"

"Cut off his fucking head!"

A guard approached the crowd. "Can someone tell me what the hell is going on here?"

The irate inmate rudely took the first turn. "This bitch is pissing me off! He's acting all uppity and shit!"

The rest all agreed as Lives looked around nervously. The situation wasn't going in his favor.

"No, that isn't what happened at all, sir."

Right before he could continue, the irate inmate swung at Lives, and punched him in the face as hard as he could. He sent a tooth flying in the process. Lives was knocked down in an instant. The crowd cheered happily. Rather than restrain the irate inmate, the cop instantly tackled Lives, and put him in handcuffs.

"Calm down, sir! No need to get violent now!"

Lives was completely dumbfounded. "He attacked me for no reason! Why the hell can't you see that? What type of guard are you?"

"That's it, into the hole you go!" He bashed Lives over the head with his club, knocking him unconscious. Lives was then sent to solitary for the rest of the day.

A day later, in the visitation room, Lives pleaded, "Father, I was set up by people I arrested in the past who had committed crimes."

Lives's father reflected on this as he shook his head. "My son, reduced to an inmate in prison. Are you someone's bitch yet? How many times did you drop the soap?"

"Hell no! I'm going to get out of this situation somehow."

"Somehow I doubt that. To be honest with you, even when you were a cop, you were a piece of shit."

Lives gasped as his father continued, "You are a shitty cop. I curse the day that your mother gave birth to you. You know, the only reason why you're even alive is because of me. She wanted to perform an abortion because you were a mistake. Goodbye, my piece-of-shit for a son." His father stood up to leave, but paused, realizing something. "Wait a minute. That's right. I don't have a son, because from this day forward, I disown you. Peace, bitch. If you want to grovel, I'll be moving into the Typical Nursing Home. That place is paradise, or so I've heard."

The older man left.

Later on that day, in the prison church, Lives said to the priestess, "I feel like just killing myself. I've never felt so much turmoil. What have I done to deserve this?"

Marpha, the priestess, gave him a concerned look. "The Lord gives us these trials in order to test us. Are you saved, sir?"

Lives shook his head no. "Sorry, ma'am. I was, but because of what's happening now, I don't believe in the Lord anymore."

Marpha narrowed her eyes at him darkly. "I see."

"The reason I came here is because the church room is the most peaceful room," said Lives. "And I needed some time to myself. Always can rely on that."

"It is understood, sir. I shall return shortly."

Officer Lives nodded, and Marpha left the room. Now he was alone. He stood up, and looked at the picture of the Lord. He sighed in contempt.

"You let me down. The reason I'm here is because of you! What have I done to deserve this? I have always been a good servant! I did all of that work in your name, and now you reduce me to this. It's all your fault!"

After his rant, Officer Lives was assaulted from behind by one of the inmate church members. He was knocked down as he tried to turn around to fight back, but was restrained by several more who were present. He was then knocked out after one of them punched him hard in the face.

Thirty minutes later, Lives awoke to find he had been stripped down to his boxers, and was tied to a cross. There were daggers against his arms and legs, like someone had used him as a human dart board.

"What the fuck is this shit?!" he yelled.

Immediately, Marpha hissed, "Silence, heretic!"

"Get me the fuck down! Now!"

"I said, SILENCE!"

Lives struggled to break free. Marpha, who was becoming increasingly irritated, said, "The Lord has told me himself that you have a lot of unresolved dark karma. At first, me and the congregation members were throwing daggers at your limbs in divine attempts to impale you, but all of us missed, so I asked him if he wanted me to kill you in his name. He told me he wanted you to suffer, so you could learn from your past mistakes."

"What?! I didn't do anything wrong! I have always been a good person!"

Marpha motions for one of the church member inmates to go toward Lives. The member took out a club, and knocked him out. He was left on the cross with his head low until a guard saw him there, and threw him violently in his cell.

A day later, in the courtyard, a young man said, "Hey, Lives. What's up?"

Officer Lives ignored the young man talking to him. He didn't want to talk to anyone anymore. "Hey, I was hoping that we could be friends. You see, the reason I'm here is because I was framed for a crime that I didn't commit."

"Fuck off."

The young man looked as he got closer. "Lives, I just want t—"

Immediately, Lives punched the young man in the face repeatedly. The inmates cheered. Lives was separated from the young man, and three guards restrained him and placed him in an empty room. Lives glared at the three as they chuckled at him.

One of them spoke. "You think you are a big man for messing with someone that much younger than you, don't you?" Lives stayed silent. The guard continued, "Well, do you think you're a man?" Silence. "Didn't think so. You are a piece-of-shit, washed-up, ex-cop who is now a criminal." The guards then immediately took turns beating up the inmate gleefully until five minutes later. The sound of the emergency sirens filled the room, which caused one of the cops to yell, "We have a riot on our hands!"

———

In the courtyard, an inmate yelled to the crowd in front of him, "Alright, bitches, this is how it's going to be. Now that we have the guns, we plan on getting out of here. If any of you aren't cooperative, then you will be shot in the head."

Some of the inmates chuckled at this. The riot leader looked down at the ones who were laughing. He motioned for someone to give him a gun, and then shot one of them in the head, killing him. The others stopped in their tracks. This obviously wasn't a joke.

"Good. Now you all understand. This is the plan: We demand to get out of here safely, and if our demands aren't met, then every thirty minutes we shoot a guard."

The inmates began to cheer, except for Lives, who remained silent.

Thirty minutes later, the leading inmate yelled, "All right, bitches. We gave our demands to the mayor thirty minutes ago, which means that one of you must die."

The leader beckoned for his cohorts to hand him a guard. The victim struggled as he tried to break free, but was met in the stomach with the hilt of the gun. The leader raised his pistol, and then held the gun to the guard's head.

Lives narrowed his eyes, and yelled, "Stop it! Now!"

The leader paused, looking toward Lives. "Who the fuck said that?!"

"It was me!"

Lives emerged from the crowd, walking toward the riot leader, who allowed him to come close.

"And who are you?"

Lives proudly crossed his arms. "My name is Fuxup Lives! I am the hero who's going to stop you, and free these people!"

The inmate chuckled at him. "You?! By yourself?!"

The former cop rushed at the man and tackled him, but was somewhat surprised when his opponent didn't struggle. The inmate whispered in his ear, "We got the memo from Abraham. Keep playing along, but try not to hurt me too much."

"Roger that."

Everyone began to cheer. A couple of the inmates tried to pry Lives off of their leader. He kicked one in the chest, but softly enough so as to not cause him any damage. The inmate played it off like he'd been kicked very hard, and launched himself back against the wall. Lives fake-punched the other inmate, who passed out after barely taking a hit. More and more inmates fought with Lives, but the false hero demolished everyone. Those who were wielding guns began to shoot at Lives. He held out his arms to shield himself, but soon realized the bullets were duds.

Lives proudly puffed out his chest like a superhero. "Your

bullets can't harm me! I am a hero!"

This caused a cheer from the observers. Lives rushed to the men with guns, then fake-attacked them. A few minutes later, Lives had single-handedly taken out the gang, and ended the riot. The guards cheered for him as they handcuffed the inmates who had started the whole thing. This whole incident had been broadcast on the television, much to Michael's dismay. Fuxup Lives was now considered the hero of Harshtown. In a week, his court hearing would commence.

A week later, Fuxup Lives arrived to the courtroom, and sat down at the defendant's side. He looked over at all of the people who had helped put him in jail in the first place, as they glared back.

Once everyone was settled, the judge said, "We are gathered here today to settle these accusations against our beloved hero, Officer Fuxup Lives. He is accused of holding these people hostage, and being a corrupt officer."

Most of the audience began to boo in response to the last few things the judge had said.

"Calm down, people. I know, I know. I feel the same way. He's our hero, and couldn't possibly have done what he had been accused of. Even though that's the case"—the judge motioned toward Michael's crew—"we gotta give these people their chance to make fools out of themselves, so let's get started."

Thirty minutes later, during Jason's Testimony, the lawyer asked skeptically:

"So...you really don't know what happened, do you?"

Jason crossed his arms and looked away. "I already fucking said what I said! I got run over, people came to me and didn't help me, and then shortly after, Officer Lives arrested me without analyzing the situation."

"Yes, you told me this six times, and it was the same, but

you don't have any recollection of the events. You based this off of dreams." The defense attorney turned to the audience. "Dreams, people! That is his evidence! Dreams!"

Everyone began to laugh. The judge chuckled a little as well, and shook his head. Jason glared at the enemy's helper.

"This stuff really happened! The only reason I couldn't remember it when it happened is because it happened so fast! If you got hit by a car that came out of nowhere, then got knocked unconscious, you wouldn't remember it either."

"Indeed I wouldn't! As a matter of fact, nobody would if that happened to them—but that isn't what happened! You smoked some weed, then went out for a little walk. Then you saw Marisol's car, took a pipe, and bashed the vehicle! You then passed out in the street because you were too high, and the witnesses, as well as Marisol, saw the damage that you'd done!"

A gasp came from the audience, and many of them nodded their approval.

"Fuck you, fuck this court, fuck you all, and fuck this society! I fucking hate you motherfuckers, and hope you all die of Hyper Cancer, you insensitive fucks!"

The judge banged his gavel. "Order! Order!"

Fifteen minutes later, during Tony's Testimony, the prosecutor observed Tony with concern, then he looked over at the lawyer and said, "Please be easy on him. He is only ten years old."

The lawyer nodded as he looked at Tony. Surprisingly to him, the boy was calm. "Tony, you stated that your class believed in the Illuminati, and they accused you of being a reptilian, and were willing to kill you?"

Tony nodded at him. "That's right, sir."

The older man sighed and shook his head. "You have one heck of an imagination, kid, but I guess that's normal for your age."

The child shook his head no. "Not really. That's how it happened. We talked to Officer Lives, and he said he would take care of the situation, but he didn't. He pretty much sided with them, and believed what they said, and then left it at that. I had to fend for myself for the most part, sir. Surprisingly my teacher was able to provide me some support in the end."

"What exactly did Officer Lives tell you?"

"He said that he went to one of the parents' houses, and was shown an article about a woman who interviewed a reptilian. He then said that he thanked the kid, and moved on from house to house, learning things he never knew about. He stated that his eyes had been opened. He then said that my problem was taken care of, and hung up the phone—just like that."

The older man gave him a skeptical look, and asked for the details of the time and date, but Tony told him the exact information. The man asked Tony to explain his story again, but it was exactly the same, no matter how many times he inquired.

An hour later, Tony said while clearly annoyed, "And that's what happened, for the seventy-eighth time, sir. Are you that much of an idiot? You'd get along well with Lee, since you both share the same level of retardation."

The lawyer looked rather upset that Tony hadn't slipped up at all. Tony said curiously, "I got a question for you. Are you happy, sir?"

"What?"

"Are you happy, sir? Because you look awfully stressed out. What's the matter? You thought that just because I'm ten years old, I would slip up? That I'm making this whole thing up? That you could easily make me look like a fool?"

The defense attorney stuttered, "I-I...but—"

Tony interrupted him. "Well, you are the one who looks like a fool. You got nothing on me. You tried every trick in the book, and got completely outclassed by a ten year old. You probably should just quit your job, or better yet, kill yourself, especially since you're defending Mr. Fuxup Lives."

This made the audience laugh. The judge banged his gavel. "Order! Order!"

———

The court sessions continued, and Hector gave his testimony.

"It was because of my religious beliefs, sir. They assaulted me in church, and placed me on a cross. There is no telling what they would have done if Officer Lives hadn't come."

The lawyer raised a brow. "So you are saying that Lives saved you?"

Hector shook his head no. "Nope, after he arrived, he was going to arrest Abraham, but Abraham bribed him, so Lives left it at that, and arrested me for no reason!" The audience booed. "Here is the proof right here."

Hector took out a video tape, and placed it on the podium. "This happened right after I tried to leave the church."

Hector played the tape. They watched the whole scene unravel, as church members beat the hell out of Hector in the parking lot. The proof was concrete.

"I still find it hard to believe that a church would do something like this, especially a church as renowned as Abraham's," said the lawyer, continuing, "If this was such a major problem, then why didn't you show it to the police off the bat? It's like you waited for this moment. You waited for an opening to blackmail Officer Lives!"

Hector glanced over at Michael for a moment, then turned to the lawyer. "We tried to explain this to the cops, but as I said before, ABRAHAM BRIBED THEM AGAINST ME! Michael showed them the tape, but they didn't care!"

"Or maybe you're just acting, and you did it purely to frame poor Officer Lives, here! Your video-editing skills are piss-poor!"

The crowd booed Hector off the podium.

Ten minutes later, during Cecil's Testimony, Cecil pleaded, "That's what happened, sir. I was trying to be polite, but the man still remained hostile to me. The crowd beat me up as well. Knocked me down, and kept kicking me repeatedly. I tried to explain this to Officer Lives, but he didn't care, so he arrested me and Fatima."

"Your story is strange," said the lawyer.

"Pardon?"

"You want to know why? It's because it is completely the opposite of this guy's story!"

He pointed to a person in the crowd. Shortly after, Andre, the man who had been irate with Cecil, approached the podium. Cecil narrowed his eyes at him as the young man strutted over coolly.

Andre looked over at Cecil, and said, "Yo. What up, dawg? You mad, bro?"

Andre took his position. He looked at Cecil, his former victim, with a smirk, and then looked at the lawyer.

"Andre, tell us what happened based on your perspective."

Articulately, Andre stated, "This is what happened, sir. I was walking down the street, and then this guy walks over to me. He spits on my new shoes. I asked him what the issue was, but he started to go berserk, and then he made weird animal sounds, and jumped from tree to tree like a monkey. The people who were in the area came to my rescue, and then we subdued him after he started throwing feces at us! He then got some backup from that woman, who also went berserk. Officer Lives arrested them, and saved us."

"That isn't what happened at all, you fucking liar!" yelled Cecil.

Hector yelled out of the blue, "You're fired!"

The judge banged his gavel. "Order! Order!"

Andre looked over to Hector as he tried to remain professional.

"Sir...I...I'm just attending this court session to give my testimony. I do apologize, boss."

Hector glared at him as the young man's demeanor gradually returned to normal.

"I-I-I...need this fucking job! Who the fuck do you think you are? I hope your ass gets real Hyper Cancer, and your head fucking explodes, motherfucker!" Andre moved from the podium to get in Hector's face. "We robbed yo' fuckin store when you passed out, you dumb bee-yotch!"

Hector laughed at the young man. "You're a stupid motherfucker for admitting that in court...and it isn't the first time you robbed me. Either you pay me back the amount you owe in a week, or go to jail for five years."

Immediately, the guards grabbed Andre, who was screaming, and then took him away to prison.

Ten minutes later, during Mark's Testimony, Mark calmly said, "That's what happened. He kicked me out of the house as soon as I turned eighteen. He didn't give me a chance to graduate from school."

The attorney reflected on this. He turned to Officer Lives, and whispered, "Now, if what your son is saying is true, then... that's really fucked up. I would *never* do that to my son!"

Lives remained silent and cold.

"Well, Mark, technically by law you are the one who committed a crime, not him. It isn't something that I agree with, but the rules are rules. You turned eighteen, and legally became an adult. He felt that you trespassed, so he exercised his right to bear arms. You got nothing on him, man."

Mark looked down, and then left the podium. The lawyer felt like it wasn't necessary to go harsh on Mark. He actually did believe Mark's testimony, but the young man was on the opposing team.

Fifteen minutes later, during Jamaal's Testimony, Jamaal finished explaining things to the attorney about his problems with Andre at the Underwater Basket Weaver's Professional Building.

"Any other questions, sir?" asked Jamaal. "Also, I was with Hector that day when he was placed on the cross, so I can vouch for him there."

"No questions, but why is it that you seem so sure of yourself? You aren't giving any proof of your testimony. All you are doing is telling us a story," said the defense attorney.

The prosecutor chuckled, "It's because we saved the best for last. Now I haven't said much until now, but here is all the evidence that you need.."

The prosecutor walked over to the table with a bag in his hands, and took out a camcorder.

"Right here is the tape with footage of all the beatings Andre gave to Jamaal. Right here is the paper work that Officer Lives did after he talked to Tony and his mother. Here is another recording. Believe it or not, there was someone who recorded the incident with Jason. Please don't ask how we found this. Also, Jamaal was present that day when Jason was run over."

The audience gasped. Officer Lives begins to sink in his chair in despair.

"Don't forget about the recording that Hector showed you. Here are two actors who saw Officer Lives in action." The prosecutor motioned to the man and woman who had acted out the robbery. They waved at him. "Along with the tape of Lives holding these eight hostage with a gun, and finally, this is a recording of the officer assaulting an elderly man in the Typical Nursing Home. The prosecution rests." He confidently sat down.

The judge reflected on all of this. "Any last words?"

The defense attorney preached. "Ladies and gentlemen! Do not focus on the evidence! Rather, focus on the testimony!" He played the tape with footage of Officer Lives stopping the riot. "He is a good man! Look at how he single-handedly stopped this riot! He did not care that he was falsely placed in jail. He still wanted to serve justice! Even though these people have evidence, do not go by the evidence, go by the testimony. He fights for what he believes in, and highly values justice. Sure, he may have made a few slip-ups here and there, but who hasn't? Nobody is perfect. Focus on the present, not on the past!"

The audience began to cheer. Michael shook his head at them in disbelief. The recording ended, and Officer Lives was given a microphone.

"Ladies and gentlemen! It has always been my dream to be a cop! Now I understand, just like he said, that I'm not perfect, but then again, who is? I have made mistakes in the past, and I own up to them. Regardless of my past deeds, I strive to do the right thing, as you see in this video of the riot. Now all I ask of you to do is do the right thing. Realize that I am not guilty, so that I can continue to be your hero!"

The lawyer slowly clapped his hands. Shortly after, the audience followed suit, and began to chant Lives's name. The judge even clapped for Lives.

Twenty minutes later, once the cheering has died down, court resumed. A member of the jury said, "Ladies and gentlemen, the jury has come to a decision. We find the defendant, Fuxup Lives…" There was silence as everyone waited patiently. "Innocent of all charges!"

Everyone began to cheer, except for the ones who were against him. Michael was completely shattered, and held his head in his hands. The rest just had blank stares on their faces because they couldn't believe what had just happened. Jason was the first person to come out of his shock. He shrugged his shoulders, told everyone that he wasn't surprised, and then left the courtroom. Eventually, everyone else left as well, except for Michael. He remained in place for a couple hours in deep contemplation.

A week later, Officer Lives arrived at in the police station. He was surprised that it was pitch black inside the building. He curiously walked around, asking if anyone was present. As soon as he made it to his desk, the lights came on.

"SURPRISE!"

Officer Lives gasped, and was surprised and happy at the same time. He saw a cake on one of the tables, and everyone welcomed him back warmly. Shortly after his reunion with his coworkers, he was called into the office. Once inside, he looked down at the sheriff who was sitting at his desk. The older man spoke professionally,

"Officer Lives, you have been a very great officer, and your service is highly valued."

Lives nodded at him. "Thank you, sir, but what is this about?"

"I'm retiring, Lives, and we all agreed that it is best to promote you to sheriff. Congratulations! You are now Sheriff Fuxup Lives!"

Officer Lives beamed. "Are you serious?! Yes! I'll do it!"

He shook his former sheriff's hand, and hugged him.

"Officer Lives—or should I say, Sheriff Lives—jail must

have been tough for you. Did you learn anything?"

Lives reflected on all of the terrible experiences that he'd gone through, one at a time, as he looked at the former sheriff.

"Yes, I did learn something—that prison food is terrible."

A couple hours later, in the parking lot, Sheriff Lives proudly walked out of the police station toward his car. It seemed like everything worked out in the end. The one thing that he regretted losing was his faith in the Lord. It seemed like God was on his side after all. As he got close to his car, he heard a man shout his name.

"Sheriff Fuxup Lives!" The sheriff turned around.

"Yes, did you need anything—" He stopped in his tracks when he saw that it was Michael standing next to Fatima. They both gave him emotionless stares.

Michael said, like he had read Lives's mind, "Just because you won this time does not mean that God is on your side. I just wanted to let you know that we are far from over. Don't let your promotion get to your head. Regardless of what position you take, you still are nothing but a piece of shit. I *will* become mayor of this town, and I *will* reform everything, and free this place from as much corruption as possible. This includes destroying the very foundation that you built yourself on. All that I request is that you enjoy yourself while you can, because once it is all torn apart, not only will your image be destroyed, but people will forget about you, and the only thing that you will have left is despair—for the rest of your life."

The sheriff was speechless. Michael simply turned his back on him and walked away. Fatima stayed behind.

"He means that, too. Also, the people will eventually catch on to your corruption. Just keep fucking up lives. It is only a matter of time." She then followed Michael, and the two continued their plans to right all of the wrongs in Harshtown.